MW01356374

# AM I REALLY CATHOLIC?

## The President's Daughter Is Surprised by Her Faith

William E. Bullis

Biblical references are drawn from the New American Bible Revised Edition as found on the United States Conference of Catholic Bishops website.

Am I Really Catholic / William Emory Bullis

TO MY MA AND POPS,
YOU KNOW MY PRAYERS.

# CONTENTS

PART I .......... 1
RISING STAR .......... 3
THE INFLUENCER .......... 11
COLONEL GARDNER .......... 14
THE HIKE .......... 16
TRAIL RHYTHM .......... 19
FATHER JACK .......... 25
SARAH EXPLAINS .......... 28
PRAYERS UPON HIGH .......... 31
STRANGER ON THE TRAIL .......... 38
FALCON EMERGENCY .......... 48
WHIRLWIND .......... 51
HIS FRIEND, THE ARCHBISHOP .......... 56
VERY IMPORTANT PERSON .......... 62
VISITOR IN THE LOBBY .......... 70
GOING HOME .......... 80
PART II .......... 83
ONWARD .......... 85
THE ENTREPRENEUR .......... 92
UNCLE RAKESH .......... 97
THE ENGINEER .......... 100
QUALITY ADVICE .......... 104
UNCLE RONNIE'S SECRET .......... 109
FIRST DATE .......... 116
MARY .......... 120
FRIENDS IN HIGH PLACES .......... 124
PRESIDENTIAL POWER .......... 129
BACK TO THE BLUE RIDGE .......... 133
JEWISH MOTHER .......... 135

COVENANT ........ 139
SILICON VALLEY ........ 147
MERCED ........ 155
SOPHIE'S FRIEND ........ 160
SOPHIE AND SARAH, JEAN AND HANK ........ 169
SILENCE ........ 173
THE BIG SHOW ........ 178
VISITORS FROM FRANCE ........ 187
WOMAN'S INTUITION ........ 193
CHALLENGE ACCEPTED ........ 197
PRAYERS ANSWERED ........ 201
SMOKY REFLECTIONS ........ 208
PART III ........ 213
CAROLINA CONFESSION ........ 215
DECISION TIME IN MERCED ........ 221
TAKE TWO, HIT TO RIGHT ........ 224
FATHER RAKESH ........ 229
MOTHER MIRIAM ........ 238
RANGER POLICY ........ 248
EPILOGUE ........ 259
A LETTER FROM SARAH ........ 261
SARAH'S PRAYER ........ 267
TEACH ME YOUR WAY ........ 269

# PART I

# 1

# RISING STAR

It had been a year since her mother Maggie's death from cancer and about the same amount of time since moving to Silicon Valley, which didn't seem like much of a valley compared to her beloved Shenandoah, where her father still lived on three quiet acres along the North Fork of the river.

To her way of figuring, the opportunity she'd received from a top venture capital firm was too good to pass up. Plus, San Jose put her within a stone's throw of her best friend, Sophie Shriram, who she had known her whole life and needed now more than she realized. Meeting her for coffee on Saturday mornings seemed to be the only reason to get out of bed, which didn't fit with her normal routine but had become her new reality over the last few months.

*You know you don't like sleeping in. Is something wrong with you?* She wondered while walking up the street from her studio apartment to the corner café. *Prolly. So what? Deal with it later. Who said time heals all wounds? What a load of malarkey...! Hey, good word. One of Grandpa's favorites!* She tightened her jacket against the morning chill and headed towards the café, hoping her good friend wouldn't notice her weary eyes - or the weight behind them.

Sophie was worried about Sarah after learning she had not

spoken to her father for two weeks. She hoped they could talk about it but worried she might do more harm than good.

After a hug and a quick order, she just came out with it.

"Sarah, it isn't good that you have not spoken to your dad for so long. This isn't like you. I get being sad and angry with what you've been through, but your dad loves you!"

Sarah avoided eye contact while toying with her bagel wishing there was a way to turn it into a biscuit. "I know, I know," she whispered.

"What's going on? Talk to me."

"He's so frustrating. He seems so confident in his beliefs. I don't understand him. Mom was so young. Why her?  How can the world be this way? It doesn't make any sense. What's the point?"

She watched a squirrel scamper across the street wishing her life could be that simple.

Sophie was determined to help her shake the malaise but was taken aback by the intensity of Sarah's pain. Then, suddenly, she thought aloud, not realizing she had spoken, "*Maybe Uncle Ronnie could help?*"

Sarah put her coffee down and smiled.

"What did you say?"

"Uh... Maybe Uncle Ronnie could help?" Sophie replied sheepishly.

"Hmm. Interesting you say that. I have a business trip next week that will take me close to his home. Maybe I could talk to him. You're right. He'll know what to do."

Sophie agreed, adding, "Uncle Ronnie loves you more than life itself. He'll have the right perspective."

"Yes!" Sarah said, suddenly animated. "You're right. I can't wait to see him!"

He met Sarah for lunch wondering why she was making a special trip over the ancient Uwharrie Mountains. They agreed to meet in the Village of Pinehurst, North Carolina, which was not far from Fort Bragg, where he had once been stationed and near where he now lived.

"Why, Sarah, you look fit as a fiddle. You're keeping yourself in shape," said Uncle Ronnie as he pulled her in close for their traditional bear hug, which they had done since she was a little girl.

"You know me, Uncle Ronnie. I'm not going to let myself go soft. Plus, I could easily beat you in a mile run, right here, right now!"

"I bet you could, girl dear. I bet you could! Let's go inside and get us some barbeque and sweet tea and catch up on things."

They talked for quite a while, but not about what Uncle Ronnie was expecting.

"I've got an idea for you girl. Why don't we go for a hike with your dad just like the old days?" suggested Ronnie.

"What will that accomplish?"

"Do you have time for me to tell you a story about your dad? This is going back a ways, but I think it might help you understand where he's coming from."

"Do I have to?"

"No, actually, you don't. You see, Sarah, you're a woman now. You are on a path, whether you realize it or not. You set the direction with what you do based on how you think and what you believe. Sometimes, God sends you a message. It's up to you to listen, interpret, decide and act."

She scowled. "What if I don't believe in God or at least the God my dad believes in?"

"Don't worry. He still believes in you!"

She sighed. "OK, what's the story?"

"I'll tell you what, you set up that trip we talked about, and I'll tell it to you while we're walking out in the great wide open."

As soon as Sarah left, Ronnie got on the phone to his good buddy, Jack Martin, who was Sarah's third "uncle." Ronnie knew he'd be essential on this mission.

Somehow, as if by magic, Sarah was able to convince her father to accompany her and her best friend, Sophie, on a weeklong backpacking trip along the Continental Divide in Colorado. Even more remarkable, Sophie convinced her father, Rakesh Shriram, to join them. He was the CEO of a Fortune 100 tech giant. He also happened to be the best friend to her father, former president of the United States, Sean O'Malley.

How the girls were able to get "Uncle" Sean and "Uncle" Rakesh to join them on this adventure is on par with many of life's great mysteries. Perhaps the men were due for an adventure. O'Malley was six years post his presidency, but still very busy teaching at the community college and volunteering with the Knights of Columbus and St. Vincent De Paul charity. He was also on one corporate board and had recently been a special envoy for the United States. Dr. Shriram was also equally busy, although he was beginning to plan his retirement from NarrowGate Technologies, which he had founded thirty years earlier.

When they learned of their daughters' plans, they immediately called each other.

"Yo, Rakesh, can you believe what these girls are thinking of having us do?" asked O'Malley laughing.

"I don't know how I can get out of it. You know me, I haven't been to the woods for years, and they think we're going to backpack for a week! They are certifiably insane!"

"I know! Don't these girls know we are distinguished gentlemen who are more at home at the country club than the backcountry?!" O'Malley laughed even harder.

"Look Sean, you've got to get me out of this!" Rakesh laughed.

"What are you talking about? I bet Sophie came up with this idea!"

"Ha ha! You know that's not true. All Sophie cares about is how many views she's getting on YouTube, or is it Instagram? Hold it! She's not going to film this damn hike! Oh, hell no. I am not going backpacking with my daughter if she's going to bring her GoPro video camera. That's what this is all about, isn't it?"

"You know your daughter better than I do. I know she's popular, but I think Sarah's been struggling with some things lately. It seems she wants some time to sort things out. I'm glad she's asked us to come along."

"What kind of things?" asked Rakesh.

"I'm not sure, but I think she's struggling with her faith."

"Hmmm. Been there. Done that. I'm in for whatever she needs. How long do we have before we go?"

"Four weeks."

"I'm screwed!"

O'Malley replied with deadpan seriousness. "Me too, but that never stopped us before. This is a mission from God."

"I'm in!" shouted Rakesh.

Four weeks later, when Sarah and her father arrived at the hotel in Denver, O'Malley was shocked to see not only his good friend Rakesh but also his two other best friends, who he'd not seen since the funeral, along with Rakesh's daughter, Sophie. He immediately knew he was in trouble when Colonel Ronnie Gardner, U.S. Army Rangers (retired), hugged him and simultaneously grabbed his butt while whispering, "Love you, bro!" and then kissed him on the cheek while emitting a loud, guttural laugh that caused all activity in the lobby to come to an immediate standstill.

Thankfully, their other good buddy, Father Jack Martin, pulled Ronnie off and extended his hand for a more normal greeting, which O'Malley could not abide by, pulling him in close and saying, "Bless me, Father, for I am about to sin!" while simultaneously grabbing his butt, too.

To which Father Martin replied, in his best fake Irish accent, "Aye, dear President, let me ask for your considerations in advance because I'm worried I'll be doing some sinning soon enough meself!"

Then Ronnie pulled Rakesh in close for a four-way, uncomfortably long love-hug, which was broken when Rakesh yelled their traditional, "Ireland Forever!"

The patrons gaped at the former president's actions.

The daughters reacted a bit more subtly, having seen this kind of silly behavior many times from these men they had known all their lives.

Sarah approached. "OK, that's enough boys. I suggest we get settled and meet back here in thirty minutes. We'll go over our plans during dinner. We've got to get an early start tomorrow."

All four men turned, came to full attention, saluted and yelled, "Yes, Master!" which they'd done many times in response to Sarah's stern leadership going back to when she was a little girl.

They all laughed and brought both girls in for an even bigger hug and then broke ranks as directed.

An hour later, at one of Denver's finest steak houses, the team came together for a pre-hike planning meal. As the food arrived, Rakesh asked if anyone would like to do the honor of saying grace, and at that instant all eyes turned to Father Jack.

"So, here we go, ganging up on the old Catholic priest again, eh?" he said with a grin.

"But, Uncle Jack, you were trained for this, were you not?" asked Sophie.

"Why, dear Sophie, all of us can talk to God, but I'll let you in on a little secret: He once said, "Where two or three are gathered together in my name, there I am in the midst of them."[1]

Father Jack said grace in the tradition he had learned from Sean's family, making the Sign of the Cross over the whole table saying, "In the name of the Father, the Son and the Holy Spirit. Bless us, O Lord, and these Thy gifts, which we are about to receive from Thy bounty, through Christ Our Lord. Amen."

Then Rakesh added, "I pray, God, who is ever capable of removing all obstacles, for your blessings and protection on this hike. Plus, if possible, could you make it so I don't break my leg!"[2]

Then all joined in with a hearty, "Amen!" except for Sophie who was trying to foil her father's silliness.

Much was discussed at dinner, including an agreement they would get an early start in the morning to reach the access point for the Continental Divide Trail (CDT) loop by midday.

Just as they were about to leave the table, a woman suddenly appeared standing directly next to O'Malley. She was about twenty-five years old, well-dressed, and extremely nervous, almost to the point of

[1] Matthew 18:20

[2] Adapted from a Hindu Prayer of Protection (to Ganesh). Rakesh had a deep affection for Hindu culture and deep respect for the faith of his Hindu friends, most especially his wife's family

distress. "President O'Malley," she said, "I want you to know how much pain you've caused me."

He gazed up at her. "How may I help you?"

She frowned. "You can't. What's done is done. But you should know what you say and do has an impact. You hurt me, and it's a pain that won't go away. You said you support women, but that is not how I see it!" Tears trickled down her face.

President O'Malley stood up. "Do you have a few minutes to talk? Perhaps we could go over to that corner table?" He put his arm around the woman and together they walked over to the bar area.

Sophie and Sarah were stunned and upset by the intensity of the woman's emotions.

Father Jack said, "Good luck to that woman. She doesn't know it yet but she's about to convert or revert to Holy Mother Church."

Sophie said, "What do you mean, Uncle Jack? That woman is really upset."

Then Uncle Ronnie joined, "Ah, Sophie and Sarah, we've seen this happen many times, and not just when your dad was president. He has an extraordinary gift for listening with love. It's why his men admired him in the Army and why he became so successful in business."

Rakesh nodded. "I always thought he would be the one of us who would become a priest, but that was not his calling. Anyway, it's getting late. That young woman is in good hands. Let's go to our rooms, as we must get an early start tomorrow."

# 2

# THE INFLUENCER

Sophie Shriram had been an influencer for years. Famous for her spot-on analysis of fashion trends, she was sought out by all the major brands. Taking YouTube and Instagram together, she had over 100 million views and counting. Educated in the finest schools, she was the beneficiary of her father's largesse as he built his NarrowGate Technologies into a Silicon Valley juggernaut.

She had traveled to many countries and counted her study abroad program in Paris as the most extraordinary experience of her young life. This was where she had developed a taste for fashion and decided to commit herself to the industry. It is also where she fell in love.

Her rugged young man from Bordeaux was the first in his family to go to university. His mother was a seamstress, and his father was a carpenter. They scrimped and saved every Euro to send him to college in hopes he could reach his full potential. When he saw Sophie for the first time, he was immediately taken by her beauty and also her gentleness.

"*Bonjour*, I understand you are looking for help," he said coming up to her at a bench near the library.

"*Bonjour*, I am sure I don't need your help," she replied dismissively.

"Ah. Forgive me. I must be mistaken then. It is I who needs your help."

"How so?" she replied with suspicion but looking up noticed this was not the typical college student, but rather a man— lean, broad shoulders, strong hands, working shoes, and smiling eyes.

"I'm hungry and have no one with whom to share my meal. Would you mind if I bought you lunch?" he replied with a grin.

And so, they had lunch and immediately found they could joke with each other like old friends. Sophie had never met a boy like him, who seemed only interested in friendship.

"So why did you come to Paris?" he asked.

"To get away from my father," she replied.

"Why?"

She shrugged. "Because he loves me too much."

"And this is a problem?"

"How can I be my own person if my father does everything for me? You see, my father is a very rich and powerful man. He's a good man, too. I needed to see how I would do on my own. But now I'm not so sure," she says looking down at her meal, which she has hardly touched because they have been talking so much.

"What are you not sure about?"

"I wish I could explain it. Wait, don't you know who I am?"

"No. Who are you?"

"I'm Sophie! I'm the girl who sets fashion trends in California! Every girl in San Francisco and L.A. knows who I am! But I guess not boys from Bordeaux."

"And this matters how?" he asks with an eyebrow raised.

"Because even though I influence and get millions of views, I couldn't care less about it. My social media persona is not who I am. It is not who I want to be."

"Let's go to Bordeaux this weekend."

"Why?" she asks, now with her own eyebrow raised.

"Because I want you to meet my mother!"

"Are you sure she would want to meet an American, of Indian descent, from California who has three million YouTube subscribers?"

"Perhaps not. But, if you're interested in fashion, do you not think it would be good to learn how to make a dress?" he replied, with a smile.

# 3

# COLONEL GARDNER

Colonel Ronnie Gardner stood at the edge of a cliff atop Otis Peak deep in the heart of Rocky Mountain National Park looking east across a deep valley. It was a crystal-clear morning, the kind you can only get high in the mountains where the clarity of the sky hints at outer space just beyond. He'd taken the Continental Divide trail loop from the west two days earlier to scout out the trail well before the hiking trip he'd encouraged Sarah to set up. He'd not been to this high spur off the Continental Divide Trail (CDT) before, and he wanted to leave nothing to chance.

He had plenty of experience on the main trail over the course of time and considered it to be the most difficult to through-hike of the eleven national scenic trails in the United States. Covering 3,100 miles, the CDT stretches from the borders of Mexico to Canada following the Continental Divide in New Mexico, Colorado, Wyoming, and Montana. It crosses deserts, high plateaus, alpine peaks, grasslands, and the Yellowstone caldera. It was not to be taken lightly under any circumstances, especially in the high country of Colorado, because the weather conditions could change within the blink of an eye.

Scouting the trail beforehand was not unexpected for a man who had been sought out for advice regarding training techniques, equipment, and strategies for outfitting elite fighting units of NATO.

While not leading elements of the U.S. Army Rangers, he was an accomplished section hiker and mountaineer having completed most of the Appalachian Trail and major sections of the Continental Divide and Pacific Crest Trails.

He was also an expert marksman and martial artist who had been deployed with special forces elements during his long and distinguished military career. Regarded as a fierce warrior, he was also known for his compassion for the enlisted men and women in his care, which was his primary reason for delving deep into military history, strategy, and tactics, where he was regarded as one of the finest minds in the U.S. Army. To his way of thinking, he never wanted to put his troops in harm's way without giving them the best tactical and strategic advantage possible.

His best friend, former U.S. President Sean O'Malley, also had a special arrangement with the Secret Service that included relying on Col. Gardner for security and protective services while on expeditions like this one. This unprecedented concession was only made possible by the reputation and track record of "Uncle" Ronnie Gardner, two-time recipient of the Silver Star, the nation's second highest award for military valor.

# 4

# THE HIKE

Sarah had chosen a circuit hike starting upon a section of the Continental Divide Trail, which touched the western portion of Rocky Mountain National Park. She desired to see the wide-open spaces above the tree line and look east to Long's Peak, the park's highest mountain at 14,259' above sea level. Their starting point would be just north of Grand Lake.

An early start averted the busy Denver rush hour as they climbed steadily along Interstate 70 to the western side of the front range of Colorado's Rocky Mountains. The western approach provided an awe-inspiring vista of the massive peaks of both Rocky Mountain National Park and the Indian Peaks Wilderness to the south.

O'Malley noticed his daughter was not saying much as they got closer to the trailhead, so he broke the ice. "What are you thinking, Sarita?"

"I wish Mom were with us," she replied without feeling staring east looking for elk or moose just as she had done as a little girl.

"Me too. She would have loved this. Well maybe not the camping part. We would've had to make sure we found a good hotel for her to stay in," O'Malley replied with a smile.

"I miss her a lot."

"Let's pray to her while we hike and ask her to put in a good word with Himself, while we're dancing up on the high plateau in her honor. I brought a little surprise for you when we get up on top of Hallet Peak, too."

"You really think you can pray to her? What good will that do?" she asked.

"I do. I'm surprised by the intensity of my prayers to her. It's as if she's on the trail just ahead of us. She's gone up and around a bend. We can't see her, but her spirit is alive, and I pray she's in Heaven face-to-face with our Lord. We can pray to her like we're talking and ask for her intercession with Jesus, Himself, on our behalf. I believe nothing makes your mom happier than hearing our prayers and asking our Lord to watch over and guide us according to His perfect will."

She replied with silence while she looked out the window at the high, lonesome peaks.

All the while, Uncle Ronnie was listening and driving and wondering about his best friend's daughter. Her mother passed just a year earlier, but obviously the pain of grief was still intense.

They got to the trailhead mid-morning, with the intent of hiking only a few miles to their first campsite, respecting the need to acclimate to the higher elevation of this rugged country. While all the men enjoyed joking about their age and fitness, indeed they were all experienced outdoorsmen, not only because of their Army training, but also because they truly loved backpacking, especially with their daughters / "nieces."

Whose idea this was became the subject of debate as they began to arrange their gear at the trailhead.

"So, who's bright idea was it to have us leave a perfectly good hotel room at o'dark thirty only to skedaddle up this cold, cold mountain?" crowed Father Jack, a Jesuit priest, an order of priests founded by Saint Ignatius of Loyola in 1540 A.D.

"Near as I can tell, it was Sarah's idea. I'm planning to blame her when my back goes out in about fifteen minutes. At least I won't be too far from the cars for when you boys have to carry me back," crowed Uncle Rakesh.

"Sarah's idea? Hmmm... Well, let's hope we don't have the Luck of the Irish rain down upon us, because from the look of those clouds over there, it might not be rain but snow up there today," warned President O'Malley.

Then Sophie chimed in. "The idea for this trip was mine. I'm not saying why right now, but if you geezers can't handle it, you might as well give up now before Sarah and I have to call search and rescue."

"This calls for a pre-hike huddle!" yelled Uncle Ronnie.

And so, the team huddled together in a circle, arms around shoulders, as they had many times before, while Uncle Ronnie said a prayer.

"In the name of the Father, the Son, and the Holy Spirit. Dear Lord, we thank you for your many blessings and ask you to overwatch our safety as we set out on this hike. We ask that our dear departed Maggie be joined with you in Heaven. Today we hike in her honor and know she will be with us in spirit. Amen."

All chimed in with a hearty Amen! Then they were off.

# 5

# TRAIL RHYTHM

The morning was cool and dry with the strong smell of ponderosa pine in the air. No clouds were apparent through the treetops, but this was certain to change as the day brought southwesterly winds up from the desert across the high mountain peaks.

Sarah and Sophie set a fast pace, moving out ahead of the geezers to get a little alone time. "How is Jean? *Where* is Jean? When will you see him next? Tell me everything, Sophie!"

Sophie sighed. "I don't want to talk about it right now. Can we just hike?"

Sarah frowned at Sophie and turned her gaze to the trail in front of her knowing it would soon become more difficult, given their starting elevation above 8,000 feet. If all went well, the team would bag a few peaks along the divide, topping out above 13,000 feet. Starting at the north inlet trailhead made for an easy opening stretch, albeit through a burn area that looked like a ghost forest.

Taking on the CDT Loop in late September allowed for less crowds but brought on the possibility of freezing weather and accumulating snow, although these hazards can present themselves at any time of year at the higher elevations. The treeline is quite high in this part of the country at approximately 11,400', and spending time above it was Sarah's objective. She longed to meditate, think and reconnect with herself in the wide-open expanse.

Altitude sickness was a real possibility, for they all lived and worked close to sea level. In fact, all of them had experienced it at various points in time during their many deployments, hikes and backpacking trips. The signs and symptoms were well known to them, and they were prepared to deal with the challenge if it presented itself by truncating their trip and moving down to a much lower elevation, knowing this condition was not to be taken lightly.

The silent hiking lasted all of a minute. Then Sophie couldn't help herself.

"OK, here's the thing. I'm mad at Jean. Well, not really mad at him. It's not easy being apart from him. He's gotten a good job near Paris with a good engineering firm, and now I'm back in California running my clothing business. We're both so busy, and I know it will be no time before one of those French tarts sinks her claws into him. You're like my big sister, so tell me. What am I supposed to do!?"

"This all started when Jean told you he didn't want to move in together, right?" asked Sarah.

"Well, yes, and also the fact that he didn't want to move to California, at least not without establishing himself with a good job first," Sophie explained while starting to huff and puff with the exertion. "He became different when I asked about moving in together. He was never the same after that."

"Did you talk to him about it?"

"I tried, but he would simply say how what I was asking was not in line with his faith. Then he said something about it also not being manly, whatever that means."

"Unmanly? What's up with that?" asked Sarah.

"Yeah, I know, right? I got mad at him, but he said, 'You can get mad all you want, but if you think I'm going to compromise my faith or follow you around, then you ought to find another boyfriend.' I've never seen him more... what's the right word? Stern! That's it. He was mad and disappointed in me at the same time. Ever since then, he's been different."

"He sounds like my dad."

"Yeah, or mine."

"Well, why don't you move on? You're in California. He's in France. You've got an amazing business going. You're well-known in the industry, too," Sarah said positively.

O'Malley yelled from behind them. "Hey, Sarita and Sophie, can you girls slow down a little?"

"What's wrong, Dad, you having trouble keeping up with a couple of women?" Sarah yelled back.

"Um, uh, yeah! You walk faster than a mountain goat who just got done grazing in a pepper patch," laughed O'Malley, while huffing and puffing at the same time.

O'Malley caught up with them, and they continued chatting for the better part of the afternoon until they arrived at camp.

With camp set up and the sun setting early due to a high ridgeline to their west. Sarah found a good spot to lean back and relax.

Her Uncle Ronnie settled on a nearby log. "Talk to me, Sarah. How are you liking this hike so far?"

"Loving it. I'm looking forward to reconnecting with my inner spirit."

"Dang. Sounds complicated. How do you know when you've '*connected*'?"

"Well, first, I must try to reach a state where I am not thinking about anything, where I'm emptied out and totally relaxed. Then I'll be able to re-connect," she said sitting up straighter and getting energy from Uncle Ronnie's interest.

"So, let me get this straight. You're going to try to empty yourself out in order to find yourself?"

"Uh, huh. But when you put it like that it seems like you're making fun of me. Are you?"

"Not at all, girl dear. I'm trying to understand your process and objective. So, let me ask a question. Why do you think you lost your connection to yourself?"

"It is hard to explain. I guess I just feel empty inside," she said quietly.

"How long have you felt this way?"

"A while. I don't know when it started."

"Can you describe how you feel using a word other than empty?" asked Ronnie.

"Mmmmm. That's hard. Aimless, maybe. Or maybe pointless is how I'm feeling," she said with her eyes closed.

"How old are you now, Sarah? 27?"

"Yup."

"What happened to that boyfriend of yours? What was his name again, Brady?"

"Yeah, that didn't work out. He turned out to be a guy whose main concern was himself on most days."

"Got it. Good riddance then. That's what dating's for anyway. Turns out it doesn't take much time to get a read on people. I'm not sure why your generation dates and then lives together for so long and then maybe gets married sometime down the road, but that's for another day."

"Hey, Uncle Ronnie, can I ask you a serious question?" Sarah was fully herself and comfortable with Uncle Ronnie.

"You know you can."

"How come you never got married?"

"That's a good question! I'll tell you why, and it's pretty simple. It just wasn't my vocation."

"What do you mean by vocation?"

Then, suddenly, all hell broke loose. Her question was interrupted by a massive crash in the trees, and Uncle Ronnie was immediately spinning on one knee, weapon drawn. The forest was dense. They could feel something crashing through the brush, but it was too high up in the air for their sensibilities.

Rakesh came round a tree yelling, "Run away! Run away! It's a freaking monster. Sasquatch himself!"

Uncle Ronnie lowered his weapon and stood up, realizing what was about.

"You idiot," he said to his lifelong blood brother.

"Moose!" Uncle Rakesh grunted between breaths.

"Let's hope it doesn't come back looking for your Boston beans," Ronnie said calmly.

"I can't believe that was a real animal! It was sooooo huge!" cried Sarah.

"Bull moose, I reckon," said Uncle Jack walking up to the trio, drinking a cup of coffee.

"What'd I miss?" asked Sophie, coming out of her tent.

"Oh, nothing, Sophie," her dad replied. "Sasquatch or a bull moose came crashing through our camp. I almost died, but what concern is it to you if your dear olde father departed before his time?"

"Hey, where's my father?" asked Sarah.

"Spread out, everyone. Search outwards from here, but don't go more than one hundred feet. Return here immediately, when done," commanded Uncle Ronnie.

Each person took a direction and headed straight out from the camp in various directions, roughly covering the four points of the compass.

One minute later Sophie cried out, "I've got him!"

The whole team converged on her voice to find O'Malley sitting Indian-style on a rock, smiling.

"Didn't you think to come check on me, Sean? I could've been dead," Rakesh whimpered dramatically.

"I would've known you were dead by the way you claimed to be chased by Sasquatch. Reminds me of another time, when we got chased by someone a heck of a lot more real, you buffoon!" crowed O'Malley laughing so hard he almost fell off his pedestal.

"What are you doing over here, Dad?" asked his daughter.

"I was praying a Rosary when I was rudely interrupted by a bull moose and Uncle Rakesh."

"Ugh..." Sarah grunted, then turned and walked away.

# 6
# FATHER JACK

Camp was set up easily and with minimal discussion, each being well acquainted with their own setups, albeit with varying philosophies on gear. Father Jack Martin was easily the most maniacal about being "ultralight," claiming his base weight was only nine pounds, not including his food, fuel, water, and essentials for conducting Catholic Mass.

He informed the team while they were setting up, "Hey, everyone, if you want to join me for Mass tomorrow morning, I'll be saying it at dawn, which I think will be around six a.m.. It might still be dark then because of these hills; we'll play it by ear."

Sophie replied, "Uh, er, don't wait for me, I might need my beauty sleep."

"No worries, everyone. There is no obligation."

Sarah thought, *What business is it of the Church to set obligations for us, anyway? Mass on Sundays. Confession. Ugh!*

Father Jack Martin had joined the Army right out of college but had not gone into the officer candidate school, instead preferring to join the enlisted ranks like his pap and grandpap before him. Serving in the military was an "honor and a privilege that came with being citizens of these here United States," according to his grandpap. So, even though he was the first in his family to go to college, there was a strong expectation he serve in the Army, regardless.

He didn't mind. He wasn't sure what he was meant to do anyway, and setting up for the Army, along with his college buddies, took some of the pressure off deciding. It also gave him time to see if his Catholic questionings, which had begun during college, would wear off, because he wasn't sure how he was ever going to explain converting to his family back in Wytheville, Virginia.

Nevertheless, convert he did, and not only did he convert, he also became a priest of The Society of Jesus, partly because of Jesuits who were stationed at the Neuman Center at his college, whose example of faith he could not shake during his tour in the Army.

Of course, all of this was enabled by his goofball friends, who also happened to be Catholic. During that time, Rakesh, whose family was from Southwestern India, was a cradle Catholic which was highly unusual for an Indian. Ronnie Gardner was also raised in the Faith, but his parents were divorced, and he had not been in the habit of going to Mass when they first met. However, Sean O'Malley was a cradle Catholic and rigorous about adhering to the strictures of the Faith, albeit with the limited understanding of a college kid.

Being surrounded by these three "weird Catholics" made it nearly impossible for Jack to miss some of the differences between his version of Christianity and theirs. More importantly, he noticed their joy and interest in serving others seemed imbued in their personas.

Serving in the Army seemed natural to them, especially Ronnie Gardner, who claimed it as his chosen profession early on in college. During his tour in Iraq, Uncle Jack reached out to the Military Chaplain to discuss his questions about the faith and his possible vocation to the priesthood. Having been raised in the Baptist tradition, he'd had many concerns, all of which had been answered the more he delved into the history of Christianity, which took him to the writings of Church Fathers like Irenaeus, Polycarp, and Clement of Rome. He became especially fond of St. Athanasius, a diminutive monk and Doctor of the Church from the Egyptian desert, who took on the Arian heresy at great personal expense.

His decision was made one night in Iraq when Sean O'Malley happened upon him. They had both been in some tough action and had reconciled themselves to being as good as dead.

Then Sean asked, "Jack, you're the most devout guy I know. What's keeping you from joining the Church?"

"I don't want to disappoint my pap and grandpap and all my kin back in Virginia, is all."

"OK, so you don't have any squabbles with the teachings of the Catholic Church?"

"Nope. I used to think you yahoos worshipped Mary, the Pope was the anti-Christ, and that you didn't believe in the Bible, but that was a bunch of hogwash that I now know ain't true," replied Jack in his most beautiful Southern drawl.

"Is the cost of your family being mad at you worth not partaking in the Sacrament of the Eucharist?" asked Sean.

"Think about it from my end, O'Malley. I love my folks. And my grandpap and I are really close. I don't want them to disown me. I love them! I miss them like crazy."

"Yeah, I get it. But what if they became Catholic too?" O'Malley wondered aloud.

"Man, that would be awesome, especially with me bein' a priest and all!"

"Hold it! What'd you say?" yelled O'Malley.

"Woops," Jack replied with a wink and a grin.

# 7

# SARAH EXPLAINS

The sun set quickly on their camp and the cold came on fast reminding them they would have to provide for their own survival. They were able to get a fire going, and the men turned in early leaving the girls to themselves with some hot coals to keep them warm.

Sophie glanced at Sarah, then poked at the fire with a long stick. "How's it going with your dad?"

"Good. I guess."

"You sure? You didn't seem happy with him after the moose."

"Yeah, well, why does he have to pray a Rosary every day?"

"That makes you mad?"

"Maybe. Not really. I just don't get it." Sarah looked up at the sky hoping to see some stars. "Mom has only been dead just over a year, and he seems happy."

"So, you're mad that your dad is happy?"

"Well... Like, I guess so."

"Come on, Sarah, talk to me."

"OK, I'm mad. I'm really, really angry. I don't get it. My mom was only sixty and now she's gone. Just like that. No more. Gone! It's not fair!"

After a long while, Sophie responded, "Yeah, it isn't fair. Your mom was awesome. She was my hero. So positive. And, beautiful, too!"

"My dad just moves on. How can he do that?"

"Maybe it is because he's got faith she is in Heaven."

"Yeah, what's that?" grumbles Sarah.

"What do you mean?"

"What is faith? What is Heaven? Why did my mom have to die so young?" Sarah sobbed.

Sophie leaned in, wrapped Sarah in her quilt, and held her close.

The next morning, while Father Jack prepped for Mass, Ronnie approached. "Hey Jack, did you hear the girls last night?"

"Yep."

"What'd ya think?"

"That girl sure loves her mother. This'll be a stern test, but she's made of solid stuff."

"Indeed. Indeed." Ronnie sighed. "Not sure if there is anything we can do."

"Let's dedicate this Mass to Sarah's faith."

"Roger that."

The two buddies celebrated the liturgy together, dedicating their prayers accordingly. Sarah approached them when they were finished.

"Have you guys seen my dad?"

"I heard him a while ago. He seemed to be going over to that rock he favored last night," replied Father Jack.

Sure enough Sarah found her father praying a Rosary. He stopped when she approached.

"Hola, Sarita. Would you like to join me as I finish this Rosary? Today I'm contemplating the Sorrowful Mysteries." Her father seemed like he had been awake for hours.

"What do you get out of saying a Rosary? Why do you waste your time?"

"I started praying the Rosary regularly after your mom died. I made a pledge to God I would say the Holy Rosary every day for one year in hopes your mom would avoid or be released from purgatory and be in Heaven with the Lord."

"It's been more than a year."

"Well, now it's a habit, and I love it. Once I start, I get in the zone and you'd be amazed at how relaxing it is. Most of the time I don't want it to end."

"Purgatory. Seems like a load of bull to me."

"I thought the same when I was your age," he replied getting up off the rock.

"Aren't you going to finish your Rosary?"

"I'll finish it on the trail. I think you could use some of my world-famous trail coffee. You seem grumpy."

"Yeah, well, I don't know why you're so happy all the time."

"I used to cry every day. Now it's more random. Your mother is in my thoughts and prayers constantly. So are you."

"Yeah, well, I wouldn't waste your time on me."

O'Malley tried to give Sarah a hug, but she shook him off violently and skulked back to the camp, noticing the sky was brightening, but it still looked awful dark toward the west, perhaps due to storm clouds, though it was still too early to tell.

# 8

# PRAYERS UPON HIGH

Sarah had to admit to herself that 'trail coffee' was one of her favorite traditions going back to when she was little girl backpacking with her father who taught her to savor black coffee.

"I'll make the coffee, Pops. You make it too weak."

"OK, Sarita. You are the boss! Plus, I love your coffee. How 'bout I cook up some sausage and oatmeal for everyone?"

It had been a while since they had all backpacked together, but it didn't take long to recall the traditions that had been established going back to 1979 when the four men had met as college students in Virginia.

"Anyone want some of these Pop-tarts?" asked Rakesh, with a chuckle, knowing everyone thought it preposterous he brought such things on a backpacking trip.

"I'll take one, as long as it's not broken. It'll hit the spot along with Sarah's coffee!" Jack cheered while packing up his gear, knowing the chances of getting an unbroken Pop-tart were negligible.

The team consumed their breakfast and struck camp efficiently wanting to get a jump on the day's hiking to allow time to summit one of the tall peaks to the east. It was a cold morning, and everyone looked forward to getting a move on to warm up. They ascended past the treeline after two hours of steady hiking.

O'Malley and Sarah breathed in the fresh morning air, Sarah sighing at the serenity of the quiet morning. The sky to the east was clear as a bell. They hoped to be on the summit of Hallet Peak before noon, as this was a mountain they had climbed together with her mother Maggie, well before Sean had gotten into politics.

Walking along in silence was more than Uncle Rakesh could abide, so he asked the group an important question. "Hey, Jack, did you see that horse manure back there? It looks pretty fresh, no?"

"Uh, yup."

"How much would it take for you eat some of it?"

Jack cast him a disgusted look. "What the heck! Are you serious?"

"Completely!" yelled Rakesh.

"Daddy, stop!" cried Sophie.

"Why, Sophie? Do you want first dibs on the horsey pie?" her dad asked, trying to be as serious as possible while hiding his face so she couldn't see him laughing.

"If you'll give me $50,000, I'll take a bite," she replied.

"What?! You wouldn't! Would you?" her Daddy asked.

Sarah waved her hand in the air. "I'll eat two bites for $25,000."

Rakesh laughed. "Hey, that's a good deal compared to Sophie, the capitalist!"

"I've eaten horse crap," Father Jack added without emotion.

Sophie turned and looked at Father Jack. "Wait! Hold it. You're not serious?"

"I'm not proud of it," added the good Padre.

Sarah laughed. "You've got to tell us the story!"

"No, you don't. I forbid it!" yelled Uncle Sean.

"Free country, Mr. ex-President. Go ahead and tell 'em, Jack!" chuckled Uncle Ronnie, trying to stir the pot.

Uncle Jack refused to tell the story in deference to his friend's request. And so, the debate over how much money it would take to eat some horse manure went unanswered, although it appeared Father Jack ate some without compensation back in the day.

Eventually, they came within view of the high peaks of the Continental Divide, first Taylor Peak, then Otis, and eventually Hallet at 12,720 feet above sea level. They made steady progress across the high plateau, angling eastward towards the crest of these mountains that formed the western side of an amazing valley bordered on the east by the Long's Peak massif.

Climbing Hallet Peak was not technically challenging, as the approach from the west was more gradual than the nearly vertical eastern face. Rock scrambling was the order of the day, and it was only a matter of time before the group was on the summit looking eastward and down to Bear Lake.

Upon reaching the summit, Sean asked everyone for a moment of silence in honor of his dear, departed Maggie, then blessed himself with the sign of the cross and said this prayer:

"In the name of the Father, the Son, and the Holy Spirit.

"Dear Lord,

"On this day, at this time, it is good we find ourselves here in your glorious presence.

"In these mountains, where Sarah and I were here with your daughter Maggie many years ago. At that time, I prayed to you in thanks for your many blessings, especially Maggie, who became my wife, which enabled us to become father and mother to Sarah, our most precious gift.

"This was our true vocation – husband, wife, father, and mother! I thanked you then, and now I thank you again today for the blessing of my time with this wonderful, amazing woman, who you called home according to your own perfect will.

"Today I pray Maggie is with you in paradise.

"Today I pray she is also with her parents, my parents, and her sister, Peggy.

"Today I pray also for faith, courage, and understanding for myself and my dear daughter, Sarah. It is not easy to fathom why our Maggie was taken so young, but we trust in your goodness and mercy.

"I also wish to pray for your blessing upon my friends, and my brothers, Jack, Rakesh and Ronnie, and wonderful Sophie, who join us here today in the glory of your creation.

"Finally, I ask that I be made worthy of the promises of your beatitudes, for I do not wish for a long life but instead desire that I should be reunited with my dear Maggie according to your plan and not mine.

"Amen."

After completing his prayer all joined in unison exclaiming, "Amen!" Sarah noticed Uncle Ronnie had tears in his eyes along with her father.

By this time the sun was high in the sky, and all looked for a good sitting rock to enjoy lunch.

Then Sarah asked Uncle Jack, "My dad keeps praying for my mom to be in Heaven. What's up with that? How can this do any good?"

"Let me make sure I am answering the right question. Are you asking me, "What good is prayer?" Or are you asking me, "Where else could your mom be besides Heaven?"

"Yes," she replied.

"Got it. Let me take on the second question first. There are three possible destinations for a soul upon death. One is Heaven. One is Hell. And the third option is Purgatory. I assume you are wondering about Purgatory, right?"

"Yes."

"Understood. And to be clear, no one who knows your mom has any concerns about that second option, as she loved God and desired to live according to His commandments. Therefore, to my knowledge, she did not choose to alienate herself from God by choosing herself as her own god or desiring to separate herself from God, which is why souls of humans and angels end up in hell. Thus, we trust she is either in Heaven or Purgatory.

"Let me then take on the idea of Purgatory by asking you a question, 'If you died today, would you be able to be in Heaven without sinning? In other words, are you already holy enough to be in God's presence and to be with Him without sinning for the rest of eternity?'"

"Ummm... Errrrr... I doubt it. I've been thinking some pretty angry, evil thoughts lately when it comes to God and my mother dying."

"So, then you might see the dilemma we face when we die. Our soul may be desirous of Heaven. We may truly love God deeply, but we might not be holy enough to be with Him. We may have some vestiges of sin that require atonement, and our souls may need further purification and grace.

"Remember the scripture, 'Nothing unclean will enter the presence of God in Heaven.'[3]

"This makes sense, no? Imagine coming into the presence of God. Imagine being face-to-face with the creator of all things seen and

[3] Revelation 21:27

unseen! This is serious business, no?

"When we die, we will undergo a particular, individual judgment. In Paul's letter to the Hebrews it states, 'it is appointed for men to die once, and after that comes judgment.'[4]

"So, now imagine what your dad is thinking regarding your mom. She has died. She has been judged. We cannot know the result, unless we suspect a miracle has occurred through her intercession, which requires the process of Beatification and Canonization.

"Therefore, because the Catholic Church takes very seriously the notion that nothing unclean or unworthy shall enter Heaven, and because we cannot be sure of your mother's status, it is prudent to pray on her behalf.

"Indeed, our prayers for those in Purgatory can be very helpful towards the cause for the purification of their soul and entry into Heaven.

"The great thing about all souls in Purgatory is they will eventually go to Heaven. How long the process of purification takes is not for us to know.

"Is this making any sense? Does it help you to understand why your dad prays the way he does for your mother?" asked Father Jack.

"Yes. I understand, I guess. Is this stuff in the bible?"

"Yes, it is, although the word 'purgatory' is not found in Scripture, but neither is the word 'trinity,' so don't let that trouble you. However, going back into the Old Testament, we see in Second Maccabees an example of praying and making atonement for the dead so they might be absolved of their sins.

"There are also many other passages in the New Testament that point out the process of purification and expiation of sin in language

[4] Hebrews 9:27

that is to be taken quite seriously, which the Church does.

"This is why Masses are said for the dead. In fact, we have a feast for 'All Souls' that occurs on second day of November, the day after the Feast of All Saints."

He paused a moment, and then said, "Can I make one other point about Purgatory, before we go on?"

"Sure. I never really understood Purgatory. I'm still trying to wrap my mind around the concept."

"I find as I get older, and therefore, closer to death, the notion of purgatory makes more and more sense. Why? Because I keep sinning. Of course, I go to Confession to ask forgiveness. I do penance. And then, despite my best efforts, I still sin. Hopefully, Lord willin', my sins are becoming less frequent and less hurtful to God, as I continue to aspire to holiness, but I still mess up. Thinking about it realistically, I'm glad God has a plan to make me worthy of him, if I die before I'm fully ready."

"And you think that's what my dad is worried about with my mom?" asked Sarah.

"Yes, but your dad has told me how holy and good he thought your mother was. So, I think your dad also prays on her behalf out a sense of duty and responsibility to your mom because he loves her deeply and would do anything for her. She's still alive in spirit. She might be in purgatory. So, he prays."

"Thanks, Uncle Jack. This helps me a lot. Can we talk about the prayer part later. I think we better get moving to not risk running out of sunlight on the way down."

"You got it! Anytime," he replied with a smile.

# 9

# STRANGER ON THE TRAIL

The group descended in the early afternoon with storm clouds building all around them. Sarah had looked forward to this part of the trail because it was an easy plateau called "Flattop," which was wide open to 360 degrees of scenery, but more importantly because it was where she and her mother and father had danced together in the sun when she was a little girl.

She gazed at the serene view and prayed to God that He have mercy on her mother and grant her the grace to be with Him in Heaven.

And, then she thought, *Am I praying? Yes. I'm praying!*

Suddenly she was startled to hear, "Coming through on your right!" from behind her.

She turned to see a man about her age coming fast with a full pack. She had no time to react before he blasted by her. She lost her footing momentarily, and said, "Thanks for the warning!" with full sarcasm.

He stopped, turned, looked directly into her eyes, and said, "At ease, Ma' am. I'll be in the general area all day. Smoke 'em if you got 'em!" Then he winked, smiled, turned, and continued on.

As he approached Uncle Ronnie, he had to slow down because Col. Gardner was not giving him any room on the trail to pass.

Ronnie stopped and turned to inspect the stranger.

"Army or Marines?" quizzed Gardner.

"Army," said the stranger.

"Unit?" demanded Gardner.

"Rangers. Who's asking?"

"Colonel Ronnie Gardner, U.S. Army Rangers, retired."

"Did you say Ronnie Gardner?"

"Yes."

"Woah! I've heard about you during some of my training."

"What's your name, son?" demanded Gardner.

"Hank Carson, sir."

By this time the whole group had stopped and was listening to the exchange.

"Let me introduce you to this rag-tag assembly. This is President Sean O'Malley and his daughter, Sarah, who you almost knocked over when you came rushing past. Next to her is Rakesh Shriram and his daughter Sophie, from California. And, hiking point is Father Jack Martin, from Virginia."

"Nice to meet you all. As I said, I'm Hank Carson. I grew up in California, served in the Army, and now I live back home near my mom. Sorry, I almost knocked you over, Sarah."

"You're forgiven. Where are you headed?" asked Sarah now noticing Carson's ruggedly handsome features and smiling eyes.

"Down over the hill to camp tonight. I'm doing a circuit starting from Bear Lake."

"Good luck, Hank. Perhaps our paths will cross again," said Gardner.

"I hope so," said Hank looking in Sarah's direction.

Carson continued at a pace that was far too fast for any of them to consider.

Sophie giggled. "Hey, Sarah, that guy was *good looking*! And, he had his eye on you!"

"I won't deny it!" said Sarah with a smile.

"What? Sarah's not angry anymore? Is that all it takes?"

*Maybe. Maybe...,* thought Sarah.

Then she said to the whole group, "Hey everyone, would it be okay if I hung back for a bit. I'll join you at camp. I'm just hoping I can hang out up here for a little while by myself."

"You know the camp and have it on your map, right?" asked Uncle Ronnie.

"Yup."

"Don't be too long Sarita. Seems like a storm is brewing. You know how it is up here this time of year," beckoned her dad, with mild concern.

"Yes. I won't be far behind you."

So, the group split, leaving Sarah to herself, knowing this was one of the big reasons she wanted to go on this journey.

She had spied a soft, relatively flat area just north of the trail and went to it. She spread out her thin foam pad and sat with her back to the sun facing southeast towards Long's Peak. She saw lightning hit the summit and hoped no one was up there, but the sky was clear above her, and it looked like the storm clouds were breaking apart and heading south of her location.

For a few minutes she took it all in. Then she thought, *OK, now I need to relax and let it all go. I need to empty my mind and allow myself to just be.*

So she tried and kept thinking, *Just be. Just be. Just be. Just be.*

And then she thought, *Be what?*

She tried to suppress this and went back to her mantra, *Just be. Just be. Just be. Be what?*

*Slow down.... Take your time... Just be. Just be. Just be. Just be. Be what?* And then she thought, *Why God? Why is my mom dead? If you exist then why did you let this happen? She was so good! There are so many evil bastards you let live. Why her! She didn't care about herself, only me and dad and her parents and her friends and her church and her community. Why did she have to die, when all she ever wanted to do was to be a mom and a good daughter and a good friend and sister?*

*I wish I had more time with her to tell her how much I love her. Why is this taken away from me? She won't see me get married. She's going to miss everything!*

*I miss her so much. I didn't do enough for her. I didn't thank her enough. I miss her! I miss her! I miss her!*

*Please let her be in Heaven with you, Dear Lord!*

*I have to trust you now! Help me to learn how to trust you. To have faith.*

*Help me to stop being so angry!*

Then she thought, *Did I just pray again?* Then she just let everything go as the tears and sobs overtook her out on the high plateau of the Continental Divide.

Sarah arrived at camp after a time and was met by a big hug from Sophie.

Father Jack stepped forward. "Hi Sarah. I see you found us. Everything OK?"

"I prayed. I was trying to "find myself," but instead I asked God to help me. I didn't expect it, but it was good."

"God bless you, Sarah," said Uncle Ronnie.

Sarah smiled, then wandered off to set up her tent. Once it was ready, she went and found her father and asked, "How do you pray the Rosary, Dad?"

"Let's do one together, Sarah. It's the best meditation I've yet to come across, plus it's a prayer, too, and it helps me understand the Gospels. Today we're doing the Glorious Mysteries."

When they were finished, they returned to camp and were met by an excellent fire and the smell of fresh coffee brewing.

"You know, I think I saw where that young man is camping," exclaimed Uncle Rakesh.

"Really? We should ask him to come up here to have some dinner with us!" cheered Sophie, winking at Sarah.

"I'll go ask him," said Sarah, to everyone's astonishment.

It took her about five minutes to reach his camp. As she got close, she called out, "Hi, Hank, it's Sarah coming into your camp."

"Come on in! I'm just getting ready to boil some water to heat up some of this freeze-dried stuff. I'd offer you some, but I only brought enough for myself. I do have some extra electrolyte sweet water I just made up."

"No, thanks. How about you come over to our camp. We've got a fire going and were just getting ready to cook up some dinner. You'll be surprised by what my Uncle Rakesh has in store for us. He always says, "When I go camping, I eat like a king!" And he does, and so do we all. It's tradition."

"Are you sure? I don't want to intrude, plus you probably don't have enough."

"You'd be surprised. Let's go!"

As they started back up the trail, Hank asked Sarah, "Where are you from?"

"I'm from Virginia, but now I live in California, near Silicon Valley."

"Really? I live in California, too, but I'm east of you. Mom and I could never afford living in Silicon Valley."

"I understand. I can't afford to live there, either. I'm just doing it for the experience. I'm living paycheck to paycheck, basically. You mentioned your mom. What about your dad?"

"My dad left us when I was a little kid. I don't remember him. Ever since, it's just been me and Ma, aside from when I was in the Army and then college."

"Hmmm. I kind of understand. Now, it's just me and my dad."

"Yeah, I read the news about your mom. She was a *real* First Lady. True class. Sorry about that."

"Thanks. Looks like we're here."

Uncle Rakesh greeted them with a grin and an outstretched hand. He shook Hank's hand vigorously while looking him square in the eye. "Howdy, Hank. Have a seat on this log. Can I get you a hot dog?"

"Sure! I'd love one!"

Dinner was simple and the conversation flowed easily, with Sophie keeping a keen eye on Hank to ensure he felt comfortable.

After a while she asked, "Why are you hiking up here alone, Hank?"

"Good question. I love the mountains. None of my friends like backpacking. Hiking, yes. Outdoor stuff, yes. Backpacking, not so much. Plus, I figured it would be good to be alone and reboot.

"I wasn't sure what I wanted to do after I got out of the Army. I joined a small construction company and have been learning the trade. I think I love it but have been wondering if it's right for me. So, I guess I came up here partly to think but mostly to see this great Rocky Mountain National Park."

O'Malley said, "I recall when I got out of the Army, I did the same, albeit I was in the Blue Ridge. When I got home, my dad asked me, 'So, Sean, what'd you learn up on top of that thar Blue Ridge?'

"I hate to say it, but I didn't learn much. I learned I needed a job. I learned I liked hiking. I learned I didn't know much about praying. But mostly I learned I couldn't get my mind off of this pretty young lass named Maggie. I knew I loved her then and figured I'd have to get myself squared away so I could ask her to be my wife.

"Actually, I guess what I learned was when I thought about Maggie I was happy. When I thought about other things, I kept coming back to her."

Father Jack chimed in. "You know Sean, that's a pretty good way of describing "discernment" in the Ignatian way of thinking."

Hank asked, "What do you mean by Ignatian way?"

"Ah... I'm a Jesuit Priest, or more correctly, I am a priest of the Roman Catholic Church who is a member of a priestly order called the Society of Jesus, which was founded by Saint Ignatius of Loyola back in the mid 1500s. Ignatius was a soldier who was injured in battle. While recovering, he discovered a way of discerning his true vocation by imagining himself to be like a saint versus being a soldier. Over time he realized he was much more energized and happier imagining himself as a priest or holy person and thought, 'Why don't I do that instead?' So, he did."

"Very interesting. How did you all come to know each other?" Hank asked looking in Ronnie's direction.

"Ah. Now that is a good question. Sean, why don't you give him the short version."

"Hank, I've known these three guys since we were eighteen years old. After forty-seven years there isn't much we don't know about each other. We met at college. We became brothers during a backpacking trip in Shenandoah National Park during our first fall break.

"I met Rakesh and Ronnie because we all went to Mass

together. Jack was my roommate, although he wasn't Catholic at the time.

"I suggested we go to the mountains because it turned out we were all big fans of the TV show *Bonanza* from back in the 1960s. In fact, we cowboy camped, meaning we had no tent. That wouldn't have been so bad, but our sleeping bags were incapable of providing any warmth. We were dumber than the rocks we were sleeping on!

"I'm not proud of it but the camping trip included four cases of Schlitz beer, Swisher Sweet cigars, mooning an elderly Japanese couple, lying to British ladies about our mountaineering skills and pretending to be injured next to Skyline drive so we could pull off our best Monty Python and the Holy Grail impressions. In other words, we were idiots." It was clear that O'Malley was enjoying himself immensely as he took a deep draw from his trusty Peterson pipe.

"Monty Python?" Hank looked confused.

"And the Holy Grail!" Jack added.

"I highly recommend it. One of the greatest movies of all time!" Rakesh chimed in.

"I was lying next to Skyline Drive pretending to be injured. Rakesh hid behind a stone wall. Jack and Ronnie were back down at the base of the mountains because I decided injuns would go straight up the mountain without using a trail. Rakesh was with me because... well that is still a mystery.

"Then this *elderly* couple pulled over in their convertible Ford mustang to check on me. They must've been at least thirty-five. Haha! The woman asked me if I was OK, as I'm writhing around faking like I was in serious pain. Then Rakesh jumps up on the stone wall howling like a banshee and bends over pulling down his pants to expose his 'full moon' yelling 'Run Away! Run Away! It was an African Swallow!'

"I hop up, clearly not injured, and look directly at the lady and say, 'Wise guy, eh! Woob! Woob! Woop! Woop! Woop!' doing my best impression of *Curly* from the *Three Stooges*. The look on the lady's face... I still see it today. She was in shock and looked at me with equal parts pity and humor. I think the man was laughing, but we didn't stay around long enough to find out.

"The next thing I know we jumped off the wall and ran down the mountain howling like wolves." O'Malley stopped fully satisfied he'd set the right impression with Hank.

"*Soitanly*!" Hank replied, perfectly imitating Curly, himself!

"Hooohah!" Ronnie grunted.

"And you all are proud of this because?" Sophie asked incredulously hoping to poke the bear.

"Proud? Maybe. Lucky! Amen! I found I had three brothers during that trip and haven't looked back since," O'Malley replied.

"Yeah, and I found out I had a better fake Irish accent then Sean, himself! Plus, I was good at mooning, which was definitely an asset, if you know what I mean," Rakesh added laughing using his best Irish brogue.

"It's also when we all decided to join the Army together after we graduated." Jack added.

"You guys sound like me and my buddies back in the day. Best thing that ever happened to me was joining the Army, but I knew it wasn't for me long-term. I kept imagining being back home near my mom, hopefully making some good money," said Hank.

"So, money is your main objective?" quizzed Sophie.

"Not really. I want to be an expert at something, hopefully building houses. Mom and I didn't have much while I was growing up. So, yeah, I wouldn't mind having a reliable truck, too. I could also use a good sleeping bag. The one I brought up here is from when I was a kid. I didn't realize it was going to be so danged cold in September.

Speaking of September, I better get back to my camp and get some sleep. Thanks for the grub, Mr. Shriram. I'm much obliged. I plan to get an early start, but maybe I'll stop by before I head out tomorrow, if that's OK?" he said looking over at Sarah.

Father Jack replied, "Hank, I'll be saying Mass at about six a.m. You're welcome to join me."

Hank replied, "Thanks, Father, but I haven't been going to Mass for a while. Kind of lost touch while I was in the service."

Father Jack replied, "No worries. You're still welcome to join me. It's the great prayer and sacrifice of the Church. I'll be happy to show you the ropes."

"Sounds good. I'll bring my coffee pot and show you all how to make some good trail coffee if you're open to it." He stood headed down the trail in the dark with his headlamp lighting the way. Everyone got up to go to their tents, with Sophie following Sarah closely.

"Now that's a real man, Sarah. What do you think?"

"Uh huh," she mumbled with a smile and a giggle.

"You like him?"

"Maybe. I don't know yet."

# 10

# FALCON EMERGENCY

Sarah was awakened from a deep sleep to the sound of Uncle Ronnie's commanding voice.

"Falcon emergency! Falcon emergency! Come in Command Center. Over."

She shot up immediately but was completely disoriented. Realizing something was seriously wrong, she exited her tent to see Uncle Ronnie leaning into her father's tent on his satellite phone.

"What's wrong?" she cried as she ran over in distress.

"I don't know, yet. Your dad is having a medical emergency."

"Falcon, this is Command Center. Advise, regarding your emergency. Over."

"This is Gardner. Falcon is having a medical emergency. He's vomited, incoherent, and apparently fell. I'm evaluating for other injuries. Over."

By this time everyone was up and had O'Malley's tent surrounded. Sophie said, "I'm going to get Hank. We might need his help." She immediately headed down the trail without waiting for a response.

"Falcon. Standby. Over," replied the Secret Service's command center.

"What happened?" asked Sarah.

"I heard your father fall. When I came to his tent, I found him incoherent. Then he vomited. He may have broken his arm in the fall, or it could be a bad sprain."

Sophie returned with Hank, who said, "Hey, Colonel Gardner, could I get in there and have a look? I trained as a medic."

Hank took over, while Uncle Ronnie communicated with the command center.

"I need a straight, clean branch about two feet long," demanded Hank.

He took O'Malley's vitals and called them out to Col. Gardner. "His speech is garbled. Pulse rate, one-hundred fifteen. Breathing is rapid and shallow. I suspect he is having a stroke."

He then used the branch as a splint to immobilize O'Malley's left arm. Rakesh and Jack went to look for aspirin.

"This is Command we have picked up your emergency signal and know your location coordinates. Prepare Falcon for helicopter extract. Will confirm ETA. Over."

"Roger that. Good copy. Falcon may have a broken left arm. Symptoms appear to be a stroke. Please advise best course of treatment asap. Over."

Hank took control of President O'Malley, cleaning the vomit, raising his head slightly, splinting his arm, and wrapping him in his sleeping bag. Rakesh offered aspirin, but Hank declined saying it might make things worse. O'Malley had lost consciousness, anyway. The command center informed Gardner the helicopter would be inbound to their location within two hours. Together the men took O'Malley to a clearing near their camp to prepare him for extract. Then suddenly the wind came up and it began to hail.

"Oh no! How can they get him in this storm? What are we going to do?" cried Sarah.

Hank turned to Rakesh and Jack. "Gather firewood and make a fire."

"Hang in there, Sarah. I've seen evacs in worse conditions. We're not too high. Plus, the conditions might change by the time they get here," comforted Hank.

"What else can we do? Is it really a stroke?"

"I think so but can't be sure. I'm going to turn him on his side, away from the hurt arm and keep his head elevated. Let's watch his breathing and take care if he vomits again."

"Falcon, this is Command. Over."

"Good copy. Over."

"Helo in-bound to your pos. ETA 10 mikes. Over."

"Good, copy. Falcon ready for extract. Be advised, Falcon is unconscious. Over."

"Everyone, gather round. OK, a National Guard helo will be here in 10 minutes. Sarah, you and I will go with your father. Everyone else will have to make their way back to the trailhead. We will keep you informed via text regarding details and see you at the hospital when you're able. I assume we'll be going to Boulder but will confirm and let you know. I know you won't get any of our messages until you can get a good signal back at the trailhead," advised Ronnie.

"Understood, Colonel. I'll take your gear down with me. We'll divide the rest amongst us and meet you wherever you determine ASAP," said Hank.

Sarah looked at Hank in astonishment, and then she heard the faint sounds of a helicopter.

Meanwhile, Father Jack prepared to administer the Sacrament of the Anointing of the Sick and asked all to gather around O'Malley to pray with him.

# 11

# WHIRLWIND

It was a nightmare. A whirlwind. Yet it was real. Sarah and Uncle Ronnie were now awaiting word in the hospital waiting area. Where the rest of the crew was could only be imagined. They'd had no time for planning, coordination, or discussing contingencies. Speed was the order of the day, and that is what the National Guard and Secret Service delivered.

A stroke seemed likely but they were waiting for this to be confirmed with a CT scan. *Would he die? Would he have permanent impairment?* Both seemed like real possibilities.

The Secret Service had mobilized a response team concurrent with the National Guard rescue. They were now assembled at the hospital. The President had also been informed.

Meanwhile, Sarah and Uncle Ronnie sat, prayed, and waited.

"I feel so guilty. This is all my fault. The altitude. The hiking. It was too much," lamented Sarah.

"I feel the same. I should have made him take a physical exam beforehand. I'm going through my checklist and can't believe I missed this," groaned Uncle Ronnie. Just then, the surgeon arrived looking grim.

"OK, we've stabilized him. The CT scan revealed a hemorrhagic stroke, meaning blood flow was blocked to a portion of his brain. I was able to remove the clot with a stent retriever. It was a large clot. We're preparing him for an MRI angiography exam to assess the full extent. We also want to do a deeper examination to ascertain the cause of the blood clot.

"Right now he is resting and sedated. We can't do much more until we get the results of the MRI. It is good you got him here as quickly as you did, especially considering you were deep in the mountains when this occurred," said Dr. Mark Stevens, head of Neurosurgery at the University of Colorado Medical Center.

"What is your prognosis, Doctor?" asked Col. Gardner

"It is too early to tell, Colonel. This is a critical time, and we have two objectives: find the cause of the stroke and limit the damage done."

"Can we see him?" asked Sarah.

"Yes, but please be quiet. Just a few minutes. Then I suggest you get some rest. You've had a long night."

The head of the Secret Service detail came into the waiting room and provided an update on the security measures put in place. He informed them things were ramping up rapidly as the press had already been informed of the situation, with news crews beginning to assemble in the parking lot.

Uncle Ronnie and Sarah went to O'Malley's room and shared words of encouragement with him along with a prayer. Then they began to discuss their friends, who were still in the mountains.

"Uncle Ronnie, how long do you think it will take them to get to the trailhead?" asked Sarah.

"I figure they have eight to ten hours of steady hiking. I doubt they went back to sleep and likely struck camp immediately after our departure. That would put them at the trailhead around noon to two p.m.. They'll have a two- to three-hour drive to get here, depending on traffic. I'll text them and let them know where we are."

"OK. What should we do?"

"Let's find a hotel and set up our base of operations. We can get cleaned up and get some food. Then we'll come back here ASAP."

As they exited the hospital, they were met by many reporters wanting to know the condition of the former U.S. President.

Uncle Ronnie took command. "President O'Malley is in stable condition under the expert care of this university hospital's medical staff. The nature and extent of his injuries is still being assessed. Thus far, he has been treated for a broken forearm and hemorrhagic stroke. We ask for your prayers as we hope for a complete recovery."

"Was it true President O'Malley was out in the mountains when this happened?" yelled a reporter.

"Yes. And we would like to thank the Secret Service and Colorado National Guard, who responded quickly and expertly to extract us and bring us to this hospital," responded Gardner.

"How did he break his arm?" yelled the same reporter.

"You will be provided with a full report in due course. We've had a long night and request your consideration as we see to the care of my dear friend. That will be all."

With a nod to the crowd, they got in a Secret Service car and went to the hotel.

Once back at the hospital, they learned the extent of damage to O'Malley's brain was significant. Just as concerning, the source of the blood clot appeared to be a tumor inside his heart, which meant another surgery to treat the heart and remove the tumor. Recovery would be long and difficult, with no certain outcome.

Just as they were finishing with the doctor, they were met by the head of President O'Malley's Secret Service detail.

"I've been informed the President of Russia is on his way to the hospital. He was in Mexico City for a G8 meeting, heard about the President, and immediately determined he will come to lend support. His visit, of course, will cause a significant increase in security and complicate things. A team is coming in from D.C., and the Denver office is now taking charge," explained the head of President O'Malley's secret service team.

"Damn. I'm surprised by this, but it makes sense. I don't think there would be much that could stop President Petrov, knowing his good friend is in trouble," replied Gardner.

"President Petrov and Daddy are good friends?" asked Sarah with much surprise.

"You don't know the half of it, girl dear, but you will soon enough," replied Uncle Ronnie.

Just then, they received a call from Uncle Rakesh. They were inbound from the mountains and looking for advice regarding what to do next. Uncle Ronnie directed them to the hotel and suggested they come to the hospital after they got themselves cleaned up and fed.

Upon arrival at the hospital, Uncle Rakesh said, "It has been hell not knowing how he is doing. Give us the latest update, and please don't spare any details."

So, Ronnie and Sarah gave them a full download. Interestingly, Hank was still with them. After a time, he approached Sarah.

"I'm so sorry about your dad. Please let me know if there is anything I can do."

Sarah placed a hand on his shoulder. "Hank, I can't thank you enough. The doctors said your splint was as good as they could've done, and you did all the right things. How you were able to do it so calmly is beyond me. I was a total wreck."

"That's to be expected. He's your dad. Plus, I've had plenty of experience during my time with the Rangers. I'm just glad the Guard was able to get him out as they did."

"I don't know what I'll do if I lose him." She sighed and looked down at the floor.

"Don't go there, Sarah. Pray! Stay positive. Talk to your dad. He'll hear you. I'm sure you and Col. Gardner will make all the right decisions. He's in good hands here," replied Hank, moving closer and putting his arm around Sarah's shoulder.

Looking up, she saw his eyes full of concern and kindness. "I'm sorry we messed up your hike."

"Hmmm. Yeah, my hike did get kind of messed up, but I got to meet you, didn't I?"

"Will I see you again?" she asked, noticing he hadn't stopped holding her.

"I hope so, but until then I'm going to skedaddle because you've got a lot to attend to, with the best support in the world. I'll just be in the way. One day soon, you'll look up and see me, and until that day, 'May God hold you in the palm of his hand.'" And with that he let her go, turned, and left the hospital.

Then Sophie came up to her. "Sarah, you would not have believed what Hank did. He took charge once you and Uncle Ronnie left. The amount of gear he carried down the mountain was amazing. He's incredibly strong, but what I can't get over was how positive he was. It was like he was carrying us all down the mountain himself."

"Hank Carson...," breathed Sarah, absentmindedly looking out into space.

Uncle Ronnie arrived and waved a hand at them. "Hey, girls, let's gather up and go back to the hotel for some dinner. It is going to be a long night."

# 12

# HIS FRIEND, THE ARCHBISHOP

When they returned to the hospital, they found a priest sitting on a chair in the waiting area near the president's room.

Seeing them enter, he stood. "Good evening. I'm Archbishop Joseph O'Rourke of the Diocese of Denver. I heard the news about your father and my good friend. I came as soon as I could."

Sarah responded for the group. "Thank you for coming, Bishop. It is an honor that you are here. How do you know my father?"

"You must be Sarah. Your mother and father told me about you long before you were born. That might sound odd, but I will explain soon enough. Would you all have time for a wee bit of a story? If so, would it also be possible for us to get some tea and biscuits?"

The group proceeded to the cafeteria and gathered around a table.

"Ah, so, I came to know your father when he was working here in Denver. I was a young priest, and he and Maggie were then married but a few years. One day I happened to see him at daily Mass and introduced myself.

"He told me he was from Virginia; had served in the Army and started his own construction business here in Denver, because he liked the Rocky Mountains. He also said he was praying for himself and his wife because they were struggling to have a baby.

"I suggested he and Maggie visit me so I could administer a blessing and pray together with them, and so we did.

"Over the years your father and I became good friends. He grew in faith and maturity. Then one day I needed his help.

"You see, I saw your father not only as my parishioner but also as a good friend who I could confide in. I would often seek his counsel because he came at things differently, especially differently than priests do.

"There was a time when I sought his advice because I was struggling with how to handle a very concerning situation. A young man had come to me telling me he was sexually abused by a priest in my parish. The bishop wanted to follow the established, slow, methodical protocol for handling this, but there was something troubling about this priest, and my instincts told me to go much faster.

"So, I went to see your father. His response was not what I expected, and let's remember this was over thirty years ago. We didn't know as much about this diabolical situation as we do now.

"Your father asked me two questions. First, 'Do you know any reason why this young man would seek to harm this priest?' I said no. He seems genuine and credible. Second, he asked, 'Have you ever seen a bad situation become better by waiting?' Again, I said no.

"Then, he said, 'Let's go.' I was stunned, but, together, we went to this priest's residence. Along the way he told me of a similar situation he ran into during his time in the Army. He suggested we follow his protocol and so I obliged, knowing my superior would be furious, and it could cost me dearly.

"We arrived at this priest's house at about 1am. It took a while for him to answer the door, and when he did, we simply walked in and had him sit down. Your father took control sitting on a stool directly in front of the priest only inches away from him.

"He first asked him, 'Do you
believe God exists?'

'Yes.' The priest's eyes were darting back and forth between me and Sean. They indicated a mix of confusion, anger and terror.

'Do you fear God?' he asked pushing closer still to the priest.

'Yes.'

'Why?' Sean's face was only inches away from the priest.

'Because he is all powerful, all knowing and all good.'

'Then how are you going to handle the fact that you molested a young man of your parish?', Sean hissed.

The priest hesitated.

Your father's intensity increased. I would say at this point his presence was quite menacing.

'Do you fear The Lord?' he shouted.

But the priest was silent. Then your father grabbed him by the shoulders and pushed his chair backwards landing on top of the priest who was now pinned beneath him on the floor.

Then your father said, 'I care as much about your soul as I do the young man you molested. I fear God. I fear if you die tonight you will go to Hell. You have a choice to make, right here, right now. Make it!', he whispered into his ear.

I didn't know it at the time, but your father had grabbed the man's hand and was pressing on a nerve that was producing unbearable pain.

The priest was now crying not so much from the pain as from the guilt. He looked up at me, and I simply stared back at him with pity. He had no idea who this person was kneeling on his chest but suffice it to say your father has a way of getting to the heart of the matter in any situation. Plus, he was big and very strong. For all this priest knew, he was an assassin sent by the Church to do its business. I kept silent.

Then the priest said, 'I need to confess my sins. I don't want to go to Hell.'

Then your father said, 'Do you confess you molested this boy?'

The priest was silent again.

Then I said, 'Father, if you hold back a mortal sin you'll surely go to Hell. You'll have chosen to alienate yourself from God for all eternity. There will be no going back after you die.'

Then I added, 'This may be your last night on earth.' I don't know where that came from, and to this day I regret lying, but your father got me stirred up into the moment and so I embellished a little and did my best to be menacing, too.

The priest then admitted to molesting the boy.

Your father pressed for more, whispering into his ear, 'Who else did you molest?

Do not hold back, or you risk perdition.'

The priest then admitted to molesting two other young men.

Then your father did something that was completely unexpected for me. He called the police. I tried to stop him, but he would hear none of it. I'll never forget what he said to me.

'Joe, now that we know this man has molested three boys we have to hand him over to the police. This is a serious crime. If you hold back now, you risk your soul and mine, too. Remember what I asked you earlier, 'Have you ever seen a bad situation get better by waiting?' Let me ask you another question, 'Have you ever seen a mortal sin get better by keeping it in the dark?'

The Bishop was furious with me! Then I said to him, 'Why

don't we discuss this with Sean O'Malley.'

The Bishop asked, 'Who is Sean O'Malley?'

To which I replied, 'He's like Jesus in the temple driving out the money changers. His zeal for justice is beyond compare. You should listen to him and follow his guidance regarding how to handle these kinds of situations. Doing otherwise risks your soul.'

From then on, our diocese was on the vanguard for how to handle priestly sexual abuse. We pushed the Vatican hard on these matters, which was necessary for the time. Regardless of all that, I was always amazed your father told that priest how he cared about his soul, too. That never left me."

Sarah then chimed in, "I never knew any of this. I find it amazing to know of your friendship with my father. You also said you knew my mother and you knew of me before I was born. How can this be?"

"Ahhhh... Your mother, Maggie, may she rest in peace. She was the perfect complement to your father. They were a match made in heaven! She was so smart, too! So, how did I know about you before you were born? Well, that is easy. Your mother asked me to say a prayer she had written, in hopes she could get pregnant.

"I still have it and have brought it with me today and give it to you for your safe keeping and edification. But, before I do, I'd like to say it with you all tonight because I think it will be helpful to the cause of your father's recovery.

"So, if you will allow, let's all pray together in Jesus' name.

"Dear Lord, tonight, I join Sarah and her friends here and also in Heaven, especially her mother, Maggie, to pray for her father, Sean O'Malley. May he be cured and recover completely according to your Holy Will.

"Thus, we remember, in a special way, his wife, Maggie, who we pray is with you in paradise and also interceding with her prayers on her beloved Sean's behalf."

He gazed at the group gathered in prayer. "Now I will recite Maggie's prayer written for me long ago in hopes it might have a positive effect on all of us, including our good friend Sean. Here goes:

> "Dear Jesus, my Lord, I pray to you that Maggie O'Malley might become a mother.
>
> "If it be your will she asks for a daughter and will name her Sarah, after the wife of our patriarch, who you allowed to become pregnant by Abraham at an advanced age.
>
> "And, if they are blessed with a boy, they shall call him John, after Sean's father and their good friend Jack Martin who were named after your Apostle, who you loved.
>
> "Dear Lord, I know I ask you much in this cause so Maggie may pursue her vocation. I know Sean and Maggie will follow your holy and perfect will and accept what comes.
>
> "But, if it is possible, I ask you allow them to become parents and in so doing become more holy and closer to you.
>
> "Please never allow them to stray from your path. Please give them the necessary grace so they may see your face and be with you forever in Heaven.

"Thus, tonight we join our prayers with Dear Maggie, in hopes our beloved Sean may fully recover trusting our Lord's Holy Will. Amen."

Then Archbishop O'Rourke handed a tattered piece of paper to Sarah saying, "I said this prayer every day for five years until you were born. I consider you a great gift not only to your mother and father but also to me. I hope you will allow me to be your friend, too."

Tears trickled down Sarah's cheeks as she accepted the prayer, and passed it to Sophie for safekeeping, worried her tears would ruin it.

# 13

# VERY IMPORTANT PERSON

The waiting continued into the next morning. Sarah arrived at the hospital by herself before dawn. Soon, she heard a commotion and noticed the Secret Service moving in her direction. Behind them was a tall, distinguished-looking man who appeared to be in his early seventies.

He approached and said, "Good morning. My name is Victor Petrov. I am a good friend of your father's. I heard he was ill and arrived as soon as I could."

"Hello, President Petrov. I am honored and surprised that you are here. Please follow me and let's go into my father's room. It will be good for him to hear your voice, even though he is still unconscious."

They went in and President Petrov said, "Hello, old friend. This is Victor. I got here as soon as I could. I know you can hear me, and I want you to fight hard. We are praying for your complete recovery. Until then, know I will abide by our covenant and watch over Sarah."

After a time, they left the room, and Sarah asked, "What did you mean by 'our covenant'? And how is it you came to consider my father as your friend?"

"Ah, dear Sarah, this is a long story, but we have time while we await your father's recovery. So, let me tell you about how I came to know your father.

"I had been president of Russia for many years when your father was elected President of the United States. It was no secret our countries had been adversaries since the end of World War II.

"I was quite surprised that he asked to meet me within his first month in office. He traveled to Moscow. I remember it like it was yesterday.

"He came to my office and walked straight up to me, and looking directly into my eyes, he asked, 'Are you an evil man?'

"I was stunned and immediately angry. I considered this amazingly disrespectful.

'Who are you to ask me this?' I demanded.

"He replied, 'I am a doorway; a guide for you, if only you would escape the evil you have succumbed to.'

"'What is this?' I asked him. 'You are my judge?'

"'Your actions judge you,' he replied. 'You sanction assassinations. You imprison meek people who disagree with you. You steal money and use it illicitly. You wage unjust wars. You do whatever you want whenever you want.'

"He continued: 'Let me ask you a question, "Do you believe in God?"'

"I replied, 'Why do you ask me this?'

"'Because I cannot trust a man who thinks of himself as God. Some men succumb to evil and become evil themselves. I need to know what kind of man you are!'

"To which I replied angrily, 'You'll find out soon enough.'

"Then he surprised me. He said, 'President Petrov, I have only one concern. I worry you will not go to Heaven when you die.'

"With that he turned and left my office and flew back to Washington, D.C.

"I was left stunned. I was angry. Very, very angry. I felt disrespected.

"I was unable to sleep that night. I kept wondering, 'Am I evil?' I also had nightmares where my dear grandmother, my Babushka, was sobbing uncontrollably. You wouldn't know this, but she was a devout Jew whose brothers and sister were killed in the Holocaust.

"A few months later, I met with your father while visiting the United Nations in New York. I arranged for a secret meeting, just the two of us, in my suite.

"I asked him, 'How would I know if I was evil?'

"He replied, 'This could be very challenging. The Devil is amazingly powerful. You can fall into a pattern of evil that can be hard to overcome. You can discern if you have succumbed to evil by evaluating your conscience. What does it tell you?'

"I said, 'Ever since I met you, I can't sleep. I wake up in the middle of the night and wonder if I am evil. My gut hurts all the time. It is telling me something. I must admit I believe in God and He would not like the things I do,' I replied.

"Then your dad asked me, 'Is there ever justification for the president of a country to violate one of God's commandments, which we can think of as the natural law?'

"I replied, 'I think yes when it is necessary for the good of his country.'

"Then Sean said, 'I think not. When we think we can justify violating God's law, the natural law imprinted into our hearts, and our conscience, then we risk making ourselves our own God. This is how we succumb to evil.'

"'But, what about our obligation to our country?' I asked while pondering his strange perspective.

"He replied, 'Is your country more important than God? You

see if you operate and lead your country as if God does not exist, this does not change God. Simply ignoring Him or reasoning His non-existence does not annihilate Him. His law still operates, and the effects are as real as His physical laws. For us, it is easy to see the effect of gravity, isn't it? Is not the effect of sin just as apparent?'

"What amazed me during this exchange, Sarah, was that your dad seemed to genuinely care about me. I was simply amazed! He was not condescending. Far from it! He simply spoke the truth, plainly, without embellishment. He was on a quest to know if he could reason with me. More than that, he wanted to save my soul!

"I was deeply embarrassed, and he sensed this.

"'Victor,' he said, 'can I tell you a story to help you understand where I am coming from?'

"I said, 'Let me pour us some vodka. It is a nice night. Let's go out on the balcony and take in the city.'

"Then he told me a story from his youth. It would be for him to tell it to you, but it involved some rough people, and he became aware he was on the wrong path when he realized how ashamed his mother and father would be of his actions. This hit me like a lightning bolt. I knew my Babushka, my father's mother, would be very disappointed in me, and this I could not bear."

"You must have loved your grandmother very much."

"More than life itself. She taught me about her Jewish faith from a very young age."

"What was her name?" Sarah asked.

"Anna. She was my rock. I knew I could not disappoint her anymore, but I didn't know how to get out of the pattern. Your father told me getting back on track took time and required him to leave his supposed friends and start over. He prayed hard and found strength in scripture and going to Mass and most especially the Eucharist, but I did not understand these words.

"Then he said another thing that struck me as odd. He said, 'The more I find myself conforming to God's laws the happier I feel. His laws make me free; not the other way around.'

"You must understand, Sarah, how incredible this sounded to me. Consider my perspective. I am the President of Russia with incredible authority. What I say goes or else. I was taught by my father to lead with ferocious power. Yet I was isolated and sullen. It never occurred to me that giving up power and following someone or something else would make me happy. I had long forgotten about happiness or joy. Then I thought, *If Sean can do this, then why not me*?

"We talked about these things deep into the night. Two presidents, but really, we were simply two men, two husbands, two fathers, who were on the way to becoming friends.

"Then one day, almost a year later, I got a call from your father. He said he wanted to talk, and we looked for an opportunity to meet privately like we had that night in New York.

"We met in Paris, which isn't a bad way to go. This time he brought a bottle of American whiskey, you call Bourbon. I now call it 'nectar of the gods,' but I cross myself after I say it because there is only one God.

"Your dad asked me, 'Victor, what is keeping you from becoming Catholic?'

"'Well, Sean,' I said, 'it could be that my grandmother was a Jew!'

"Sean replied, 'I know that, but is there something *you* are finding to be a stumbling block?'

"I have to say I was quite happy that was what he wanted to talk about instead of tariffs or stolen patents or other political matters.

"Then I asked, 'Why do Catholics pray to Mary and treat her

like she is equal to God?'

"His reply startled me. He asked, 'Imagine you are God and were considering creating the Universe. What is the one thing on your list of things to create that you would ensure did not get forgotten?'

"I immediately replied, 'Vodka! And, bourbon, too!' laughing hard as I did so.

"'I could not agree more!' he laughed. 'And, how about a mother?'

"'What are you getting at, Sean?' I asked.

"He said, 'I could be way off here theologically, but I believe one of the primary objectives incorporated into God's design of the whole universe is His desire to have a mother,' he replied.

"He, Himself, is one God and at once a unity of three persons—Father, Son, and Holy Spirit, which is a great mystery, and I have my limits in understanding it. Regardless, I accept it, and some days I feel like I'm understanding it more fully, but then on others, it seems to elude me.

"I imagine God by Himself, creating the Universe, which continues to unfold to this day, knowing I cannot come close to realizing how powerful He is, and yet in the midst of it all, He creates His own mother, and I must conclude God wanted a mother. He also got Himself a real honest to goodness father, too, in Joseph, albeit he was His foster father.

"Is it possible God created everything visible and invisible simply so he could have a mother and be part of a family? Is this not what Love would do?

"I don't know the answers to these questions. I'm out on a limb theologically, which is dangerous considering I'm really a construction worker playacting as a president.

"So, let me answer your question directly. Catholics do not

worship Mary. We only worship God. We *venerate* Mary! We think deeply about her and her role in our salvation. Likewise, we think deeply about her spouse, Joseph, who said nothing in all of Scripture, but is considered the second greatest saint next to Mary, and the patron of the Church on Earth. This Tradition reflects the deep understanding of the Church.

"'Do you remember the story about the Wedding at Cana?', he asked me.

"I do."

"Remember the exchange between Mary and Jesus when they were informed the bridal party had run out of wine?"

"Yes. She said to the head waiter, 'Do whatever he tells you.'"[5]

"Was this not all it took for Jesus to perform his first sign, turning water into wine? We Catholics imagine the relationship between a mother and son and think deeply about how holy and powerful this could be when the two people involved are God and the Queen of Heaven, namely his mom, Mary.

"We pray to saints and ask for their prayers, just like we ask living friends and family for help and prayers when we need them. We don't see their being dead on Earth as a barrier to us asking for their intercessions, because we know they are still alive in spirit, hopefully in Heaven. When we ask Mary for her intercession, it is similar to the headwaiter going to her with no wine. We hope she turns to her son on our behalf.

"'Does that help?' he asked me.

"To which I replied, 'Will you be my sponsor and be there on the Easter Vigil when I join the Catholic Church?'

"Then we drank a lot of bourbon!"

[5] John 2:5

"How come my father never told me any of this! What about your covenant?" exclaimed Sarah.

"I think I know the reason, but let's keep that for another day. Where is his doctor? I want to speak with him!" President Petrov demanded, more to his security team than to Sarah, and with that, he got up to ensure his good friend was receiving the best care.

# 14

# VISITOR IN THE LOBBY

President Petrov met with the doctors and consulted with his own personal physician and felt fully satisfied the doctors treating his friend were fully competent.

One of the Secret Service team members approached Sarah. "Ms. O'Malley, there is a young woman in the lobby asking to see you. She's insistent that she speak with you. Her name is Melissa Powell. We've run a background check on her and find no concerns. It is your call if you would like to meet her."

"I'll go to the lobby. Thanks for letting me know."

In the lobby, she saw a young woman who looked familiar, but she could not place where she had seen her. "Hi, I'm Sarah. I understand you wish to speak with me?"

"I'm Melissa Powell. I appreciate you coming to see me. I heard about your father and had to come here."

"How do you know my father?"

"I'm the woman who came up to your group in the restaurant a few days ago in Denver. I was really upset, and your dad took me aside for a private conversation."

Sarah nodded. "Now I remember. You said something about my dad hurting your feelings."

"That's right. I happened to be in the restaurant and saw your father and instantly became upset. I wasn't thinking straight and figured I'd give him a piece of my mind. Little did I know he would ask to sit with me and talk."

"What happened?" Sarah asked.

"I told him I disagreed with his position on a woman's right to choose and the actions he took to limit it during his presidency."

"That's funny. I've done the same."

"He asked me why I disagreed. I told him neither the government nor anyone else has the right to interfere with a woman's right to choose. A woman is to be in charge of what happens to her body. It is her decision to make.'

"Hmmm. I made the same argument."

"Then he asked me, 'On what authority do you base your position?' I was not sure what he meant, so I asked him to clarify.

"He replied, 'Which human authority on faith and morals are you basing your opinion and on what are they basing their determination?'

"Then I understood and replied, 'I don't go to church much. I'm a Democrat and pro-choice.'

"He seemed to challenge me. 'So, the authority you are relying on is your own intelligence, experience, and logic bolstered by others who share your opinion?' I said yes but pushed back because he seemed to be painting me into a corner. I told him the way he was saying it seemed as though he was belittling me.

"His reply was not what I expected. He said something like, 'My apologies Melissa, I do not mean to come across that way, sometimes I get frustrated. Your argument is based on what you believe is common sense, your gut instinct. This is to be respected. My position on this topic is derived from the teaching of the Catholic Church, which is my source for guidance and direction on matters of faith and morals.

Arguing against your opinion isn't going to do either of us any good."

"That made me mad, but I could tell he was genuine. So, then I asked, 'How do you know the Catholic Church has authority on this?"

"He replied, 'I've studied history, scripture and educated myself on the Catholic Church. Yet, in the end, I must have faith.'

"I asked, 'Where does your church derive its authority?'

"He replied, 'Jesus.'

"I was stuck at this point, and your dad knew it. You should also know he was smiling and trying to make me feel comfortable, which wasn't easy. He even asked if I wanted to order a drink. I asked him what he was drinking, and he said it was Scotch. So, I asked him to order me one, too. It was my first time drinking Scotch, and he taught me how he liked it, especially avoiding the big single ice cube that does no good, according to him.

"Oh, yeah. He's given me the whole Scotch tutorial. It took me a while, but I might be just starting to like it," replied Sarah while looking away trying not to think of her father's condition.

"Please don't tell him, but I hated it! Anyway, he continued to ask me questions about my religion and my church's teaching. Then he asked me, 'What is a human being?'

"I answered, 'A human is a person – man, woman, or anywhere in between.'

"He then asked, 'What is the nature of a human person?'

"I asked, 'What do you mean?'

"He asked, 'Who creates a human person?'

"I replied, 'A human person is created when a man and woman have sex and the woman becomes pregnant.'

"Then he asked, 'So, the man and woman create the person's soul, too?'

"'What do you mean?'

"I think he could sense I was genuine, but I also had the real sense your dad cared deeply about me.

"He continued, 'According to the Catholic Church, the nature of a human person, Melissa, is we are a body-soul composite. We are unique creatures bestowed with characteristics that are in the image and likeness of God. Thus, not only do we have a physical body, but we also have a soul that is joined completely to our bodies.'

"'Thus, we must then ask, who creates the soul? Is this done simply through the physical act of the man and woman? If not, then who creates it and when is it joined to the body? The Church answers this by telling us God creates each human person Himself, through the action of the man and woman and by His own direct action creating the soul and imparting it into the body. We know from science the physical process of creating a human being commences at the moment of conception, but when is this new person's soul created, Melissa?'

"Your father was looking directly into my eyes in a way I can only describe as caring. He was not arguing with me. He was calm and sure.

"I replied, 'I am not sure. I've never thought about it before.'

"He continued, 'According to the prophet Jerimiah, when the Lord called him, He said, "Before I formed you in the womb, I knew you."'[6]

"'I love the Book of Psalms in the Bible. Are you familiar with them?'

"'I said I was not.

"'He continued, 'The Psalms are great songs, or prayers of worship and praise of God. Seventy-three or so were written by King David. There are one hundred and fifty in total, and let me tell you,

[6] Jeremiah 1:5

they are mysterious and wonderful. I have been trying to muster up the courage to write one myself. We'll see if that happens.'

"Then he pulled out his phone and went to a particular Psalm.

"He said, 'Melissa, this Psalm has great meaning for me, especially regarding our nature and relationship to God. It starts:

'Lord, you have probed me
You know when I sit and when I stand
Where can I go from your spirit
From your presence where can I flee?
You formed my inmost being
You knit me in my mother's womb.
I praise you because I am wonderfully made
Your eyes saw me unformed
In your book all are written down
My days were shaped before one came to be.'[7]

"Let me stop for a second and tell you that your father was not lecturing me. Far from it. I felt his gentleness. He was like my own father. He was tender and looking into my eyes the whole time.

"I asked him, 'Why do you tell me all of this? Why do you care about me?'

"His reply startled me. 'Do you believe in God, Melissa?'

"I said, 'Yes.'

"'Then he asked, 'Do you fear Him?'

"'What do you mean?

"'Have you ever heard of the notion called "fear of the Lord"?' he asked.

"'Not that I recall,' I replied.

"'Aha, let me ask you then, do you believe in gravity?'

[7] Psalm 139 verses 1, 2, 7, 13, 14, 16

"'Of course.'

"'It's a law of nature, right? It can't be seen, but whether you believe in it or not, does not change its existence, correct? Gravity does not require you to believe in it, no?'

"'Correct,' I replied, wondering where he was going.

"'Suppose you're climbing a mountain and come to an edge with much exposure where if you slipped and fell you would die. You would fear this place, right?'

"'Yes.'

"'One of my favorite books in the Bible is the wisdom book called Sirach or The Wisdom of Ben Sira. Here is how it begins:

"'All wisdom is from the Lord.'[8]

"It continues, 'Before all things wisdom was created.'[9] 'The beginning of wisdom is to fear the Lord; she (meaning wisdom) is created with the faithful in the womb.'[10]

"I've always found it strange the wisdom book writers, and the Church to this day, use the term 'fear of the Lord' rather than 'respect the Lord.' Why does wisdom begin with 'fear of the Lord' rather than simply respecting the Lord? It's got to mean something much more than this, no? Reverence, awe, respect, and fear, too. Maybe it means more than all of these things combined when it comes to our limited understanding of our infinite God.

"Let's come back to gravity, which we commonly refer to as a law of nature. You said you believe in God, then you would agree He is the creator of these laws. There are other natural laws He created. Some we can observe and some we cannot. Some are physical laws like gravity. Others are moral laws.

[8] Sirach 1:1
[9] Sirach 1:4
[10] Sirach 1:14

"We observe physical laws in nature. We feel moral laws in our consciences. When we violate a physical law, we can observe the result, like falling off a cliff. When we violate a moral law, we feel it in our conscience in the form of guilt. Violating a physical law has direct consequences for our bodies and our world. Likewise, sin, which is what we do when we violate God's natural moral law, has real consequences, as well.

"But we're hardheaded, and God took steps to reveal His moral laws to us. Eventually through His great prophet Moses, He made them plain in the form of the Ten Commandments.

"These include the first four which relate to God Himself and loving Him with our whole hearts, minds, and souls – you shall not have other Gods beside me, you shall not worship false idols, you shall not use the Lord's name in vain, and you shall keep holy the Sabbath.

"The next six relate to loving our neighbor as ourselves, with the first focused on the foundation of society, which is the family, 'honor your father and mother.'

"The rest express how we relate to each other: 'You shall not kill. You shall not steal. You shall not bear false witness.' The final commandment, 'You shall not covet' relates both to how we relate to each other and also how we live our internal lives given God's grace bestowed on us.

"These laws are just like gravity. They were created by God. They cannot be seen, and they do not require us to believe in them to exist. They are different than gravity in that they were imprinted into our hearts by God, and we know them in our consciences. We also know them through His revelation, but do we really believe in them?

"Violating these laws has consequences for our souls, just like tripping near a cliff has consequences for our bodies due to gravity. In fact, we see the consequences apparent throughout the whole world due to our sins. We can't hardly fathom the impact sin has had on the world, our bodies, our relationships, with each other, and with God.

"So, why do I care about you? Why do I share all of this with you? I have a responsibility to you as my neighbor, to love you as myself and to reflect Christ to you.

"If we were climbing a mountain together, surely, I would warn you of a dangerous spot and help you to be safe because of the consequences of gravity.

"Similarly, I should warn you of the dangers that exist when one aborts an unborn human person, because it violates God's law, 'Thou shalt not kill.'

"Just as importantly, I must also warn you of the dangers that exist when one justifies such killing by arguing it is the mother's right to choose, for you violate another natural, moral law, 'You shall not worship false gods' by setting yourself up as equal to God and acting as though He does not exist or that your own moral code supersedes His natural laws.'

"Then he asked me if any of this made sense, and I said yes, I guess so, but the way he came across when he was in office seemed so hurtful.

"His response made me cringe in fear. 'Are you sure it hurt because of the way I came across or because you sensed you were out of sync with nature? Were you mad at me, or were you feeling guilty?'

"I sat there silently, then he asked, 'Dear Melissa, do you know you still have a path to salvation?'

'How is this possible?' I asked, stunned, wondering how he could know so much about me.

'First, you must admit to yourself and to God that you have gravely sinned. Then you must repent of your sin, confess it through the Sacrament of Reconciliation to a priest of the Catholic Church, and do penance.'

'Yes, but will this rid me of my guilt?'

'Melissa, God's love for you is awesome. Like Jeremiah, he knew you before he formed you in your mother's womb. He loves you more than you can imagine, and His mercy is beyond our understanding.

'Jesus left us a Church to administer His sacraments, which are real and efficacious. There is a path for you to follow to restore your relationship with God. Perhaps your guilt and anger are a sign of God's spirit within you. Perhaps you fear Him, which means you have wisdom within you.'

"By this time I was crying. I didn't know what to say. Then your dad held my hand and began to pray.

'Dear Lord, please help Melissa come back to your path through the Sacrament of Reconciliation and all it entails. Help her, through your sacraments, to restore her relationship with you. Amen.'

I didn't know how to react. I'm not even Catholic! Your dad was so sure of what he was saying. He wasn't preaching. He was teaching. I wanted to be mad or at least embarrassed, but instead I felt something I hadn't felt for as long as I can remember." Melissa looked away.

"What was that?" Sarah asked.

"Hope," Melissa whispered.

"Oh."

"After that I went to my local church and spoke with a priest. It was good, but I've got a long way to go. When I heard your dad had a stroke, I just had to come here and pray for him. I just had to!" Melissa was crying.

Sarah also had tears in her eyes. "Let's go to my dad's room to pray."

As they got up, they were met by Uncle Ronnie, Uncle Jack,

and Uncle Rakesh.

Uncle Jack took Sarah's hand and said, "Please sit down girls. We have some sad news."

# 15

# GOING HOME

Time seemed to stop for Sarah. One day she was praying on a high Rocky Mountain plateau and the next she was preparing to bury her father. She was now an orphan with no family left in the world.

Many people expressed their condolences. Most were probably even heartfelt. Being an ex-president of the United States made everything more grandiose and complex. Sarah wanted to have a simple funeral service at her father's local parish, but the wisdom of the day dictated he lie in state at the Capitol with a funeral Mass at the Basilica of the Immaculate Conception, which is one of the largest Catholic churches in the world and just a few miles from the center of power in Washington, D.C.

Father Jack and Archbishop O'Rourke concelebrated Mass. President Petrov provided a moving eulogy. The entire world was in shock! Sarah was supported by her friend Sophie, who took control over all the details and ensured Sarah's wishes were upheld throughout.

Sarah was simply stunned and grief-stricken. Some well-meaning politico proposed O'Malley be buried at Arlington National Cemetery, which would have meant her mother would have to be exhumed and moved, but Sophie intervened and ensured the arrangements were made to bury her good "Uncle Sean" with his beloved Maggie at their diocesan cemetery in Virginia.

After the burial, Sarah and her tight-knit circle of friends gathered at a small pub near Front Royal, Virginia, which had been both her father's and grandfather's favorite place. She was pleasantly surprised to see Hank Carson arrive at the cemetery. She assumed Sophie had prompted him. She was also pleased Jean Macron had flown in from Bordeaux. These two young men were good support.

Prior to supper, Father Jack asked everyone for a moment of silence and to say grace in advance of the meal. Then Uncle Rakesh rose to say a few words.

"Dear friends," Uncle Rakesh said, "thank you for coming to help us bury our dear friend and Sarah's father, Sean. It is good we are here in the shadow of his beloved Blue Ridge Mountains in Virginia. This is where I met Sean decades ago. I have many stories I could tell you about this wonderful man, but there will be time for that later. Those of us who knew him as a friend, a husband, and a father know what kind of man he was. As he always said, 'What part of *God is real* don't you understand?' For us, this meant we got everything he had whenever we needed it. His love, his friendship, his faith, his wisdom, advice, and support. Words cannot express what this man meant to me and how much I admired him. Today my prayer is this: May I live up to Sean's expectations until we meet again."

Turning to Sarah he said, "Dear Sarah, I am convinced your father died of a broken heart, so deep was his love for your mother. Therefore, since he has gone on to Heaven ahead of me, I tell you of the vow we made to each other, imagining something like this might happen to him or to me.

"From this day forward, you are to be under my care as my own daughter, as requested by your father, until I depart this earth. I know this is not sufficient, as no man can replace your father, but it will have to do. You are my Goddaughter, and I will do my very best for you as your Godfather.

"Now, I'd like to propose a toast to our dear, departed Sean O'Malley, 'Erin go brah! Vivat Jesus! Vivat Sean!'"

After dinner, Hank and Jean approached Sarah and Sophie.

"Want to go for a walk?" asked Jean.

So, they did, talking deep into the night.

# PART II

# 16
# ONWARD

It was not hard for Sarah to get back into her old routine. Oddly enough she flew back to her apartment in San Jose, California, only to learn she would be flying back east for a new assignment to assess a potential acquisition candidate called E-Fly LLC, which was working on new solid-state batteries intended for personal flying vehicles.

With her boss and colleagues' support, getting back to work helped immensely to take her mind off her father's death. She'd uploaded her backpacking photos onto her computer and loved how they filled the screen when it went into "screen saver mode," Reviving memories that seemed ages old, even though only a few weeks had passed since she'd been in the Rockies. Remembering the smell of pine, trail dust, and cool clean air was something she savored.

Her schedule was packed with activities mostly related to work. When she wasn't traveling, she was preparing to travel. When she reached her destination, she was on highly engineered schedules designed to maximize her exposure to the acquisition target and limit her personal time. Evenings usually included dinner and drinks with the executive team and her colleagues. She was a morning person and usually made time for a good long run before breakfast, which gave her time to see the new city or town in a way that can't be done via car.

Time at home consisted of resting and recharging her batteries

– literally and figuratively. Then one Saturday morning, she ran into an interesting man at her local Starbucks. He was just in front of her in line.

"I'll have my usual upside-down caramel macchiato with a double shot of expresso," he said.

Amused by his order, she couldn't resist speaking to him. "Are you sure you need the double shot? One wouldn't do it?" He turned, and stunned by her beauty, he smiled. "You're right!" He turned back to the barista and demanded, "Make it three shots!"

She stepped forward to order. "I'll take a Grande dark roast, no room for cream."

While waiting for their orders, he asked, "You must really like coffee because what you ordered is about as boring as it gets."

"I don't like coffee. I love it! I call it the nectar of the gods." Then she made the Sign of the Cross, remembering President Petrov as she did so. "That's why I don't add cream or other things. I want to savor it for what it is rather than making it into something else."

He laughed and said, "I love it! I'm going to try it as you suggest next time. Hey, I'm Trevor."

"I'm Sarah. Nice to meet you." Then she noticed he was wearing a Rolex and was stylishly dressed for a Saturday morning. He was also about six-foot-two and looked very fit.

He glanced toward the huge windows at the front of the restaurant. "Want to join me at a table outside? It is a glorious morning."

"Sure." She judged him to be in his early to mid-thirties and quite sure of himself.

Sitting down he asked, "So, Sarah, are you from around here?"

"I am. Well, I live here now because of work, but I grew up in Virginia. How about you?"

"I'm from L.A., born and raised. I have a place up here now because I started a business and wanted it to be in Silicon Valley."

"What kind of business?"

"We're working on a new technology to print propeller blades for personal flying vehicles. My engineers think they've found a new geometry that can enable them to be much more efficient, but so far, we can only achieve this design by printing them with a new metal dust material. I guess you could say we're an aerospace additive manufacturing start-up."

"Are you an engineer?"

"No. I'm a serial entrepreneur. I like to think of myself as an enabler of new ideas."

"Sounds fascinating. I would love to fly 'personal flying vehicles' one day."

"Me too! In fact, I hovered in a prototype from another company about six months ago. I was only allowed to go about two meters off the ground. I can't wait for this to become real. That's why I got involved with this new start-up."

"Well, I hope you're successful because I want to fly to work instead of driving! Speaking of flying, I've got to get going. It was nice to meet you. Maybe I'll see you around," she said and got up abruptly.

Trevor was left wondering if he had done something wrong. Meanwhile Sarah was wondering why she didn't stay. Later that day she called Sophie.

"I met a guy this morning, but I couldn't bring myself to hang out with him," she confided to Sophie. "He seemed really nice, but..."

"But, what? Talk to me."

"I feel guilty being happy. Plus, I don't want to get involved with anyone right now."

"Do you mean anyone other than Hank?" Sophie asked

seriously.

"I don't know." Sarah sighed. "I haven't had a chance to think."

"When's the last time you spoke with Hank?"

"In Virginia after the funeral."

"What? You two haven't spoken since then?! What about Snapchat, texts, or email?"

"Nope. Plus, Hank told me once he doesn't really do those things. He mentioned something about being old-school, whatever that means."

"Sarah! You seemed to really like Hank."

"Yeah, well, if he likes me then he can call me."

"That's true, but maybe he's shy or doesn't know how you feel."

"Well, maybe I don't know how I feel, either."

"What are you doing this weekend?" asked Sophie, knowing she had to change the subject.

"Not much. I have to fly back to Boston on Sunday. So, my weekend is basically only Saturday."

"OK, how about if I come over and we hang out. Maybe we can go for a drive somewhere and get out into the country. Plus, I've got some big news!"

A few days later the two best friends were driving north towards Napa on a beautiful Saturday morning.

"What's this big news you were teasing about, Sophie?" asked Sara with a curious smile.

"Jean is moving to California! He got an engineering job with an aerospace startup and will be moving here in a month. I can't be happier!" cried Sophie. Her eyes were wide with excitement.

"Wow! This is like the best news ever. I'm so happy for you.

What made him decide to move here?"

"He said he asked my dad if it would be okay if he courted me when he was at your dad's funeral. My dad gave him permission. He also said he felt somewhat established as an engineer in France and confident he could do well in the U.S."

"Are you serious? Is he that traditional?"

"What do you mean by traditional?"

"I guess I mean he's conservative and careful. I don't know what I mean. I guess I'm not used to a man thinking he has to ask permission to court someone. What does "court" mean, anyway?"

"The funny thing about Jean is this is all his own doing. His mother and father are really laid back, but he is very sure of himself and says, 'I always try to do things right, and to do the right things.' I think I heard of courting in an old movie or something. What Jean tells me is courting is more serious than dating. It means he wants to marry me, and we are to take our relationship beyond friendship towards engagement. I am sooooo happ-eeeeeeeeeeee!" yelled Sophie.

"This is amazing! Does that mean he's going to move in with you?" asked Sarah.

"Ha ha!" Sophie was laughing hard, and Sara worried she would lose control of her car. She hoped the Tesla's autopilot might help somehow.

"Why are you laughing?" Sarah inquired knowing the answer already.

"You know Jean. He's C-A-T-H-O-L-I-C! Right. He would never do that."

"I know, but aren't you worried you would marry him and not have lived with him beforehand?"

"Nope."

"Seriously?"

"Think about it Sarah. If a man respects his faith and me so much as to ask my father permission to court me, how much risk could there be?" she asked joyously.

"Good point, but what if he's a big slob? What if he walks around naked? What if he snores?" Sarah was laughing hard at herself.

And, so it continued until they arrived at a nice Napa Valley resort called Silverado just in time for lunch.

Afterwards they went for a walk, and Sophie asked, "How are you doing?"

Sarah stopped in her tracks and looked down, then turned and gazed into Sophie's eyes.

Sophie saw her pain. Real pain.

Sarah turned and continued walking.

After a few minutes Sarah said, "After the funeral in Virginia, Father Jack told me to think of it this way. He said, 'Imagine you and your dad are walking along a trail in the Blue Ridge. You're talking and having a grand old time. Then you get distracted by a flower or something just off the trail and stop to investigate, but your dad continues walking.

"After a bit, you turn back to the trail and continue walking, but now you can't see or hear your dad. He's gone over a rise and around a bend on the trail. You continue without concern, knowing you'll catch up to him shortly, as you are sure he is just ahead of you. That's how it is with your dad today. He's on the trail just ahead. You can't see or hear him, but just as sure as you would be if you were walking together in the woods, he's alive in spirit. Just because you can't see or hear him doesn't change this fact.'

"His explanation has helped me a lot, not just on that day, but in all the days and weeks since. I think about him being at my side, still with me. Still, sometimes I hurt so much. I miss my dad and mom, and

I wonder why God took them. It doesn't make any sense. I didn't get to say goodbye to my dad. There were so many things I wanted to ask him. Now, who do I turn to? Where am I going? What am I doing? What's the point?"

Sarah had tears in her eyes but was not crying. She wasn't even sure how to define her emotions. Sometimes she felt mad and sometimes she felt hopeless, but most of the time it was hard to tell the difference.

Sophie did the only thing she could think of doing. She hugged Sarah tightly. At the same time, she thought of something else she could do, but it would have to wait until she got home.

# 17

# THE ENTREPRENEUR

Somehow Trevor managed to track her down and asked her to go on a date, which she did. He picked her up in his Porsche, and they went to a fancy restaurant nearby. Afterwards, they went to a dance club, and Sarah was surprised by how well he danced. He seemed at home on the dance floor and at this club. The music was loud, so they couldn't hear each other well, and it was a work night, so Sarah asked if they could go home when it reached 11 p.m., but Trevor seemed like he was just getting started.

Regardless, he took her home and was a complete gentleman walking her to the front door of her apartment building and saying goodnight. As she turned to leave, he asked, "Would it be okay if I called you again?"

Sarah said, "Sure," but wondered at how they had spent several hours together yet knew very little about each other. "Do you golf?"

He said, "Yes. I love it, too. Do you golf?"

"Yes."

"OK, I belong to a club. How about I set up a tee time?"

A week later they were preparing to tee off at Trevor's prestigious private country club. They were paired with two longtime members, one of whom was the club president, having recently taken the position after retiring from a successful career in business. The other player was the U.S. Congressman from that district, who no doubt arranged to join the foursome given Sarah's father's prominence.

The three men teed off and then proceeded to Sarah's tee box. The congressman asked Sarah, "How long have you been golfing?"

"My father taught me when I was a little girl."

"Really? That's great. My father taught me to golf, too."

With that, Sarah teed off and striped her drive straight down the middle. Her ball flew past all three men's drives and gave her a perfect angle to the green.

On the next tee box, the president of the club asked Trevor, "You didn't tell me this young woman was an ace golfer. How are you going to keep up?"

Trevor laughingly replied, "I'm just now finding this out myself. As for keeping up? I guess I'll have to cheat!"

They all laughed. Then the club president said, "You know, Sarah, a lot of the members at this club are not comfortable with women joining or even playing on the course."

"I'm used to it. My dad didn't belong to a private club. There weren't any near where I grew up, but he took me to a few, and we would play in tournaments as a team. I enjoy being underestimated, even in golf," she replied with a smile.

A few holes later, the Congressman said to the club president, "I won't be able to play next week. I've got to go to Mass during our usual tee time. My apologies in advance, but my wife sets the schedule. Seems her good friend's granddaughter is receiving First Communion."

The Club President responded, "Yeah, the Catholic Church is a disaster and responsible for a lot of problems in this world. Good luck with all that."

To which Sarah asked, "Can you give an example of a problem caused by the Church?"

The Club President was put off balance but quickly responded, "The Crusades. And The Spanish Inquisition."

She asked, "Does anything else come to mind that is more current?"

He replied, "Priestly sexual abuse and not allowing gay marriage."

She responded, "Got it. Thanks. Just wanted to know what you were thinking regarding the Catholic Church." Then she shanked her wedge into a bunker and double bogeyed the hole.

Sarah thought, *Why am I put off by this guy thinking the Catholic Church is behind a lot of problems in the world? Is he right about that?*

They finished the round, but Sarah decided she wanted to go home afterward and kindly declined their offer to sit on the veranda and have some drinks at the nineteenth hole. She also decided not to date Trevor again, not because he wasn't nice, but because he used his "foot wedge" a few too many times for her liking.

When she arrived home, she checked her mail and found an envelope addressed to Ms. Sarah O'Malley with a return address from Hank Carson. She could hardly wait to open it.

Once inside, she sat down to read the letter:

> Dear Sarah,
>
> I know it has been a while since we talked, but this does not mean I haven't been thinking about you. I wanted to give you space knowing how difficult it must be during your time of mourning.
>
> Your father was a great man and a hero to

many, including me. It was my great fortune to run into you, almost literally, on the trail in the Rockies. It would be my honor to meet you again, although I do not know when this will be.

If our paths do cross, I would love to go for a walk with you in hopes of getting to know you better.

Sincerely yours,

Hank

She was so excited she could hardly contain herself and called Sophie right away.

"What should I do? How should I respond?"

"Hellooooo! Earth to Sarah. Earth to Sarah! Why don't you give him a call?"

"But he hasn't called me. He wrote me a letter instead and sent it in the mail. Is he from the stone age, or what?"

"Maybe, but you're not. How far away does he live from you?"

"Looking at his address, it seems he lives in a trailer park near Merced, which ought to be about two hours away."

"Perfect! You could go for a drive out there and meet him but just call him and set it up."

"OK. OK. I will."

But she didn't call him, instead opting to write a letter in response. It said:

> Dear Mr. Carson,
>
> Thank you for your nice letter. I appreciate your consideration during my time of mourning. I too have thought of you often since we met.
>
> If you desire to take me for a walk, then you should inquire and seek approval in advance from my godfather, Rakesh Shriram.
>
> Sincerely yours,
>
> Sarah

A week later Sarah received a call from Uncle Rakesh. He asked her to come to his house for the weekend to talk.

# 18

# UNCLE RAKESH

Uncle Rakesh's wonderfully quaint two-story home was in Palo Alto, within walking distance of Stanford University. Sarah arrived just ahead of "post time," which is what he called 5 p.m., when it became "legal" to have a snort of his favorite scotch or bourbon.

Knowing this, Sarah presented him with a twelve-year-old bottle of Macallan scotch, which was her father's favorite.

"Ah, Sarah, a girl after me own heart!" he yelled in his best Irish accent, grabbing her into a big bear hug. "It's post time. Will you join me?"

"Of course! You know I can't let you drink alone."

"How have you been? Tell me what is going on with my favorite goddaughter," he said as he prepared their drinks with the perfect amount of small ice cubes and healthy amounts of the bronze nectar of Scotland.

"I've been soooo busy. Flying all over doing due diligence for various deals. I haven't had much time on the weekends because a lot of my projects have got me going to Boston or Minneapolis," she moaned as she sat on a leather couch in Uncle Rakesh's cozy den.

"And, so, you aren't going to tell me why I received a call from

Hank Carson out of the blue?" he queried with a wry smile, continuing to speak with an Irish accent, which he had honed to perfection over the years, if he didn't say so himself.

"I figured that's why you asked me over. I received a letter from Hank after many weeks of not hearing anything from him. I responded with a letter back and told him if he wanted to date me he would need to seek your permission. I got the idea from how Jean asked you if it would be okay if he courted Sophie."

"Ahh, I see."

"What do you think of Hank, Uncle Rakesh?"

"You want my honest opinion?" he asked, now back in his normal Boston-American accent. "Before you answer you must know that I have hardly any experience with him and must rely on my intuition. However, you should also know my intuition is rarely wrong on these matters."

"Yes. Give it to me straight, but before you do let's do a toast."

"OK, you make the toast this time," he said approvingly.

"Take two and hit to right?" she yelled, recalling her father and grandfather's favorite saying for when things got rough.

"Amen!" he replied while clinking her glass. "Hank doesn't know it yet but he's on his way to becoming a true gentleman. He's honorable. He's a man's man."

She grinned. "So, you like him?"

"Yes, very much."

"What do you mean by man's man?"

"He's his own person and does not adapt his personality to fit others' expectations. What I mean by "man's man" is that he has virtue, integrity, and courage. Plus, he has the physical strength to back it up. These gifts all come naturally and are God-given."

"What do you mean by 'on his way to becoming a true

gentleman'?" asked Sarah with genuine interest and high respect.

"This is very, very important. A gentleman is honorable and seeks to fulfill a higher calling. Hank is a young man and still has a lot of maturing ahead of him. However, I can tell he was raised right by his mother. He doesn't seek to gain advantage with his strength, good looks, and intelligence. Instead, he seeks to put them to use in hopes he can help others. He's very humble, which is the mark of a true gentleman."

"So, you like him?" she asked with interest.

"Yes. I think he is a man of good character."

"Will you approve him to court me?"

"Only if you want me to. On the merits, he meets my expectations for the kind of man who is worthy of you."

"Then I only have one thing to say, Uncle Rakesh. Let's hope I'm worthy of him too."

"I don't worry about that, my dear. Your buddy Sophie tells me often to 'stay in my lane,' but if you would be OK, I would like to give you some advice."

"Sure." she responded while sipping her Macallan.

"Don't worry too much. Just be yourself and be friends first. If you find yourself respecting him, then it will be all downhill after that."

"Sounds good. I'll drink to that!"

Just then Mother Miriam Shriram came into the den. "OK, you two, enough of that nectar-of-the-gods stuff, time for dinner!"

# 19

# THE ENGINEER

Hank Carson was busy at his job site when he received a phone call from an unusual number. Normally he would have let it go to voicemail, but this number looked like it was coming from outside the country. He answered it warily.

"Hello, Hank, this is Jean Macron calling from France. Do you have time to talk?"

"Hey, Jean. It is great to hear your voice. Of course I have time to talk."

And, so they did, with Hank learning Jean would be arriving in California for an engineering job, with hopes of courting Sophie. He wanted to know if Hank was available for him to visit, as he was the only other person he knew in the States. They made arrangements to meet up a week later.

Jean arrived at Hank's home, which was situated in a mobile home park on the outskirts of Merced, California, a small city in the San Joaquin valley of California situated between the Sierra Nevada mountains to the east and the lower coastal ranges to the west. His small "mobile" home was exquisitely maintained with many plants lining the border with his neighbor. His hardworking Ford F-150 pickup was parked neatly out of the sun under an aluminum roof.

"Welcome to California, Jean!" Hank greeted him with a firm

handshake.

"Great to be here, Hank! I've never been to a mobile home park before, as we don't have them in France.

"I don't have the money to afford a more expensive place. In fact, I'm renting this from my mom, as I'm trying to save up money. She's the manager of this park and over the course of time she's bought some of the units as investments."

Jean could sense the respect Hank had for his mother. "I hope I can meet her," said Jean with a smile.

"You will and sooner than you think. We're going to her place for lunch. I hope you're hungry."

"Did you say food? Let's go!"

They walked down the middle of the small street inside the quaint, well-kept mobile home park. Within five minutes they arrived at Hank's mom's unit.

She greeted him with a smile and a firm handshake. "Come in, boys! Hello, Jean. I'm Mary Carson. Nice to meet you. Welcome to Merced.".

"*Bonjour*, Mrs. Carson. It is good to be here. Do I detect an Irish accent?"

"Well, you surely aren't hearing a California accent! I was born in County Roscommon, Ireland, in a little crossroads called Castleplunket. I came here in the 1980s because my father was working with a U.S.-based company at the time. Eventually we came to California and never left. What brings you to California?"

"Hmm. I want to say I'm here to gain experience and credibility as an engineer, but the real reason is a girl named Sophie Shriram, who I met while at university in Paris two years ago," he replied sheepishly.

"Aye, but that is the best reason possible! Engineering can be done anywhere, but love, if that's what you're claiming, is by far and away the most important thing we have in this life. So, why not go halfway around the world for it?" she replied looking directly in his eyes while taking his shoulders into her hands.

"That's what my mom said. She taught Sophie to sew and developed a great relationship with her. She thinks she's special. That's good enough for me."

"Aye, yes. If your mom likes her then you can't go wrong. She'll know. She'll know, indeed." She sighed, released her grip, and looked away. "Shall we get lunch going, then?"

After a fine lunch of fresh fish, salad, tea, and biscuits, Jean asked Hank if they could go out for a walk, and so they did.

"Hank, I don't know how to go about things with an American girl. I want to marry Sophie, but I need time to get myself established here in the States. I'm struggling with when the right time will be to ask her."

"Hey, you're asking the wrong man about this kind of stuff. I'm a construction guy just starting out myself. I don't know a thing about women. I haven't found the 'one' yet, so I can't give you much advice."

Jean suddenly stopped in his tracks. "Are you sure you haven't found the one?" he asked with a knowing smile.

"What do you mean? Sarah? Are you crazy? She is *way* out of my league!"

"What do you mean, 'out of your league'? I do not understand this term," Jean asked seriously.

"She's upper class!" He gazed down the road. "Her father was the president. She works for a high-end Silicon Valley company. She knows the President of Russia, an Archbishop, and her 'uncles' are a colonel, a priest, and the CEO of a big-time company. Me, I'm trying to make it by renovating houses. I get by with my hands. She's super smart. What would she want to do with an ex-army grunt like me?"

"Well, according to Sophie, you've made quite an impression on Sarah. I think you might underestimate yourself. Likewise, you underestimate her. All those things you said about her are true, but wasn't her father also ex-army? Did he not start out in the construction trades? In fact, didn't he refer to himself as a construction worker playacting as president? Perhaps you have the wrong impression of where Sarah comes from, no?"

"Yeah, well, she's impressive on every level. I'll admit I haven't stopped thinking about her."

"Then why don't you call her and set up a date?" Jean asked raising an eyebrow and a smile.

"Um...er...aargh."

"Hank, you are an idiot!"

"Guilty! OK! I'll call her, but first I have to get permission from her Uncle Rakesh, according to a letter she sent me," he said with a grin.

"Letter! What letter? You mean you've already contacted her?"

"Uh-huh." He raised his eyebrow, then said, "Let's get a beer at the local bar, and I'll tell you all about it."

# 20

# QUALITY ADVICE

The boys arrived at Scruffy's, a dimly lit pub with a pool table at one end and a bar at the other. In between were tables and chairs strewn randomly on ancient hardwood planks. The place was well known to the locals for its excellent, cheap steaks and amazing salads piled high with shaved carrots, perhaps due to the dark surroundings or maybe because they were just fun.

George Lynn, the bartender and owner, better known as Scruffy, approached as Jean followed Hank's lead and sat at the bar.

"Afternoon, Hank. Long time no see," Scruffy laughed.

"Yeah, well, Scruff, I can't come here every day, but this is a special occasion as my friend, Jean Macron, has just arrived from France and intends to try and make his way here in the good old U.S. of A."

"Welcome aboard, Jean. Whereabouts are you from in France?" asked Scruffy as he gave Jean a firm handshake.

"Bonjour, Scruffy! I hope it's okay to call you this. I am from Bordeaux but most recently was working in Paris as an engineer."

"Sure, its fine to call me Scruffy. I forgot what my mother named me long ago. Bordeaux you say? I hear they have some second-rate wine coming out of that region. Of course, everyone knows the best wine comes from California! Ha ha!"

"You might be right," Jean said with a smirk, "although I think many of your wineries learned their trade from my homeland, but what do I know? I'm a carpenter playacting as an engineer."

Then they heard a comment from somewhere down the bar. "Yeah, well, Frenchy, if you want to make it in the U.S., you got some learnin' to do."

The tone was matter of fact and not friendly. Hank knew immediately who said it and turned towards the sound. "Are you saying you could teach him a thing or two, Johnny?" Hank stood up and moved toward the man.

Johnny also got up and looked at Jean. He was as big as a bear, about sixty years old, six-foot four and two-hundred-twenty-five pounds with hardly an ounce of fat on him. He was bald with hardworking hands that looked like a catcher's mitts.

Hank went right up to him, and for a moment it looked to Jean as though they were going to fight until they bear-hugged each other, with Hank putting his arm around Johnny and bringing him to their end of the bar.

"Jean," Hank said, "I would like you to meet Johnny Cavanaugh. He's a concrete contractor who operates out of this area." Hank moved out of the way so they two men could shake hands.

Jean rose from his chair and extended his hand. "Nice to meet you Mr. Cavanaugh."

Johnny grabbed his hand firmly and looked Jean straight in the eye. "Nice to meet you, Jean. Please call me Johnny. Welcome to America. It would be my honor to buy you a beer."

"*Merci.* Oh, I mean, thank you, Johnny. That would be great."

"Three beers, Scruffy. You know the way," crowed Johnny.

Hank then explained that Scruffy's was a place that most, if not all, of the local construction business owners went to after work to meet and talk. It was not unusual for them to work things out over a beer or two. Sometimes fists were involved, but they were usually reserved for the irresponsible types.

"Johnny, you said I have some learnin' to do to make it in the U.S. What do you mean?" asked Jean with genuine interest.

"How old are you, Jean?"

"I am twenty-eight."

"Tell me about your experience."

"Well, I followed my father into the carpentry trade after school and did this for several years. I was always interested in what my father did, so this was natural for me. Plus, he always seemed happy and enjoyed showing me his finished work, which seemed to be everywhere in Bordeaux. He is my hero.

"I loved this work, too, but my mother encouraged me to get a university degree. I guess she saw something. So, I went to the university in Paris to study mechanical engineering. It seemed to me I was the oldest person in the program, but this was OK, because I had good experience working on building projects where I had a reputation for solving difficult problems."

Johnny asked, "So, in that time, did you ever run your own business, or did you always work for someone else?"

"Mostly, I worked for others. While I was in Paris, I did small carpentry jobs for people to help pay for expenses while at the university," replied Jean.

"What's the most money you ever made from one of those projects?"

"They were mostly small projects, usually about 500 euros. My biggest project was 5,000 euros," Jean answered.

"I see. I see. This makes sense. You're just starting out, and I assume you're working for a big engineering firm here in California?"

Johnny asked.

"*Oui*. Woops. I mean yes," said Jean.

"No need to apologize. French is your native language, and your English is damned good. Here's the thing I was thinking when I said 'you've got some learnin' to do.' You're a young man in a new country. Everything is new, which is great. The only question is when you will learn the importance of quality and honor."

"What makes you think I don't already know this?" asked Jean sitting up straighter.

"Your age," replied Johnny, also sitting up straighter and leaning in to close the gap.

"Johnny, you don't know me. You don't know where I come from. My father is a self-made man. My mother is built out of bedrock. They taught me the value of hard work and strong faith."

"You're working for one of those Silicon Valley startups, right?" asked Johnny with a knowing grin.

"Yes. We are developing a new battery-powered personal aircraft."

"Let's see if you can maintain your honor and integrity working with one of those kinds of outfits in that valley, but my first impression is I wouldn't bet against you. Just be careful to watch out for their shenanigans," advised Johnny.

"What do you mean by shenanigans?" asked Jean with genuine concern.

"What I mean is this: Sometimes those companies say one thing and promise the world when deep down inside all they're trying to do is turn the company over for sale to make a quick buck. So, watch out that you are not wasting your time with a company that says one thing but hides what its real intents are."

"Got it. *Merci*," said Jean.

Hank chimed in, and by that time, Scruffy and several other construction entrepreneurs had gathered around for an impromptu "debrief meeting," as was their habit. "Jean, Johnny is one of the best, if not *the best* concrete man in northern California. He's done projects near and far, big and small. Didn't you do the all the concrete for the new San Francisco football stadium, Johnny?"

"Yeah, but if you're up for it, Jean, I'll share one piece of American advice for you to consider while we sip our beers."

"Of course, *si vous plait*, I mean, *please*," responded Jean with interest.

Johnny was looking him dead in the eye. "No matter how big or complex the job, whether you're working for someone else or not, handle it as if it were your own, like you did on your $500 jobs back in Paris, doing the best you can for your customer, being able to look at yourself in the mirror at the end of each day, and you'll do just fine in America."

"*Merci*, Johnny. May I propose a toast?" asked Jean.

"Go for it."

"*C'est en forgeant qu'on devient forgeron*! What this means in English is 'it is by forging that we become a blacksmith.' For me this means, 'I am here in California to do engineering, and this is how I aim to become a good man.'"

Hank chimed in, "Amen! Cheers, everyone!"

Everyone clinked their beers together and savored the nectar of German monks.

# 21

# UNCLE RONNIE'S SECRET

Two hours away in San Jose, Sarah was finishing her morning jog when she was approached by a very handsome man. He introduced himself with a flair that signaled his maturity and global experience. She took it all in without concern, noting how easy it was to meet such men in her neighborhood.

Meanwhile, Uncle Ronnie was making the rounds with Father Jack and Rakesh, checking in with them and getting their perspectives on Sarah, as it had been several months since her father's passing. While their reports were positive, he decided it was time to see her firsthand.

Calling her, he found her to be in good spirits. He learned she would soon be in Northern Virginia, and he also had good reason to go there, so they planned to meet at the Vienna Inn, which was a well-known icon near to the power of the nation's capital.

Sitting in a dark corner of this 60-year-old family-oriented dive bar, he ordered two beers and two chili dogs, with hopes of hearing the truth.

"You want the truth, Uncle Ronnie? Well, here's how I'm feeling. I'm numb. I'm going through the motions. I've got a good job. I've got a great friend in Sophie and many good friends, but nothing to look forward to. I get up early. Exercise. Work. Eat. Sleep. Repeat. I've got no one to share anything with. My mom is gone. Now my dad, too.

Sometimes I get very mad at him. We lost a lot of time as a family because he became president. That seems so selfish to me, especially now that his life was cut short."

Colonel Gardner (Ret.), aka Uncle Ronnie, was not surprised in the least by Sarah's candor nor her anger and sadness. "Let's finish our beer and dogs and go for a walk out on the bike trail next door. It's a beautiful day here in Virginia. It'll do us some good to stretch our legs. Then I'll tell you a story about how the last thing your dad wanted to do was become president."

"What?! Are you kidding?"

"Nope. Eat and drink, then I'll tell you all about it."

"OK, but let me ask you something first. How are you doing, Uncle Ronnie?"

"Hmm."

"Yeah, me too."

Sarah breathed deeply as they left the Inn while taking in the small Civil War era storefront near the bike trail they were now walking on. Before the Civil War the town of Vienna, Virginia was a crossroads on the way to Washington, D.C. She savored the stories her father once told her about the Civil War in this part of the country, with neighbor rising up against neighbor, some supporting the South while others the North. Her dad had loved going into details about the Battle of Vienna, one of the earliest of the war, fought along a railroad track that connected it to the town of Alexandria, fifteen miles away.

Walking westward on the trail they soon found themselves along a small unnamed stream feeding Difficult Run between a mixture of 1970s suburban developments and newer, more spectacular homes that were overtaking the town, as it "benefited" from the urban sprawl of the nation's capital. For Gardner, it was not hard to remember earlier, quieter days when this area was mostly forests and dairy farms.

"So, tell me why my father didn't want to be President. This is news to me," Sarah queried with skepticism and irritation.

"Have you ever read the celebrated book of poetry by Rita Dove, '*Thomas and Beulah*?'" Col. Gardner asked.

"No."

"I highly recommend it. Now to answer your question directly, and then I'll give you the backstory. The idea for your father becoming president was your mother's. Your father wanted nothing to do with it."

She stopped and stared at him. "What? Are you serious?".

"Dead."

"I can't believe this. My mother wanted my dad to be president?"

"Yup," he replied coyly.

"Why?" She was still not walking.

"Your mother told me she felt that he should. She noticed the idea of your father being president kept coming to her not once, not twice but many, many times over the course of years. It came in dreams. It came to her while praying. It came to her in the middle of the night while she was lying in bed awakened by who knows what.

"She couldn't explain it succinctly. It was a feeling, an instinct that I think was borne out of her whole experience with your dad, but also coming to her from her guardian angel, is what she told me."

He continued. "When she put things together, she thought, '*The country needs a good man to manage it onto a different path. Who better than Sean O'Malley, ex-army sergeant, now owner of a successful construction company who was known to be fair and results-oriented?*'

"Your dad wanted nothing to do with it, but your mother convinced him the idea was not hers but from the Lord and asked him to pray on it, and so he did.

"Eventually, together, they discerned this path and took steps to realize it. All the while, your dad was worried this could put him on a path to perdition. He knew the risk of gaining so much power and was terrified he would succumb to evil temptations.

"One day before the election he told me, 'Ronnie the only thing that's going to save my soul is fear of the Lord.'

"That was his attitude going in. He felt the calling your mother discerned, but he was always worried he was doing wrong by you, as he considered fatherhood his first and most important vocation."

"I can't believe this! I'm stunned. I always thought my mom went along with it, but you're saying the idea was hers! Are you for real?"

"Yes. First your dad became governor of Virginia. Then he gave 'The Speech' on one of those daytime talk shows. The next thing you know he was president of the U.S. He didn't even finish his first term as governor! Hah, jokes on you, Virginia!"

"I guess I was too young to have the proper perspective," she suggested.

"That is true, but your parents also wanted you to have as normal a childhood as possible. However, they knew they were also making you sacrifice something, too. Nevertheless, their discernment was strong. They also conferred with Father Jack and their local pastor."

"Were you surprised by my dad becoming president?" she asked, looking him dead in the eyes.

"Yes! Your dad hated politics. He was always about results. I remember going to Mass with him one time when he told me he always sought the 'takeaway' from the readings and the homily. For him to understand something he had to act on it; try it out; see what worked and what didn't. He was even results-oriented with Catholic Mass! So, yes, I was mightily surprised when he told me he was going into politics.

"Then again, I wasn't surprised when he was successful at it. He tried his best to be a one-term president, too. His whole idea was to get in, get some things done, then get out, but your mom convinced him he should stay for the second term."

"I'm kind of struggling knowing my mom was behind this whole thing. I've been mad at my dad, but now I'm wondering if I should be mad at my mom."

"You know, girl dear, it's okay to be mad when one is in mourning. It's a process, and I find it to be a confirmation of love. I think, with time, you'll understand more about your parents and come to love them even more deeply."

"I'm not sure it's possible for me to love them more, or miss them more," she said looking up at her dear Uncle.

"Can I tell you a story about how I came to be friends with your dad?" asked Uncle Ronnie, as he went to sit down on a bench near the trail.

"Sure! I would love that," Sarah replied as she joined him on the bench.

"One day at the university, I was about to get into a fight. Your dad came upon the scene and got between me and the other guy. I'd only met your father a few times, but we seemed to have a good connection. I was surprised when he got involved. This guy I was about to fight was a bully, and I'd had enough of him.

"Your dad noticed there were several other guys siding with the bully. So, he said, 'This is going to be a fair fight, and if any of you jump in, you'll be dealing with me.' Then the bully and I went at it. I'm not sure who won, but I got some good licks in. Heck, let's admit no one really wins in those kinds of fights.

"Afterwards, your dad and I hung out in my dorm room. He asked me if I was all right and I told him I was thinking of dropping out. His reply startled me. He said, 'Ronnie, I know you're gay.'

"You must know this was a different time, Sarah. Very, very few men were open about their homosexuality. It was common to be made fun of and get beaten up or worse if you were suspected of it. So, I said to your dad, 'I'm not gay!'

"He said, 'Ronnie, I'm going to be more than your friend. I'm going to be your brother. From here forward, you should know that's how it's gonna be.'

"Then he shook my hand, got up and left.

"A few days later we were drinking beer in a local bar, and I confided to your dad that I thought I was gay. That he was right, and he was my only friend. All he did was put his arm around me and gave me a big bear hug and said, 'I got you brother. I got you.'

"We were great friends after that. I miss him so deeply it hurts." He finished with tears in his eyes.

"Uncle Ronnie, I never knew..." Sarah sighed, also with tears in her eyes.

"I'm old school, Sarah. I am homosexual, but that's only a part of who I am and not nearly the whole story. I learned so much from your father. Heck, I guess I learned if he could accept and love me, then why couldn't I do the same? I stayed in school. Joined the army with him and made a career out of it. It turned out I was pretty darned good at leading...and fighting," he said getting up from the bench to continue their walk.

"I remember one time my dad was talking about you, not too long ago. What he said makes even more sense now. He said, 'Sarita, your Uncle Ronnie is like a brother to me. He has more class, guts, and character than anyone I've ever met.'"

With that, Uncle Ronnie went down on one knee weeping inconsolably. Sarah knelt by his side holding him in a big bear hug on a trail that was once the scene of neighbors fighting each other in a war.

# 22

# FIRST DATE

Two weeks later, Sarah was set to go on her first official date with Hank. He was to meet her after work at the bar of a high-end steak house in downtown San Jose.

He said he wanted to treat her to a good steak and then walk around and talk, which sounded fine to her.

Sarah watched Hank approaching from her window seat at the bar. He was wearing a navy blue sport coat, tie, and khaki slacks. She couldn't get a gauge on his shoes until he got closer. Suddenly he changed direction, and she wondered if he'd gotten cold feet.

She could see him digging his wallet out of his pocket, kneeling down and giving some money to a man who was sitting at a bench across the street at the edge of a park. They spoke for a few minutes, and then Hank proceeded to the restaurant.

"Hey, Sarah," Hank said with cheer in his voice as he approached the table. "It's good to see you."

"Long time no see, Hank. Uncle Rakesh tells me you have his permission to date me. So, here I am."

"Ah, Uncle Rakesh. He made me visit him before he gave me the OK. What's funny is he told me straight away I had his permission and then proceeded to pour me a bourbon. We smoked cigars too," Hank said as he sat down. "What a great guy."

"He is a great man indeed. Did you meet his wife, Miriam?"

"I did. She was extremely kind. Very quiet. She also seemed to love that we were smoking cigars, which surprised me."

"I think cigars remind her of the younger days. My dad told me that he and Uncle Rakesh would smoke something called "Swisher Sweets" and drink Schlitz beer. She met them both through Uncle Ronnie. So, she knew my dad when he was very young. I love her like my own mother," explained Sarah.

"I'm not sure how my mom would feel about me smoking cigars, but I'm fixin' to find out. I loved that one I smoked with Uncle Rakesh. Best I ever had. He's cool."

"Sarah, can you tell me about yourself? We only met for a short while and under unusual circumstances. I would like to get to know you better," Hank asked.

So, Sarah told him about herself, all the while thinking how interesting it was that he wanted to know her better. He asked her many questions, including her favorite music, books, places to visit, things to do. Time flew. They made it through the final course agreeing to skip desert and go for a walk in the park. Then she realized he was not talking much about himself.

"Hank, can you tell me about yourself? How did you come to join the Army?"

"Sure. But, if it's OK, I need to stop at that automated teller machine over there because I'm plumb out of cash and need some to pay for my parking. It's on the way to the park."

While Hank was getting the cash out of the machine, he asked Sarah, "Are you a fast runner?"

Curious, Sarah replied, "I guess so, maybe. Why do you ask?"

"Stay focused on me right now. There is a man coming our way. If we need to, we're going to run up the sidewalk to our right. Take your shoes off now if you have to. Be ready to follow my lead."

The man approached, and just as Hank predicted, he was after their cash and more.

Hank put himself between the man and Sarah. Then she heard him demand, "I want her watch and ring too."

Suddenly Hank pushed the man and threw his wallet to the ground next to his feet. He said, "Run." In a firm voice. Sarah took off and did not look back, but she sensed Hank was not right behind her. After a bit she stopped and turned around to find Hank jogging at brisk pace.

Out of breath she said, "Damn, you just got robbed. I'm calling the police."

He replied, "Good idea, but I don't think they're going to be able to do much. Plus, don't worry. I just gave him my burner wallet with ten $1 bills in it. It also has a note telling him what he should do with himself, which I won't repeat."

"Are you serious? That's crazy. Weren't you scared?" she asked, still trying to catch her breath.

"Yes. Definitely. I'm glad it didn't get more serious. Let's go inside this store and call the police."

So, they did. It took the police a while to arrive. They simply took a report and said they would be on the lookout for the 'perp.' Hank apologized and walked Sarah to her car saying goodnight and asking if it would be okay to plan a second date, because the robber wrecked their first date.

"Hank, that guy didn't wreck our date, but yes, I would like to see you again. Let's make plans and ensure we go somewhere safer, although up until tonight I thought this place was pretty safe."

The next day she called Uncle Ronnie and asked if she should be concerned that Hank had her run instead of fighting.

Uncle Ronnie chuckled. "Girl dear, that's exactly what I would have done. Not only is that boy smart, he's also well-prepared. It is clear to me his first priority was your safety. Fighting that guy would have put you both in grave danger. I have no concerns at all with how he handled it. In fact, just the opposite. I reckon that robber was lucky you were with Hank. Otherwise, he might be in the hospital right now. In a real way, your presence may have saved *his* life."

Shocked and pleased, Sarah hung up thinking how little she knew about Hank.

A week later, Sarah met Hank and together they joined Jean and Sophie to go to San Francisco for some authentic Chinese cuisine. The day was wonderfully warm with sunshine and much hustle and bustle in the Chinatown area of the city. While walking along a steep hill to return to their car, the girls separated so they could talk.

"What do you think of Hank?" asked Sophie.

"I'm still feeling like I don't know him. He's so quiet. What do you think?"

"He's HOT!" giggled Sophie.

"Ha ha! Come on, Soap, what do you really think?" laughed Sarah.

"I'm like you. He's so quiet. I don't know him yet. He seems—what's the right word? I don't know. Solid? Yeah, solid. He seems rugged and smart too. I like him. He's someone to look up to."

"I think I'll have to go to where he can be himself and spend some time with him then. One thing's for sure. He's a lot different than the men I meet here in the valley and at work."

# 23

# MARY

The next day, Sarah called Hank on her way to the airport and asked if she could visit his home the next Saturday.

"Uh, um... Sarah, I'm not sure if it is a good idea to go to my place, but what if we go to my mom's? She lives right down the street."

"Okay, let's do it. I'll see you then," she responded with wonderment as to why he would not want her to visit his home.

On Saturday, Sarah picked up some flowers on the way to Merced and presented them to Hank's mom upon arriving at her home.

"Ah, good gracious me. Sure, these flowers are as beautiful as a clear morning on the Olde Sod. Come in, please, Sarah. My name is Mary. Hank will be here shortly."

"You have a lovely home, Mrs. Carson. I've not been to Merced before. It is good to be here."

"Please call me Mary. I'm glad you are here. I've been asking Hank about you, but getting information out of that boy is like pulling a nail out of a board," Mary chuckled.

"He's very quiet, isn't he?" asked Sarah.

"Well, that depends... that depends. Let's go to the kitchen and get lunch prepared. He'll be here soon enough."

"How long has it been since you were back to Ireland, Mary?" asked Sarah.

"I don't know. Let's see. I guess it was when we buried my dear departed mother back in 1993. Oh, how I wished she could have met Hank, but it was not to be."

"I suppose, then, your father had also passed by this time," Sarah queried.

"Yes, my dear old Pa passed on when I was just sixteen. He died in a car crash."

"How old were you when your mother passed?"

"I was twenty at the time."

"I see. This must've been a tough time, especially being in the U.S., so far away from home."

"Indeed. Yes. My Aunt Peggy came to stay with me for a while, but I was determined to make it on my own. I had a serious fella who I was dating, and I saw my future with him. He turned out to be Hank's father. Unfortunately, he didn't see his future with us. So, there's that," she recounted these things without drama or emotion. "Hank turned out to be a gift from the Almighty Himself. It was very hard in the early years makin' ends meet and all, but he gave me somethin' to live for outside of me-self. I set my mind to raisin' him the way my ma and pa would've wanted and tried to live up to their standards. So, I did."

Just then Hank walked in. "Nice of you to grace us with your presence, Your Highness," Mary sang as she curtsied and bowed in mock deference to her son.

"Ah, surin' the sun don't rise and the rain don't fall until I give them permission," he crowed and laughed in his best Irish accent, honed over time with his Ma.

"Well, then, if you're done with your boastin', set the table, me boy. Sarah's hungry, and we don't have time to waste." She turned to

Sarah with keen interest. "So, Sarah, tell me about yourself."

"Well, I grew up in the Shenandoah Valley of Virginia, which is where my mother and father were from. His father was a policeman in the Bronx. His father before him came over from Ireland and settled here due to the potato famine.

"My mother's people were Irish and settled in the mountains of Virginia. They met because my grandfather ran a grocery store after he moved to Virginia. Her family used to go there to get provisions for their small farm.

"I grew up in the shadow of the Blue Ridge, where my grandfather and father taught me to hunt, shoot, play golf, and cut wood. My mom and dad had a rough time having me, as I've come to understand, so I was their only child and did a lot of things with my dad.

"I went to the state university, where I studied business. I worked at my grandfather's store in the summer to pay my way and got a job out here in Silicon Valley a few years after I graduated. Now I am an analyst doing due diligence for a venture capital firm based in San Jose."

"Ah, Sarah, do you know where your people were from in Ireland?" Mary asked with great interest.

"Castlerea, County Roscommon."

"You don't say? This is not far from where I grew up in Castleplunket."

"Amazing, Mary. How far are they from each other?"

"No more than ten miles as the crow flies, dear," Mary replied.

"Wow! I can't believe this. My family roots are so close to yours in County Roscommon."

"Have you been there?"

"I have not, but I would love to visit there someday. I don't know when this will happen, now...."

"Would you like some tea?"

"Sure. I would love some."

The conversation continued for quite a while, with Hank keeping himself busy washing the dishes and straightening up the kitchen. When he was finished, Mary suggested they go for a walk. Instead, Hank decided to take Sarah to Scruffy's for a drink.

Just before they left, Mary held Sarah by her shoulders and looked at her directly. "It was good to have you here with us this afternoon, Sarah. I'll be sayin' a special prayer for you tonight and also for your dear departed mother and father."

While they drove to "Hank's headquarters," Sarah couldn't help feeling something she hadn't felt for a long time... Hope.

# 24

# FRIENDS IN HIGH PLACES

Upon entering Scruffy's, Sarah was immediately reminded of her visit just a few weeks earlier to the Vienna Inn, which was dark, old, and dingy, but full of life. Hank seemed to know a lot of people.

They found seats at a table, and a waitress named Angie came over to take their order. She gave Sarah the evil eye and focused all her attention on Hank.

A few minutes later, Scruffy walked over, introduced himself, and offered condolences to Sarah for her loss.

"Your father was a fine gentleman, Ms. O'Malley. It is my great honor that you are here today."

No sooner had Scruffy left than Angie arrived keeping her back to Sarah and delivered the drinks, along with a hug for Hank.

Sarah remarked, "Nice place. Angie's got the hots for you, eh?"

"Don't pay her any attention. We're just friends. This is the place where all of us construction contractors tend to meet up during the week. I figured you'd want to see where I do my business since you want to learn more about me."

Just then, a man of about forty came over to their table and towered over Sarah announcing, "Your father was a lousy president!"

Immediately he was taken down to the floor by Hank. It

happened so fast that Sarah had no time to react. Hank put the man in a headlock and proceeded to haul him out the front door. After a few minutes he returned and said, "Let's get out of here. I've got to cool off."

As they exited the front door, the man approached again, this time his head was lowered, and he said, "Please accept my apologies, Ms. O'Malley. I don't know what got into me, but that was uncalled for."

Hank did not let her respond but instead kept her moving to his truck.

"Sorry about that, Sarah. I hated to get physical with that guy, but I'm not about to let anyone disrespect you or your family."

"Thanks, Hank." Sarah was processing what just happened, wondering why Hank had gone ballistic so quickly. Did he not know she could handle herself? He didn't hesitate, though. He also seemed to restrain himself from doing more damage.

They continued driving. Hank was quiet.

Eventually Sarah asked, "Where are we going?"

"Good question. I don't know. I needed to cool off. Now I'm over it. What do you want to do?"

"Let's go somewhere where we can walk and talk and maybe hold hands." As she said this, she thought she saw Hank smile, then he looked away.

Hank and Sarah developed a rhythm of hanging out together on Saturdays, sometimes with Sophie and Jean, sometimes with other friends. They hiked and biked and went sightseeing to wonderful places like Fisherman's Warf, the Golden Gate Bridge, Monterey, and Carmel by the Sea.

Sarah conferred with Uncle Ronnie regarding the run-in at

Scruffy's and Hank's reaction. He confirmed that Sarah should be unconcerned with what happened but instead admire Hank's sense of responsibility and courage.

Then one day Sarah asked Hank to attend Saturday evening Vigil Mass with her. He agreed. Afterwards they went to a Mexican restaurant for a nice meal and talked deep into the evening.

"I can't believe I'm going to say this. I liked going to Mass. It's been a long time. My mom wants me to go, but I rarely do," Hank said while sipping his Modelo cerveza.

"I don't go regularly, either. I'm too busy, I guess. My dad used to go a lot, at least weekly and then more often after he retired. He said it was essential for a guy like him to go to Mass because it kept him on the 'straight and narrow.'"

"Hmm. That's saying somethin' for him to feel that way." Hank took another drink.

"The other thing he used to say about Mass was, 'I wouldn't be here today, as I am, if it weren't for the Eucharist.' He really believed in its power to change his life."

"I wish I had his faith," Hank replied with genuine interest.

"Me, too. I guess we should pray that we get some."

Hank said, "Want to try it right now?"

"What?" asked Sarah.

"To pray for faith."

"Um, er, sure. I guess. How do we start?" Sarah asked.

"I'll try first." Bowing his head, Hank said, "Dear Lord, I'd like to ask you for a favor. Could you give Sarah and me more faith, please? Amen."

Then Sarah said, "That sounded good. Let me try one." She blessed herself in the name of the Father, the Son and the Holy Spirit, then she said, 'Hail Mary, full of grace, the Lord is with thee. Blessed art thou amongst women, and blessed is the fruit of thy womb, Jesus. Holy Mary, Mother of God, pray for us sinners, now and at the hour of our death. Amen."

They were silent for a moment, then Sarah said, "I don't know where that came from."

"It felt good to pray with you like that," Hank said looking into her eyes while reaching across the table to hold her hand. "It sure can't hurt to ask Mary herself to pray to her Son for our cause, can it?"

The next day, Sarah received an early morning call from an unusual number.

"Hello Sarah, this is Victor Petrov. How are you?"

"It is an honor to hear from you, President Petrov. I am doing fine. I've been very busy at work, and I've met a very nice young man who I am getting to know."

"Excellent. I am glad to hear this, Sarah. It is very important to me that you know I am thinking of you and praying for you and your parents. This will continue for the rest of my life."

"Wow! Thank you, I am amazed by this, Mr. President."

"You are a very special woman, Sarah. Your father and I had a relationship that runs very deep for me and will never end. You may call me at any time on this number, and I will be at your service. I look forward to our next visit knowing it will be under better circumstances. I do not know when, but if my travels take me to your country, I will ensure we meet. If you find yourself coming to Europe, then perhaps you can come farther east to Russia to visit me and my wife in our home."

"I would enjoy this very much. May I ask you a question? When we were in the hospital together you mentioned something about a covenant. Can you explain this to me?" Sarah inquired.

"I would love to, Sarah. But we must do this in person. Let's keep in touch and plan to get together sooner rather than later." With that, he ended the conversation.

The next day all the major news outlets reported Russian President Victor Petrov was making an unscheduled and unprecedented trip to the United States in three weeks. Both parties tried to spin it to their advantage, but only Sarah knew the real reason for such a bold move.

# 25

# PRESIDENTIAL POWER

Sophie could not believe what Sarah was telling her. "Are you for real? The reason the President of Russia is coming to the U.S. is to meet with you regarding a covenant he made with your father?"

"Let's keep this on the down-low, Soap. I know this is nearly impossible for you, but you've got to keep your mouth shut," Sarah said laughing hard.

"Yeah, well, I might as well admit I'm going to tell Jean, my dad, my mom, and a few other friends," Sophie said seriously. "I can't keep this to myself."

"Argh! Just them. No posting to your social media channel," Sarah growled.

"OK, I'll try. Are you going to tell Hank?"

"Not sure."

That matter was decided later that day when a secretary for the office of President Petrov called Sarah to make arrangements for their meeting. She also indicated President Petrov wanted to meet Sarah's "young man." Additionally, the secretary asked if they would be available to fly to Washington, D.C. at the President's expense for the meeting. Sarah agreed and immediately called Hank.

"Hi, Hank, I've got some big news for you," she said coyly over

FaceTime.

"OK, give it to me."

"We're going to Washington, D.C. to meet with President Petrov in three weeks. I hope you can make it. Please!?"

"What? You're not serious?"

Then Sarah explained the background, and Hank agreed to accompany her on the trip. He then asked, "Is it okay for me to explain this to my mom?"

"Of course! Please do," Sarah replied full of excitement.

"One other thing. Can we go to the Blue Ridge and see your old stomping grounds?"

Sarah was stunned and overjoyed by Hank's thoughtful request. "Nothing would make me happier."

Then she called Uncle Ronnie to tell him the news. He was not surprised in the least and suggested Sarah bring a gift for President Petrov. She asked what kind of gift and was impressed with what Uncle Ronnie suggested.

"I love it. That's exactly what I'll bring. I hope he likes it."

"Oh, I think he will, girl dear. I think he will," Uncle Ronnie replied with joy and pleasure at his idea.

After the call, Uncle Ronnie arranged a call with Father Jack and Rakesh informing them of the news and seeking advice. They all agreed they should leave things to Sarah, trusting her judgment and the maturity and the integrity of President Petrov.

"Did any of you know about this covenant between Petrov and Sean?" asked Ronnie.

"I did not," replied Father Jack.

"Neither did I," replied Rakesh.

"Do you guys think this thing could be behind why things have changed so much in the world?" Ronnie asked.

"I don't believe in coincidences. For eighty years we were adversaries with Russia. Then things did an about face after Sean became president and visited Russia in his first month. Later the G7 became the G8, with Russia joining the United States, France, Germany, Italy, Japan, and the United Kingdom. Russian prisons were opened. The Russian mafia was destroyed. Our defense posture changed drastically. All this because two men made a covenant with each other?" Rakesh pondered.

Father Jack explained, "We all knew Sean well. He would have known the theological background of the term covenant. If he made one with President Petrov, it means they may have joined their families together into an indissoluble union.

"Looking at this notion biblically, we know there were a number of covenants between God and man, including those made at the Garden of Eden followed by Noah, Abraham, Moses, and King David.

"As Christians we also believe Jesus fulfilled the old covenants and established a new one. This is especially called out in 2 Samuel Chapter 7, where 'God promises to King David to "raise up your offspring, sprung from your loins, and I will establish his kingdom.' It goes on, 'I will be a father to him, and he will be a son to me.'"[11]

"The new covenant was established on the night of the last supper. What's more, Jesus established the Sacrament of the Holy Eucharist saying, 'This is my body, which will be given for you; do this in memory of me.' Then taking the cup he said, 'This cup is the new covenant in my blood, which will be shed for you.'[12]

"Our understanding of covenant must be shaped by the Semitic

[11] 2 Samuel 7:14
[12] Luke 22:19-20

cultural and biblical context which recounts the history of the whole world and the relationship between God and man in this way. A covenant is more than a contract. It is more than a legal agreement. It's a holy promise.

"It binds two together and can never be rescinded. The fact that there is more than one covenant between God and man is not because the covenants ended but because man kept breaking them, whereas God never did. In fact, each covenant strengthens and reinforces the prior one. In a real way, they form one continuous relationship where God joins us to himself, not merely as God but as our Father. In the new covenant, He joins us as a family to the unity of the Trinity in a mystical way through His promise at the Last Supper.

"So, knowing Sean as I do, if he and Victor entered into a covenant together, this would likely be done within this context. This may have real implications for Sarah," Father Jack concluded.

Ronnie gazed at him a moment, then slowly nodded his head. "This is going to get very interesting."

# 26

# BACK TO THE BLUE RIDGE

Sarah and Hank arrived in Virginia two days before their meeting with President Petrov, which allowed them time to visit her family home where she intended to get a special gift for President Petrov. Before doing so, however, she and Hank stopped at the cemetery to pay their respects to her parents.

Hank noted, "This is a good place. It is quiet with birdsong, and I love the smell of honeysuckle and cow manure."

Sarah was on her knees praying and sobbing. Hank gave her space then hugged her for a long time when she was finished.

They went to her home and found it to be in fine shape, having been under the care of a good friend who used to work for her grandfather at his store.

"I'll show you around, Hank, but first I need to get something for President Petrov.
Please wait here for a moment."

A few minutes later Sarah returned holding a crucifix. "My dad made this."

"What!? Are you kidding? It is beautiful." Hank marveled at the simplicity and expert joinery.

"Do you think President Petrov will like it?" she asked.

"Is he Catholic?"

"Yes. My father was his sponsor when he came into the Church."

"Incredible! Yes, I think he will like it a lot."

Then she showed him around the modest country farmhouse set on just a few acres, not a stone's throw from the Shenandoah River. They talked and walked and eventually wound up at Sarah's favorite spot, which was a bench her dad made for her looking east towards the Shenandoah under a large white oak. They sat quietly.

"I love to imagine you growing up in this place."

"I'm glad you can see where I am from. My family is no more, but my memories are still strong."

"I'm lucky to have met your dad for one brief moment. Luckier still to be have met the most beautiful girl in the world."

Hank held her hand and put his arm around her shoulder, which was just fine by her.

A while later, they went to supper at Murphy's Pub, which wasn't far from the house. The hostess, Tanya, came charging as soon as she saw Sarah and gave her a long hug. Many people came up to Sarah to express their condolences and pleasure at seeing her back home again. After finishing with peach pie, they bid farewell and made their way back to Washington, D.C.

# 27

# JEWISH MOTHER

"Who knows anything about Russia?" was Sean O'Malley's first question at his first cabinet meeting after taking office. Several hands went up. He selected his youngest cabinet officer, Secretary of State, Jane Goodwin to stay after the meeting.

Together they discussed Russia at length. Goodwin had studied Russian history while at Oxford pursuing her Doctorate in Political Science as a Rhodes Scholar. She was impressed by O'Malley's range of questions, which extended back to ancient times, along with queries regarding the development of Judaism and Christianity in the country.

Finally, she asked, "Mr. President, why do you want to know so much about Russia?"

"Because I think Victor Petrov may be a good man."

"What!? Petrov runs that country with an iron fist. He's cut from the same cloth as all the recent strongmen who take control of a country by being willing to kill anyone who opposes them."

"Did you know his grandmother was a Jew?" he asked looking out the window towards the Washington Monument.

"I did not. How does this change things?"

"A mother has the power to change the world. Thank you for your time, Madame Secretary."

O'Malley had his Chief of Staff make the arrangements for his meeting with Petrov two weeks after his inauguration. He went by himself, albeit with all the security provisions required by the Secret Service, telling his staff he expected the meeting to be short and to the point.

Despite being informed this was highly unusual and out of sync with diplomatic protocols, O'Malley followed his instincts to meet the leader of America's most ruthless adversary.

By the time President Victor Petrov was born, his family's Jewish roots had long been sublimated to the Communist Party and his father's ambitions during the power struggles of post-Soviet Russia. A high-ranking officer of the GRU, Russia's equivalent of the C.I.A., he sought to acquire wealth and power following the "capitulation to the West" after the fall of the Berlin Wall in November 1989. Petrov's father saw an opportunity and took it by resting control of Russia's vast natural gas resources, soon becoming one of the Oligarchs who ran the country through wealth, violence, information control, and politics.

His grandmother, who was alive until Victor's twentieth birthday, was ever present during his youth. Saddened but not surprised her daughter had married a strikingly handsome Russian military officer who was on the rise within the party, she sought to maintain the right balance in the family in hopes she could bring them to their faith in the one true God, the God of Israel.

For this goal, she was willing to die, but long before this was to happen, she realized her best bet was to play the long game through her grandson. They were like two peas in a pod, with Victor hanging onto her every word. To him, she was mysterious and fun. She was also smart, and opinionated, treated him with respect, and set high expectations.

She didn't care about the party or politics. She didn't complain about how rotten things were. Instead, she was always positive, praying and reading her beloved Tanakh. She taught him the Psalms and how to interpret them in secret, which made it even more intriguing to the young boy.

Together they went to their small living room in the afternoon when Victor came home from school.

"Let's read Psalm 25 today, Victor. Remember, we cannot let anyone know you are reading this. It must remain our secret," she would say in hushed tones, keeping their Tanakh readings hidden from his father.

Victor read aloud, "To you I lift up my soul, my God, in you I trust; do not let me be disgraced; do not let my enemies gloat over me. No one is disgraced who waits for you, but only those who are treacherous without cause. Make known your ways, Lord; teach me your paths.[13]

"What does this mean Babushka?" he asked.

"Ah, Victor, you remember the story of how Abraham had so much faith in the Lord that he was ready to sacrifice his son Issac? Was he not richly rewarded for his faith! And, then the Lord gave Moses the Ten Commandments, no? A humble and righteous man, he would become our great prophet and leader.

"The way of the Lord is the way of faith and love. His path is love. When we love God and neighbor, then we are following His way.

"You may hear and learn many things throughout your life that contradict this. In Russia, especially, power is the most important thing. Wealth and power are God. Yet, those who think this are fools! They are the ones who end up in disgrace because they do not lift their

[13] Psalm 25:1-4

soul and trust God," his grandma whispered in reply.

"What is love, Babushka?" Victor asked.

"Dear grandson, you have asked the most important question. You must spend your whole life searching for the answer. You must learn not only what love is but also how to love God with your whole heart, your whole mind, and your whole soul. No matter how hard things get, you must never stop loving, because when you love, you find God.

"I know I am on the right path because of how much I love you, my dear grandson. Sometimes when I think of you it takes my breath away.

"The 'it' that does this is love. Oh, how wonderful God is because He loves us so much! Oh, how wonderful God is because he gave me such a wonderful grandson!"

Thus, it went like this between them for many years while Victor was growing and maturing into a young man. His babushka was his confidant, his best friend, his rock until she passed away.

Once she was gone, and because his father was a very wealthy man, it was not long before he was carried away by the power of Russia and all it entails.

Who could possibly overcome such odds?

# 28

# COVENANT

Sarah and Hank arrived at President Petrov's five-star hotel in Georgetown slightly ahead of time. Before long, he met them in the lobby and asked them to join him in the exquisite restaurant overlooking the Potomac River, along with all the other guests and visitors to this charming section of the nation's capital.

After breakfast he asked them if they would like to go for a walk on the campus of Georgetown University, and they readily agreed. It was a glorious morning, cool and crisp without a cloud in the sky.

"Hank, I understand you served in the U.S. military. Why did you decide to join the Army?" President Petrov asked with genuine curiosity.

"Good question. I've wondered the same myself, especially after I enlisted. I guess the answer is—I needed it. I didn't have a dad growing up. It was just my mom and me. I was not a great student, not bad either. I just had a lot of energy.

"I was getting into a bit of trouble, and my mom was struggling with me. I was even disrespectful to her. Then I had a run-in that led me to jail for two nights. I got a lawyer and got out of it with a small fine, but I knew I was off-track.

"The problem was, I didn't know how to get back on track. Then one day, Roy, who was my supervisor at this landscaping place where I worked, suggested I go for the U.S. Army Rangers. Something clicked, and I went for it. I'm glad I did!"

"I understand you served with the U.S. Army Rangers, did three overseas missions, and after leaving the service went to a four-year university, receiving a degree in Mechanical Engineering Technology using benefits from your military service to pay your way."

"Yes, and I also started my own landscaping business to help pay my way, too," Hank added while being quite surprised at President Petrov's understanding of his background.

"Yes, and this gradually adapted to become a carpentry and then a general contracting business, where you have renovated approximately three houses and sold them for a profit. Let me ask you another question about your background.

"After the Army, you also volunteered at an organization called Big Brothers, what is this?"

"Big Brothers is an organization that seeks to help young boys who are growing up without a father. While I was in college I was paired with a few boys. We would hang out and go to parks, hike, play basketball, stuff like that. I guess I was trying to be a good example for them."

"Why did you do this?" asked President Petrov, stopping and looking directly at Hank.

"I felt I had something to give. The cause was worthy. Truth is, I got as much or more out of it than the boys did," said Hank matter-of-factly.

"Thank you, Hank. I would now like to speak with Sarah alone. I trust you can find your way back to the hotel. We should not be too long."

As Hank left them, he noticed quite a number of secret service and Russian security agents at various points across the serene campus setting.

Petrov and Sarah made their way to the Dahlgren quad just in front of the Chapel of the Sacred Heart. Together they sat on a bench. School was not in session during the summer months, so they were alone. The setting was quiet except for the twitter of birds in the trees and planes on their final approach to Reagan National Airport.

"You seemed to know a lot about Hank, President Petrov," Sarah said with a smile.

"*Da*! Of course, I had him thoroughly investigated after Rakesh informed me he had asked his permission to date you," he chuckled.

"Oh," Sarah gasped in surprise.

"Sarah, will you do me a favor?"

"Yes."

"Will you call me Victor? I want you to feel comfortable with me. From now on you will know me not as the President of Russia, which by the way I won't be for too much longer, but instead I want you to know me as your father's good friend, Victor," he said looking at her and taking her hands.

"Yes, of course. This will make me very happy. Thank you, Victor."

"Hank is a good man. I think you cannot go wrong there. Of course, it is in God's hands, but I confirm Rakesh's instincts."

A warm breeze blew, and the bells of a nearby church started their tintinnabulation. Sarah glanced in that direction and then back at Victor.

"Thank you," she said. "It means a lot to me that you and Uncle Rakesh think he is a good guy."

"After I met your father, I started doing some research into Christianity and the Catholic Church. This led me to reading the Bible, the Catechism of the Catholic Church, and writings by the

Church Fathers like Irenaeus, Ignatius of Antioch, and Augustine.

"One day I came across a sermon by St. Augustine, which went something like this:

> 'Let us suppose God proposed to you a deal and said, "I will give you anything you want, and you can own the world. Nothing will be impossible for you; nothing will be sin and nothing forbidden. You will never die, never have pain, never have anything you do not want and always have anything you desire. Except for just one thing. You will never see my face."'

"Augustine closed with this question: 'Did a chill rise in your hearts when you heard the words, "You will never see my face?" That chill is the most precious thing in you; that is the pure love of God. What good is it for a man to gain the whole world and lose his soul?'

"Upon reading this, I knew I would become a Christian. I called your father to tell him the news, but I was not able to reach him. Then I read a Bible passage regarding God's covenant with Abraham, and I learned more and more about God's covenants and thought, '*Why don't I make a covenant with Sean O'Malley, who I once hated with a white-hot passion?*'

"This was an impetuous, perhaps vain, impulse on my part, but I wanted to express my deep gratitude to your father. Being so far apart and presidents of our respective countries made it hard to get to know each other.

"Then one night in New York, after many bourbons, I proposed that we should enact a covenant. He asked immediately, 'Are you sure you mean covenant and not contract or agreement?'

"I assured him I meant *covenant*. And so, it went like this, 'I, Victor Petrov, make a covenant with you, Sean O'Malley, to be your brother and friend. Whenever you need me, I will be there for you for the rest of my life.'

"Then your father said, 'I, Sean O'Malley, join my family to yours, Victor Petrov. We are now one family devoted to Our Lord and Savior, inside His new covenant. Whenever you need me, I will be there for you and your family for the rest of my life.'

"What this means, therefore, Dear Sarah, is that you and I are family, and I will be there for you, whenever you need me, for the rest of my life."

"I cannot believe this! This is incredible! My father did not tell anyone of this, or did he?" Sarah was astonished.

"We both agreed to tell our wives. So, your mother, Maggie, knew this, and so did my wife, Sandra. Would you like to know one other implication of this covenant?" Victor asked, raising his right eyebrow dramatically.

"Yes!" cried Sarah.

"You have a brother, by way of this covenant, in Russia. He is my son, Ivan. He is about seven years older than you and has a family in St. Petersburg. The Petrov's and O'Malley's will have a special bond through you and my son, as well," Victor said with a smile.

"Wow! I cannot believe this. I am so happy. It feels so good to know you think of me in this way," Sarah was almost crying.

"Let's go back to the hotel. I have a special gift for you. I want Hank to be there, too, when I present it."

Later, that afternoon, President Petrov had Sarah and Hank meet him at the White House, where he had arranged to have a joint press conference with President Madison Saunders, the first woman president of the United States and former Vice President under President O'Malley.

Before the press conference wrapped up, President Petrov asked President Saunders if she would approve of him making an important announcement. She readily agreed and moved off to the side to give him the stage.

"Ladies and Gentlemen, today I would like to announce that I will not seek another term as President of Russia. In approximately six months, we will have our first truly free, democratic election. After this election, we will peacefully transfer power to the next president following the example set by the United States."

There were gasps and then spontaneous applause and a standing ovation. After it quieted down, President Petrov continued, "I would like to ask Sarah O'Malley to join me on stage. As all of you know, Sarah's father, former president Sean O'Malley, passed away recently. Many of us believe he died of a broken heart, for this was how strong his love was for his dear departed wife, Maggie.

What many of you don't know is President O'Malley was instrumental in my conversion to Christianity and joining the Catholic Church. He was my sponsor for this process."

Again, there were gasps in the room, which suddenly became quiet.

"During this time, he gave me a prayer, which he wrote with his own hand." He pulled out a piece of paper from the left front pocket of his navy blue blazer.

"Today I present Sean's prayer to his beloved daughter, Sarah, who I now consider to be like a daughter to me. If you will allow, I would like to pray this prayer with you all right here and now."

He looked to President Sauders for approval to proceed. She nodded her encouragement.

Then he blessed himself in the name of the Father, the Son, and the Holy Spirit.

*"Dear Jesus, please teach me Your Way! Help me to live in the present when I am scared. Remind me to be humble when I have an advantage. Help me to simplify when I am worried. Remind me of Your presence when I am sad. Let me hear Your Word when I am ambivalent. Feed me Your Eucharist when my faith falters. Have mercy on me when I feel proud. Let me appreciate Your glory when I am happy. Help me to be present, loving, and wise for all who need me. And, in everything I do, teach me Your Way. Amen.*

"This prayer, written by President O'Malley, was given to me at a time when I was not sure who Jesus was. Since then, I have said this prayer every day, which has now been for more than ten years. I will continue to recite it until I die, but today, I want you, dear Sarah, to have this copy from your father's hand, as a reminder of his great love. You will note this piece of paper is in tatters because I have kept it with me all this time. Let this also be a reminder that no matter how tattered our lives become, Jesus is always ready to help us pick up the pieces."

The press conference concluded with Sarah, Victor, and Hank leaving by a side door to proceed back to his Georgetown hotel.

Upon arriving back at his suite for drinks, Sarah announced, "Victor, I have something for you."

"Aha! Then this deserves a toast with some nectar from the work of human hands—bourbon! I bought this bottle yesterday hoping I would be able to share it with you," Victor said most pleased and relaxed.

"Hank, would you mind making the toast?" Victor asked, while providing a glass of Kentucky's best to him and Sarah.

Hank smiled. "I'll keep it short and sweet. Thanks to you both for this wonderful experience. I am glad to be here. I toast to President

O'Malley, who I didn't know but a moment. May God hold you in the palm of his hand until we meet again!"

They touched glasses and had a sip, with Victor looking quite pleased at Hank's words.

Then they moved outside to his balcony. "Victor," Sarah said, "this afternoon you presented me with a prayer written in my dad's own hand. Let me present you with something he also made with his hands." She reached into her handbag and brought out a box which she presented to him. He sat down to open it and was surprised to find a crucifix made of quartersawn white oak. "My father made the cross when I was a young girl. He sourced the corpus from Bethlehem. It was hand carved by an artisan there."

Victor could not speak.

"My father gave this to me when I received the Sacrament of Confirmation. I now present it to you as a gift of remembrance, not only for what it symbolizes, but also of my father's love for us both."

He caressed the crucifix, feeling the smoothness of the wood. He turned it over and found a miraculous medal embedded in the nexus.

"My father had a special devotion to Mary. He was not shy to say, 'I wouldn't be here if it weren't for her intercession.'" She sat down beside him. "He told me this Miraculous Medal of Mary is a symbol to remind us of her great 'Yes.' He would say, 'She is the greatest human being in the history of the world. Learn her prayer and ask for her intercessions when you are most in need.' I think he would like you to have this as a remembrance of him."

"I cannot thank you enough, Sarah," he whispered. Then he wept deeply, holding the crucifix to his chest.

# 29

# SILICON VALLEY

A week later, Hank called Sarah at her office asking if it would be okay if he came to San Jose Friday evening because he was volunteering at Habitat for Humanity on Saturday and taking his mother for brunch after Mass on Sunday. She agreed and suggested they meet at a bar her colleagues liked to go to after work, figuring it was time to introduce him to some of her work friends.

Before Hank arrived, Sarah was having wine with her good friend Amanda, who had graduated magna cum laude from Stanford and was one of the top managers at her firm.

"I'm looking forward to meeting Hank. What should I know about him?" Amanda inquired while sipping her mojito, made with extra mint.

"He was in the Army. He has an engineering degree. His mother's from Ireland, and he's a few years older than me. Actually, here he comes now!"

"Hi, Hank!" Sarah gushed, getting up and giving him a kiss and a hug. Turning to Amanda, she said, "Let me introduce you to Amanda. We work together."

Hank extended his hand. "Hey Amanda, very nice to meet you."

"Hi, Hank. Please sit down and join us."

They spoke for a few minutes and then were joined by two more of Sarah's colleagues. The first was a young woman named Skylar. The second was a young man named Bradley, who was exquisitely dressed. They seemed to be Sarah's peers at the firm.

After introductions, the colleagues quickly went about discussing the latest news at work. Hank found himself on the outside looking in but listened in hopes of getting a gauge on the kinds of things Sarah dealt with.

After a while he thought he had a bead on what they were discussing and couldn't help himself from asking, "Have any of you gone and asked him yourself, face-to-face, to learn what he is thinking?"

They all stopped suddenly and turned to Hank. Then Skylar asked, "Are you serious? This guy is a multi-millionaire who owns three companies. Plus, his headquarters is in Kansas City. So, it's not exactly easy to ask him face-to-face."

"If it were me, I'd get on a plane Monday morning and meet with him that afternoon," Hank said casually.

Bradley chimed in. "What if he wouldn't see you?"

"Then I'd have my answer," Hank replied without emotion.

"And, if he did see you, then what?" Bradley asked with interest and irritation, not knowing Hank's background.

"Then I'd ask him directly to explain what he was thinking and more importantly why."

Skylar jumped in, "OK, thanks, but you don't know the full background and history. We're in a tough spot with his company. Appreciate your advice, though. Thanks."

Amanda interjected, "I think Hank's right. I'm going to Kansas City on Monday."

Sarah, Bradley, and Skylar turned in astonishment towards

Amanda, who had a really big smile and winked at Hank.

"I'll drink to that!" Hank said, and then leaned in to touch glasses with Amanda.

Sarah wasn't sure what to think. Then Skylar sought to change the subject.

"So, Hank, tell us what you do for a living?" she asked with genuine interest.

"I have a small general contracting business in Merced. I'm renovating a historic house right now to learn my trade. My dream is to build affordable houses. I'm working with an architect on a unique design with hopes to reduce the overall total cost and environmental impact of home building and ownership, but I'm a long way from this dream," Hank replied.

"How many employees do you have?" Bradley asked.

"Two. One is my right-hand man. He's a master carpenter. The other is our helper. He's a terrific guy in every way. Additionally, I use craftsmen from the union. I also work with a local accountant and lawyer who really understand the building trades. I'm a generalist, decent at carpentry, fair at electrical, and better at organizing."

"So, how do you know so much about dealing with entrepreneurs and venture capital?" Skylar asked with a hint of condescension.

"I don't. The advice I gave you earlier came from my experience dealing with Iraqi chieftains."

"What? You were in Iraq? You dealt with a chieftain?" Bradley asked with surprise.

"I was there three different times. I learned the hard way on some deals that went sideways. The main thing I learned is you must look a man in the eye, and he has to do the same with you. Trust can't be forced. The other thing I learned is to manage my determination to win and instead set my sights on what's right, which sometimes isn't apparent until you get the other guy's perspective."

Sarah and Amanda listened with amazement.

"OK, Amanda, good luck with your Kansas City Chieftain on Monday?" Skylar chimed in hoping to be funny.

"I think I won't need luck on Monday. I'll use Hank's advice and see why Mr. Kauffman is taking the stance he's taking. Best to look him in the eye and not force something that doesn't make sense for both of us."

"Can I give you one other piece of advice before you go to KC, Amanda?" Hank asked.

"Sure!"

"If you don't like what Old Man Kauffman has to say, then before you leave, I suggest saying, 'Hey Kauffman, why don't you stick all your money up your arse if you don't have anything better to do with it.' Then take off running, yelling 'Yeeeehaw, Kaufmann!' at the top of your lungs. At least that's what I would do," Hank said barely able to keep himself from laughing.

Amanda, Bradley, and Skylar were almost falling to the floor, they were laughing so hard. Sarah was taking it all in with a smile, surprised to hear her Hank speaking so easily with her colleagues.

Hank suggested they get dinner, at which point Bradley and Amanda bowed out, but Skylar readily accepted his invitation. They moved into the dining room for dinner.

As they took their seats, Skylar asked, "Hank, what do you think of San Jose and Silicon Valley?"

"I don't know much about it. What do you think?"

"It is amazing! There are so many smart people and great companies. I love it!"

"Where are you from, Skylar," Hank asked.

"I grew up near San Francisco. I went to college at UC Berkley."

"Cool. I grew up near Merced. I guess we're both native Californians. That makes Sarah the outsider. Ha!"

"Yeah, well, why don't you ask me what I think about Silicon Valley, then?" Sarah grumbled.

"Yes, Sarah, what do you think?" asked Skylar.

"What you say is true. Great things are coming out of this valley. Well, actually, let me be more specific. Great new technology is what is being developed and pushed.

I'm from the Shenandoah Valley, where we come at things from a different perspective. My next-door neighbor ran a sawmill. He could look at a tree and within seconds figure out the best way to cut it to yield the highest quality boards. Two doors down, my other neighbor could take the same log and carve it into a cozy bear and cubs with his chain saw. I guess what I'm trying to say is technology is not an objective and should not overtake our search for beauty, be it with wood, music, words, or concepts, things that are timeless," Sarah responded, wondering where this was coming from.

"You sound like my dad," Skylar chimed in, wondering what was wrong with her friend.

"I remember working at my grandpa's store, taking in local honey, eggs, milk, and corn from our neighbors to sell. Thinking about it now, I realize he was like a hub in the middle of a wheel connecting our neighbors together, helping each other get by. They got along without the internet or smart phones, somehow," Sarah added all the while thinking, *I'm not against technology, but something seems missing out here.*

Hank asked, "You don't seem yourself, Sarah. Is something wrong?"

"You guys asked me what I thought about Silicon Valley. Here's my answer: something's missing out here," Sarah said with surety.

"What's missing, Sarah? Can you put your finger on it?" asked Skylar, slightly amused to be hearing her friend talk this way, her friend who had a degree in business and was regarded as a savvy up-and-coming venture capitalist.

"How long have you lived in your apartment, Skylar?" Sarah asked.

"Two years," Skylar answered wondering where she was going with her question.

"What are the names of your neighbors on either side of you?" Sarah asked, leaning in.

"Britney and Lacey live on my right, but I don't know the names of the neighbors to my left."

"How about the neighbors next to them? What are their names?" Sarah asked.

Skylar shrugged. "No idea."

"Yep. Not surprised. I'm in the same boat. Nice apartment. Good job. Great colleagues. Don't know my neighbors. Work in this big eco-system for who knows what, doing my part, but why? What are we aiming for? Where are we going?" Sarah asked. "Seems to me the answers aren't found in Silicon Valley."

"Then in what valley do you find them?" asked Hank.

"The Jordan Valley," replied Sarah.

"Huh? Where's that?" asked Skylar.

"Between Israel and Jordan. It's formed by the Jordan River starting at the Sea of Galilee and ending at the Dead Sea to the south," Sarah surprised herself, again wondering where all of this was coming from.

A week later, Hank arrived back at the same bar near Sarah's work, due again to his volunteering for Habitat for Humanity on the weekend. The same crew gathered, but this time another friend, Dakota, joined them.

After a few drinks, Dakota said, "I've had it with big pharma and big tech. They're evil incarnate."

Her declaration incited a heavy discussion between everyone except Hank, who listened carefully to the claims and opinions. Eventually Dakota asked for Hank's opinion.

"Have you ever come face-to-face with evil, Dakota?" Hank asked.

"What do you mean?" she replied.

"Have you ever met an evil person?"

"I guess not. Have you?" she replied sheepishly.

"Yep. Several. I'd be cautious about claiming something is evil without direct evidence. Evil scares the hell out of me. You say big pharma is evil. Have you ever tried to invent a new drug to cure or treat a disease? Have you ever tried to figure out how to manufacture enough of it to treat everyone who needs the help?" Hank asked, trying his best not to be provocative.

"No, I haven't. I haven't even thought about what all that entails. What I know is they make amazingly high profits, which doesn't seem right," Dakota responded.

"Unfair profits?" Hank asked.

"Yes. I'd say so," she replied with conviction.

"How do you know?" Hank asked.

"Well, um, I hear about it on the news."

"Well, you asked me what I think. I doubt big pharma or big tech are evil. I'm like you. I don't know if their profit margins are unfair. I'm no expert. I'm fighting like a dog just to break even, so I admire companies that are successful.

"I think if the profit is too high," he continued, "competition will help even it out. However, I do think there are evil men in this world. We've got to be on guard against them. In fact, I'm more wary about the supposed experts who say big tech or big pharma are evil. What is their angle? Who's paying them?"

Skylar sought to change the subject to something more fun. "Who's your favorite band?"

Everyone chimed in and then all went silent when Hank said, "The Chieftains."

"The Chieftains?" Skylar said with mock disdain, feeling very comfortable pushing Hank's buttons, "Is that an Iraqi band, or are they from Kansas City?"

"Ha ha! Skylar, you are a comedian, and a bad one at that. The Chieftains are an Irish band who played traditional Irish music." He flipped to his Irish accent. "My mom played it all the time when I was a wee lad growing up in beautiful Merced, I'll have you know."

"Would we know any of their songs?" asked Bradley.

"Ha! I doubt it. I'm not even sure I can name their songs me self. All's I know is they make me feel good and remind me of me dear olde Ma," he continued in his Irish accent.

Sarah listened intently, noting how easily Hank got along with her work friends. Then she wondered about his friends and suggested she join him at Habitat for Humanity the next day. He hesitated but then seemed to really like the idea the more he thought of it.

"Make sure you dress in comfortable work clothes. We'll be outside all day. Meet you at Scruffy's at 7:30 a.m. for breakfast," Hank said, then stood, gave her a kiss and excused himself in order to make the long drive home.

# 30

# MERCED

"Ah, Sarah, welcome back!" cried Scruffy, seeing her enter and indicating she should follow him to a table.

"Mornin' Scruffy. Have you seen Hank?"

"Not yet, but I'm sure he'll be here soon enough. Hey, I wanted to apologize for what happened the last time you were here. I don't tolerate that kind of behavior, ever," he said with firm conviction.

"Not your fault, Scruffy. Water under the bridge. Plus, if I paid attention to all the negative opinions, I would be living in a cave by now," she replied with a smile. "I will say I was surprised Hank took the guy down."

"Me too. I've not seen him in action like that, but I reckon he had a really, really good reason," said Scruffy with a knowing grin.

"What's that?" Sarah asked with interest.

"You!" he said with a wink then turned saying, "Coffee's on its way!"

Just then Hank came in. They ate a quick breakfast, drank their coffee, then got two to-go cups and left within twenty minutes. Hank informed Sarah the project house was about ten minutes away. They drove together in his truck.

Upon arrival, they received their assignments from the project lead and went about their work. Sarah was sad that she was not working with Hank, but it made sense once she realized skilled craftsmen were in short supply. Hank was assigned to the installation of kitchen cabinets with another carpenter, who he seemed to know quite well. The day flew by. Someone mentioned going over to Scruffy's and buying the first round, which sounded good to Hank and Sarah, so back to Scruffy's they went.

The "Habitat Team" put some tables together and sat down to recount the day. By that time, most were acquainted with each other from the day's work.

"Hey, Sarah, you carried your weight today. Well, actually you're pretty slim, so I'd have to say you carried more than your weight. Good job and thanks!" said Matt Dunham, who was the project lead.

"Yeah, and also thanks to you, we were able to get decent output from Hank for once. He seemed extra motivated," chimed Jose Santos with a wink and a smile.

"Yeah, well my output might suffer on most days due to fixing your mistakes, Señor Santos," Hank laughed.

"Them's fightin' words, Carson! Put 'em up!" Santos yelled, also laughing.

Angie, the waitress, frowned at Sarah as soon as she saw her. Sarah's first instinct was to let the situation play out in due course, hoping there wasn't more to Hank and Angie's relationship than their just being friends, as Hank had claimed.

"What should we do about dinner?" Sarah asked.

"Whoops. I knew I forgot something. My mom's cooking us dinner. She texted me and said it was in the oven keeping warm. She was hoping we could meet her for Vigil Mass and then go to her house afterwards," Hank replied sheepishly.

"What?!" Sarah narrowed her eyes at him as her face turned red.

"Are you kidding? Look how I'm dressed! My hair is a wreck. I don't have any makeup on. I can't see your mom looking this way."

"Uh. Umm. OK. I guess I didn't think about all that stuff. My fault. I'll let Ma know. It won't be a problem," Hank said, not knowing what else to do.

"No! Give me a few minutes to get myself fixed up. I hope your mom will be okay knowing I was at the project all day," Sarah muttered.

With that she left the table. Angie arrived within seconds. "She doesn't seem happy. Anything I can do, Hanky pooh?" she asked moving uncomfortably close.

"Cut it out, Angie. You and I are friends. That's it!" Hank said with determination.

"We could be so much more than that, Hanky," Angie cooed.

"Well, we won't even be friends if you keep giving Sarah the cold shoulder. Think about that."

Angie quickly turned and went back to the kitchen.

After Mass and an enjoyable dinner, Mary asked Sarah and Hank if they would like to go for a walk with her in the neighborhood. They readily agreed. Dusk had settled over the town and the air was warm with a hint of a cool breeze coming in from the west.

"So, Sarah, Hank told me about your "uncles," Rakesh, Father Jack, and Ronnie. He also told me about President Petrov. You have got four good men in your corner," Mary observed.

"Yes, I do. They are each amazing in their own way," Sarah replied as she looked up at the gibbous moon.

"They were all your father's good friends, which is quite a blessing for you. I had to make do for Hank, trying my best to fill the role of father and mother, but this is easier said than done. Luckily, he had some good role models along the way, especially his commanding officer in the Army."

Sarah turned to face Hank. "Can you tell me about him, Hank? I don't think you mentioned him before,"

"His name was Major Jacobs. He was from Georgia. He graduated from the Citadel, where he wrestled. He was highly disciplined and tough as nails.

"One day, not long after I joined the Ranger regiment and before I completed Ranger school, he took me aside and asked, 'Carson do you know why you're here?' I gave him the stock answer, and he replied, 'Your potential is easy to see. You're going to be a Ranger, and you're going to be an excellent soldier. Think of life as a journey. You're on a path right now whether you know it or not. Keep asking yourself why. Try to find the right path. Pray on it. Pray often. Then take action and work your butt off!'

"We kept talking about stuff like that. He was a devout man who cared about his soldiers. We all would have followed him to hell and back."

"Do you stay in touch with him?" Sarah asked.

"No. Well, sort of. He was killed by a sniper in Iraq. I pray to him now and then, though," Hank said looking down as he continued to walk.

"Oh, I'm so sorry," Sarah said, looking at Mary because Hank was now staring off into the distance.

"Sarah, do you have any family still living?" Mary asked.

"No. My parents and grandparents have all passed. I didn't have anyone else."

"Aye. I know this feeling, too. You have good friends. You have people who care about you and love you deeply. Despite this, it is possible to be quite lonely. So be it! This is part of life, no?" Mary had turned to stop and took Sarah by the hands. "What choice do you have but to push on? I know you will, but if ever you need a mother's advice, you know where I live." With that Mary turned around and left Hank and Sarah to each other.

# 31

# SOPHIE'S FRIEND

A week later, on a wonderfully crisp and sunny afternoon with the fog having lifted by late morning, Sophie and Jean joined Sarah and Hank at a nice outdoor café in San Francisco. Sophie informed everyone that her friend Madison was nearby and would arrive soon, which was fine by all.

"How do you know Madison?" Hank asked Sophie.

"She lives in my neighborhood. I met her at our local coffee shop, and we just hit it off. I think you'll really like her. She's fun!"

Minutes later, Madison arrived sporting long hair, loose-fitting jeans, and many bracelets and tattoos going up both forearms. Sophie waved and got her attention. She quickly approached the table, was introduced, and ordered her favorite drink—iced coffee with plant-based cream.

"It is so good to meet you all. I feel like I know you already, as Sophie has told me all about you," Madison said with a smile. "I especially feel like we're connected, Jean."

"Ah, this is good then. Sophie must have mentioned me. I was wondering if she even remembers my name sometimes, as she seems to know everyone in California and beyond," Jean laughed.

"Yes, I consider myself lucky that she graces me with her presence for coffee each Thursday morning," Madison laughed.

"Hey, enough about Sophie. How are you, Madison? What's new?" Sophie intervened.

"I'm good. All good. I'm going to a concert this afternoon with a friend," Madison replied.

"Great. Who is it?" Sophie asked.

"The Midnight Mystics. They play neo-techno meditation music."

"I've not heard of them or that kind of music. Seems interesting," Jean interjected.

"Yes. I love to listen to them when I meditate," Madison responded.

"How did you learn to meditate?" Sarah asked.

"I went to a spiritual retreat center near Half Moon Bay a year ago. It was amazing!" Madison replied with excitement.

"I've tried meditation with limited success," Sarah lamented.

"It's a process. I recommend going to the retreat center. I'll text you the information," which she did right then as they talked.

"What is your objective when you meditate?" Jean asked with genuine interest.

"I'm trying to get closer to myself. I'm trying to re-center myself to combat all the negativity out there. It helps me handle the stress."

"*Oui. Merci*. Oh. I mean, thank you, I understand, I think," Jean replied.

"Does it work?" Hank asked.

"Yes! For sure. Like, I can't believe how much it helped me. I'm so much calmer despite all the things that are going on." Madison was clearly enjoying the topic and being the center of attention.

"What things?" Hank asked.

"Where do I begin! The company I work for is driven only by profit. They could care less about us workers. The environment is on the verge of collapse due to human-induced global warming. Then there is war in the Middle East that never seems to end. Racism and the systemic oppression of African Americans. I could go on and on," Madison lamented.

"Got it. Yeah, there always seems to be a lot of bad stuff going on. I'm impressed by your sensitivity and concern," Hank responded. He did not notice Sophie's nod of approval toward Sarah, who was also impressed by Hank's response.

"So, I meditate to relieve the stress from all this stuff. That's why I do it," Madison concluded.

"How do you deal with stress, Jean?" Madison asked, turning the tables on him in a nice way.

"I'm not sure I feel persistent stress or despair like you describe. I love to run and ride my bike. I play music. I read. I pray regularly and go to Church every Sunday and Holy Days of Obligation," Jean answered directly.

"I consider myself to be spiritual. What Church do you go to?"

"Saint Thomas Aquinas in Palo Alto."

"What religion is that?" she asked.

"Roman Catholic," Jean replied.

"Oh. Like I said, I'm spiritual. I've read up on all the religions and follow my own path," Madison responded, shifting in her chair.

"Were you raised in any religious tradition when you were a child?" Jean asked.

"No. My parents were not religious. They encouraged us to find our own way and didn't want to bring religion into our lives," Madison answered.

"Oh, I see," Jean sighed.

"What are you thinking?" Madison asked.

Hank noted to himself that she seemed positive and curious.

"My father once said to me, 'Catholicism is like having fine music to play in the car while driving on a warm summer day.' What he meant was it makes life better. I was thinking how differently we were raised," Jean answered.

"Seems to me that religion makes everything worse. It causes people to fight. It causes people to be marginalized. It causes wars. The Catholic Church, in particular, is responsible for a lot of this. I'm sorry to say this because I know this is your religion, Jean," Madison seemed to be getting ready for an argument.

"Let's not argue, Madison. You are Sophie's good friend. I am devoutly Catholic, which seems unusual nowadays for people our age. I'm still learning my own religion and seeking to follow God's path. I will pray for you and ask you do the same for me, if that's okay," Jean replied.

"Sounds good."

"You know what my dad used to say in these kinds of situations?" Sarah asked.

"What?" the other four all said simultaneously.

"Take two and hit to right!"

"Yeah. I've heard you say that a lot lately, Sarah. What does it mean?" asked Sophie.

"Ha ha! Great question! It's a baseball phrase. He got it from his father, who was a great fan of the New York Giants, who we now know as being from San Francisco. What we might not realize is that the Giants were based in New York City up until 1958. The owner moved them to San Francisco because the Brooklyn Dodgers, their hated rival, moved to Los Angeles. Plus, I guess their attendance was declining. Anyway, take two' means don't swing at the next two pitches because maybe our guy can steal.

'Hit to right' means hitting the third pitch to the right side of the field, preferably into the right outfield. Hitting to the right side of the field will enable our players to advance to second base, third base, or even to home.

"When my grandfather and father said this phrase, it meant something entirely different, and knowing baseball helps reveal what they were thinking. Hitting a pitch to right field is easier said than done and can be a lot harder if the pitcher and catcher are not cooperating, which they never do!

"What's the best way to describe it… Most of the time what they meant was 'Keep going. Don't let it get you down. Deal with what comes as best you can.'

"Now I find myself saying it partly because its good advice and mostly because it reminds me of them."

"*Oui.* Sarah, I do not understand baseball, but can I also use this saying?" Jean asked with a smile.

"Absolutely!" Sarah answered with a laugh. "My grandfather and father would be most pleased."

"Are you all Catholic?" Madison asked, turning to Sophie, Sarah, and Hank.

"I am," Sophie answered.

"Me too," Sarah answered, while thinking, *Am I? Really?*

"I was raised Catholic," Hank replied. "My mom is very devout. I feel like I drifted away from the Church over the last few years. I'm not sure why. I guess I got too busy. None of my friends seem to be into the Church. Sorry for the long answer."

"Hmmm…" Madison said aloud while thinking.

"What's that mean?" Hank asked.

"You all seem so happy. Hopeful, too," Madison observed. With that, she said goodbye and left the four friends to themselves.

"Madison seems smart to me. I like her," Hank said to Sophie.

"She's super intelligent and caring," Sophie replied, happy that Hank liked her friend.

"Jean, I was really surprised you did not argue with Madison. I was equally surprised to hear you describe yourself as a devout Catholic. How did you become so convinced?" Sarah asked.

"Good question, Sarah. First, I should acknowledge that I am in God's hands, and He has blessed me in many ways, beginning at an early age. Second, I had excellent examples, especially my father, mother, all four of my grandparents, and most of my aunts and uncles. Third, and most importantly, I give credit to the Eucharist, which I have received faithfully since I was first able. I am just starting to realize the power of this Sacrament in my own life. I could make it more complicated, but I don't think it is. Mysterious, yes. Complicated, not so much," Jean answered with pleasure.

"Maybe I ought to get back into the habit of going to Mass," Hank wondered aloud.

"Mass is so boring. The priests' homilies are so long and repetitious. Plus, they treat us like we're idiots," Sophie observed while watching people walking up and down the steeply pitched sidewalk outside their busy café.

"I can't argue this. Sometimes I wonder about the homilies, too. Here is what I know. I go to Mass and feel more complete. I miss Mass and I feel like something is missing. I can't explain it," Jean responds.

"Can't we accomplish the same thing or even more if we give ourselves time to reflect and pray on our own?" Sarah asked.

"I think the answer is not going to Mass *or* personal reflection. Why not both? Going to Mass isn't helpful if it is not self-motivated. I must admit I did it out of a sense of responsibility or habit for many years. Now this is not so much the case. I used to wonder why some people loved it so much. I think I am now beginning to understand," Jean added matter of factly.

"My Ma loves going," Hank added.

"My Mom loves it, too. My Dad isn't as vocal about it," Sophie chimed in.

"I wish it weren't like being forced to go. What right does the Church have to say we have to go to mass?" Sarah asked.

"This is where I can get myself into trouble," Jean replied. "I don't feel I'm knowledgeable enough to answer your question. I don't want to argue. Here's what I know. I feel better after I go. I think it helps me to be a better person. As for the obligations and other theories, I'd leave the answer to Father Jack."

"Yeah, he would know and help us to understand. He's the real deal," Hank added.

Sarah was agitated. Not with the conversation or guilt of not going to Mass. She was wondering why she felt like she had to rebel against her parents "traditional, robotic" practice of the Faith, and now she was feeling guilty because they were gone. Her pain ached inside her.

Then she said, "I already asked him. I was trying to understand why my parents, especially my Dad, were so *rigid* about going to Mass and why they thought the Church could set obligations on them for how to practice the faith. I'll do my best to relay what he told me.

"He said, 'Going to Mass is just one part of how we can worship God and incorporate Him into our lives, and, yes, it is very, very important. Better still is to center our lives around the Sacraments. We received them as children to initiate us into the Faith – Baptism, Reconciliation, Communion, and Confirmation. In the future, perhaps there will be Marriage and Anointing of the Sick.

"Then he told me to think of my life as a sacramental offering to the Lord. Make use of the Sacrament of Reconciliation along with the Eucharist, via Holy Communion at Mass, and orient your life around these two great Sacraments. Celebrate great things in your life by going to Mass, not just on Sunday, but to commemorate great joys and to help overcome great sadness.

"Likewise, as you grow and perhaps are blessed with a family, you can center your family life around the Sacraments, initiating your children and celebrating great events with the Eucharist. Add in reading Scripture and learning more about God through education, and I think you'll be well rewarded, is how he put it.

"Then he said something that I'm still trying to wrap my mind around. He said, 'The Sacraments do stuff to us but only if we cooperate with God and want His grace to help us grow closer to Him.'"

Sophie sighed, "He makes it sound so simple. Why does it seem so lame?"

Hank replied, "In the Rangers, we would think of mission, duty, honor. I'm going to try to get back into going to Church and see what happens. I don't have a good excuse for not having the discipline. Only seems like good can come of it."

"I don't think it is an accident that Jesus left us a Church after He ascended into Heaven. It gives us good guidance," Jean added.

"Yeah, and two thousand years later we have pedophile priests preying on young boys and bishops covering it up," Sarah challenged. Then immediately regretted it wondering why she was arguing.

"Eight percent," Jean replied.

"What does that mean?" Sarah asked.

"That's the percentage of bad apostles," Jean answered.

"What! What are you getting at?" Hank asked.

"Jesus chose twelve men to be his apostles. These were his

closest disciples. He even called them his friends and taught them directly. Despite this, one of them betrayed him. So, if one of the twelve apostles did not live up to his calling, what are the chances the Church won't experience similar issues throughout its history?

"Priests, bishops, cardinals, popes, monks, and nuns all started out as kids, teenagers, young adults like us. They're humans subject to the same challenges we face. Can you identify a more diverse and global organization than the Catholic Church? I cannot. Have you ever met a bad priest? A Judas, or worse? I have not. That doesn't mean we don't have them. Of course, we do. That's when we 'take two and hit to the right,'" Jean answered.

# 32

# SOPHIE AND SARAH, JEAN AND HANK

They paid their check and went for a walk. Sophie and Sarah pushed ahead, while Hank saw a cigar shop and suggested to Jean that they stop in leaving the girls to themselves.

"Does Jean talk about religion all the time?" Sarah asked her buddy.

"That was the first time I've ever heard him talk about it. I was really surprised, but I will also say, he is very devoted to attending Mass."

Sarah smiled. "Reminds me of my dad."

"Mine too. I think we find it weird, not just with Jean, but also with our parents, because hardly any of our friends pay attention to their religion. Most of my friends are like Madison. They're spiritual."

"Yep. Plus, we're too busy." Sarah added.

At the cigar store, Hank asked the manager for some assistance.

"Do you favor a mellow, medium, or full-bodied cigar? Then may I ask do you prefer Parejo or Figurados?" asked the fully engaged manager.

"Um. I don't know what all that means," Hank replied. "Can

you help us to find a really good cigar? His girlfriend's father treated me to the best cigar a few weeks ago. I was hoping I could find something like it."

"What is his name?" asked the manager.

"Rakesh Shriram," Jean replied.

"No! You know Dr. Shriram? I know exactly what to get you, then. This is wonderful!" cheered the manager.

Sophie looked back with disgust when she saw the boys coming up the sidewalk smoking their new cigars.

"You're not serious? You bought cigars?" Sophie chided.

"Not only did we buy cigars, but we also bought the same cigars that your dad buys. Turns out the store we walked into is where he gets his supply. So, ha ha! Soap!" Hank laughed using Sarah's nickname for her.

They continued walking together. Then Sophie asked Jean, "Do you think Madison is a good person?"

"*Oui.*"

"Do you think she is wrong?" Sarah asked.

"About what?" Jean asked, but without waiting for a reply, he continued, "Madison is smart and compassionate. She is simply on the wrong path, in my opinion. Meditation to relieve stress and anxiety is good and helpful. Spirituality based on self-referenced beliefs not founded on revealed truth will likely lead to frustration."

"How can you push your agenda onto Madison? How can you think she is wrong in her approach? Who are you to say her approach is wrong, or that she is wasting her time?" Sarah demanded, becoming angry.

"I think Jean is right. I hear a lot of people say they're spiritual, but what does that mean?" Hank asked, wondering why Sarah was getting spun up.

"Yeah, well it is easy for you and Jean to say all that because you are men and the Church is run by men," Sophie weighed in, supporting her friend.

"I'm not sure what that has to do with anything, but OK," Jean replied.

Then Sophie noticed Jean roll his eyes and wink at Hank. Sarah noticed Hank did the same.

This caused Sophie to stop. She gave them both a death stare. "I guess we're a joke to you big men with your cigars,"

"No. You're not. I'm not even sure why we're arguing," Hank replied.

"Just because you're so sure of yourselves doesn't make you right," Sarah added feeling betrayed.

"I meant no disrespect. I'm disappointed you both became so mad at us. I think I'll head back home. I've got a long drive ahead. If it's OK, I'll drive you home, Sarah."

Sarah was stunned, then said, "I'll get a ride home with Sophie and Jean," becoming more determined to prove her point.

Hank turned and left, leaving the three friends to themselves.

"What just happened?" asked Jean with genuine surprise and concern.

"Don't act so innocent, Jean. I saw you roll your eyes and wink at Hank," replied Sophie, bearing down on him to get an admission of guilt.

"What? You thought that had something to do with you two?" Jean answered.

"Yes," Sarah added.

"Umm. No, it wasn't related to that at all. It was related to the fart I let loose in Hank's general direction. It was all we could do to not start laughing, but we knew if we laughed, we'd be in big trouble."

"What?! You idiot!" Sophie yelled in disgust.

# 33

# SILENCE

More than a week went by without contact between Hank and Sarah. Sophie and Jean became quite concerned. Jean suggested they visit Hank and his mom without Sarah to get a sense for how he was feeling.

Upon arrival, Jean introduced Sophie to Hank's mom and then went out to the backyard to smoke a cigar with Hank.

"Mrs. Carson, I have a question for you about Hank," Sophie started.

"Well, sure, I'm happy you're here Sophie, and please call me Mary."

"Jean and I are concerned because Hank hasn't spoken to Sarah in almost two weeks. Has he mentioned anything to you?"

"Hank has not spoken to me of this. I'm surprised to learn he has not spoken to her. All I know is he's head over heels for that girl," Mary said with alarm.

"I'm not surprised. Hank is sure of himself. Jean and I think he's wonderful. I've never seen Sarah so happy. She's proud and stubborn, too, I guess," Sophie sighed.

"Do you mind me asking what the row is about?" Mary asked.

"It's dumb, but we were in an argument about 'spirituality' and then Sarah said the Church was dominated by men."

"Hank argued against this?" Mary questioned.

"No. There was also a misunderstanding of a private joke between Hank and Jean that both Sarah and I reacted to. However, Hank withdrew when Sarah got angry. Since then neither one of them has reached out to the other."

In the backyard, between puffs, Jean asked, "So, Hank, are you still mad at Sarah?"

"Mad? No, not really. Why do you ask?"

"Because you have not called her since our argument in San Francisco two weeks ago," Jean replied, leaning in and looking up at his big friend.

"Yeah, well, she hasn't called me, either. So, I'm waiting her out," Hank argued.

"So, you still love her?" Jean asked with a smile.

"Yup."

"You idiot! You need to get over it," Jean laughed.

"Yeah. I know. I guess I didn't realize how tough she is. Plus, what do I know about men dominating the Church and all that stuff she was talking about?"

Just then the boys heard Mary calling them in for some tea and biscuits.

"Hank, Sophie tells me you're giving Sarah the silent treatment, eh?" Mary asked.

"Argh... You know I don't know how to handle women, Ma. Plus, I especially don't know how to handle feminists," Hank replied.

"Feminist! Is Sarah a feminist, Sophie?" Mary asked, stopping abruptly.

"Well, she's female. Aren't all of us women feminists?" Sophie replied.

"Dear God, I hope not!" Mary responded with alarm.

Jean jumped in hoping to understand, "Mary, what is your concern with feminists? How do you understand them?"

"You know I'd have to be an eejit to say I was against ensuring women get a fair shake, but it seems to me some people go too far with these kinds of things and throw the wheat out with the chaff. What I mean is, upholding the rights of women ought not require us to demonize men, which some feminists seem to do. What bothers me more is feminists promoting abortion and twisting the truth by using false terms like "reproductive rights", "right to choose", "reproductive health" and so forth. You know, in the past, feminists saw abortion as an evil that was meant to exploit women. Equal rights for women, of course, yes. Feminism? Aye, that word leaves a bad taste in my mouth."

"Wow! I had no idea all of this was involved. What do you think Hank?" Jean asked.

"I have no idea what Ma is talking about. All's I know is when Sarah got mad, I figured I was screwed. Sometimes the best thing to do when you're attacked is retreat," Hank lamented.

"I don't think Sarah is a feminist as you describe, Mary," Sophie added.

"I don't worry Sarah thinks like that, Ma. She's rock solid," Hank said.

"Then why don't you call her, dear boy?" Mary asked.

"I guess I will, especially if Sophie thinks I should."

"Yes!" Sophie cried. "Call her, Hank. She loves you!"

Sarah called her Uncle Ronnie to check in and see how he was doing. It wasn't long before he asked about Hank.

"So let me get this straight. Jean farted, you and Sophie got mad, and now you and Hank don't talk anymore?" Colonel Gardner asked, never one to beat around the bush.

"Yup," Sarah grunted.

"You idiot!" Gardner laughed.

"Yup," Sarah moaned.

"So, of course you know what you have to do, right?" asked Uncle Ronnie.

"That's the problem. I don't know how to get myself out of this," Sarah sighed.

"That's simply because you want to win. Then what? So, you win an argument and lose the man? You know Hank was trained as a Ranger, right?"

"Yes, and what does that have to do with the price of tea in China?" she queried.

"Rangers lead the way! They are trained to be disciplined and always learning. A Ranger is led by love, mission, and God. So, I have one simple question...."

He let a dramatic pause settle between them.

"Go ahead; what is it?"

"Have you told him how much you love him?"

"Got it. Understood. Thanks, Uncle Ronnie. I love you, too," and with that she ended the call.

Just then her phone rang, and Hank's image appeared.

"Hi, Hank."

"Hi, Sarah."

"What's up?" she asked with a smile.

"Well, um, er, uh..."

Sarah couldn't wait. "Hank, I'm sorry! I miss you like crazy."

"Me, too." Relief flooded through him. "I'm an idiot for not calling sooner."

"Can we get together this weekend? I have something to tell you," Sarah asked.

And so, they did.

# 34

# THE BIG SHOW

"Sarah, I need you to say yes, no matter what? Will you?" Sophie squealed into her smart phone.

"What are you talking about Soap? You sound crazy."

"I need you. I need you with me!" Sophie was even more excited, which did not seem possible.

Sarah chuckled. "Then of course, yes, I will be with you, even though I have no idea what's going on."

"I've been invited to be a guest on *The Daylight Show*! Can you believe it?" Sophie yelled.

"What?! Hold it." Sarah's voice climbed an octave. "You're going to be on national television? You're serious?"

"Yes! I don't know what I'm doing," Sophie's pitch climbed higher with each word. "I don't know if I can do this! It's a very popular daytime talk show! They want me there next week. I need you with me!"

"That's not much notice, but I'm with you. Let's get together and plan this out as best we can. I'm coming over right now. Wait! Do your mom and dad know?"

"Yes. My mother is cautious. My dad is very excited and encouraging," Sophie replied.

"What does Jean think?"

"He doesn't know, yet. I called you first. Get over here, and I'll call him while you're on your way!"

The girls planned the trip and speculated on what Sophie could talk about and promote for her new clothing line. Then her mother came in and asked if they would like to get something to eat, which they readily agreed to.

"What do you think about all of this, Daddy?" Sophie asked her father.

"I must be honest. I've never seen this show. Your mom has told me about it, and some of the host's names are familiar. Regardless, this is a big opportunity for your business. You're going to do great as long as you stick to one important tenet."

"I know. I know. Just be myself. That'll be plenty good enough," Sophie replied, trying her best to imitate her father's voice and Boston accent. They all laughed hard at her attempt.

"What do you think about this big news, Mother Miriam?" Sarah asked.

"I agree with Rakesh but want to caution you, Sophie, some of these women support agendas that are quite concerning and different than how we have raised you. You may be challenged and provided with an opportunity. In fact, Sarah, this reminds me of the time your father was interviewed on a similar program when he was running for his first term as President. This was when he made what is now referred to by many as *The Speech*"

Sarah answered, "I was too young to understand, but I hear many people refer to it as a seminal moment in American politics."

Rakesh added, "Indeed. I remember it like it was yesterday. What's more, I remember the reaction of the host when your father answered her question in an unexpected way. She was stunned and did not know how to continue the show. Your father told me how uncomfortable he felt at that moment."

"It is interesting to consider how skilled these pundits are at pushing an agenda and bullying people into conforming, or appearing to conform, to their point of view under pain of being cancelled. Keep your wits about you, Sophie, is all I'm saying," explained Mother Miriam.

"Yes, Mom." Sophie groaned, trying again with good success imitating her father.

"How did Jean react to the news?" Sarah asked.

"Ha ha! He's never heard of the show. He does not know any of the celebrity hosts, but he was supportive. He said it would be good for business," Sophie replied.

The week flew by with Sophie and Sarah arriving the day before the taping of the show. They took in the sites and met with the producers. Sophie had several samples of her new line that were to be modeled by professionals live in front of the studio audience. The entire process was very exciting to say the least.

The intensity increased exponentially when Vanessa Garfield, the longtime, Ivy League educated host came by to meet her newest guest.

"Hello, Sophie. I'm so pleased to meet you. We are excited to showcase your new line on our show tomorrow. How are you feeling?" asked Garfield impatiently, not noticing Sarah. Without waiting for a reply, she continued, "I'm sure you'll do great."

Sarah noticed Sophie's demeanor change after Garfield quickly moved on to her next "appointment."

"Hey, Soap. That's the style in the big city. Don't let her get to you," Sarah offered.

"She could not care less about me," Sophie lamented.

"Yes. And don't you forget it! This is a business operation. They are not in the caring business. They are in the advertising business, which means they need controversy, headlines, and intrigue to get viewers. You know what this means for you, don't you?" Sarah asked positively, while getting up to take Sophie back to the hotel.

"What?" asked Sophie, hoping the answer wasn't bad.

"Don't take the bait! Don't let them rile you. Your product is good. Plus, guess what? You have more subscribers than they do! They probably need you more than you need them!"

"You're right! Watch out Garfield! Sophie Shriram's in town!" Sophie said with a smile, following her best friend's lead.

Sophie was positioned on her chair between the four celebrity hosts of the show. Her makeup was spot on. Her outfit was one of her latest designs. She looked stunning and exuded confidence and maturity well beyond her years. Soon the director was counting down the seconds until the taping would begin... three, two, one.

"Today it is our pleasure to welcome Sophie Shriram, founder and CEO of *Sophie's*, one of the world's hottest on-trend clothing lines aimed at young women of modest means. What do you mean by 'modest means,' Sophie? Who are you targeting for your clothing line?"

"Thank you for having me on your wonderful show, Ms. Garfield. My clothing is aimed at young women who are just starting their careers, living paycheck to paycheck, in the U.S., Europe, South America, India, and beyond," Sophie replied with energy and a smile that coul melt the coldest of hearts.

"Let's take a look at some of your latest designs and then return to learn more about your company," Vanessa Garfield said.

Several models paraded in front of the audience displaying modest yet fashionable dresses and pants suits. Sophie commented that the design intent was for the clothing was to be functional and hardworking, able to withstand commutes on public transit and meetings with executives and clients.

"Getting back to your approach, Ms. Shriram, I understand your clothing is made in India at a fraction of the cost were it to be made here in the United States," Garfield posited.

"Yes," Sophie replied, noting she was not asked a question.

"How do you ensure the conditions at your factory are kept up to the proper standards?" one of the other hosts asked.

"The factory is in the town where my family originated. My uncle is the Vice President of Manufacturing, and his son, my cousin, oversees production. I trust them implicitly. I visit the operations every few months to check in and ensure our new launches are ready. I am very proud of the positive impact this operation has had on the families that support our plant," Sophie replied.

"Impressive. Can the women in your plant afford to buy your clothing line?" Garfield asked provocatively.

"Absolutely! We give a steep discount for all employees. At normal retail prices, our first and second-year assemblers would be hard pressed to afford our clothes. However, if they stay with us, they may rise in both rank and pay and then will be able to afford our clothing."

"So, you are saying some of your employees cannot afford your clothing, correct?" quizzed Garfield.

"Yes. Our clothing is mainly targeting professional women who are newer in their careers. So, it is too expensive for entry-level assembly staff," Sophie answered positively.

"Don't you find this strange or unusual? Are you worried about the optics this creates?"

"Not at all! I suppose most of the assemblers at an Audi plant cannot afford the cars they assemble, especially the high-end ones. I think this analogy holds.

"Let me go further to address your concern. First, we looked for an American location to manufacture our clothes, but those with available capacity target niche fashion items like shoes. Almost all assembly operations for products like ours are done in east Asia, especially China, which is why we chose India, instead, because I have family there whom I trust. Just as importantly, India is an up-and-coming manufacturing powerhouse and the largest democracy in the world with a well-developed legal system. Second, the reason my company exists is not for our customers or shareholders. Sophie's LLC exists for its employees. Our primary purpose is to provide meaningful livelihoods for our employees so they may raise and support their families and take care of their parents as they age.

"We are a small company. We aspire to be around for 500 years. In fact, the companies I admire most are long-standing Japanese firms that have lasted for centuries. These are my benchmarks.

"Therefore, we are retaining all of our earnings and investing in our infrastructure while we gain critical mass and improve operational efficiencies. We're also beginning to save money for hard times to support our workforce if or when they come." Sophie replied positively.

"Hold it. You are saying your company exists for its employees and not its shareholders? This is highly unusual, is it not?" asked Vanessa Garfield with genuine interest.

"Yes," Sophie replied with confidence.

"I guess this is because you are a startup and new at the game. Eventually this will change, assuming you're successful and become a public company and are sold on the stock exchange. Correct?" one of the other hosts asked.

"No," Sophie replied with confidence.

"Does this not fly in the face of capitalism?" Garfield demanded.

"Let me see if I'm understanding your concern. Sophie's LLC is a privately held, for-profit business that has been growing at 15% per year for the last three years. It is profitable and investing in itself with the aim to grow slowly and steadily over the next 500 years, all the while taking care of its employees, who produce excellent products for up-and-coming professional women around the world. What problem do you see, so that I may properly address your concern?" Sophie inquired.

"Your perspective is amazing!" exclaimed one of the other hosts, breaking the tension. "You seem to have wisdom beyond your years. I wish you a lot of success in the future."

"Thank you. I have benefited much from my mother and father's guidance. When it comes to business, my father is my hero and mentor. I am lucky to have him in my corner." Sophie continued positively with calm energy.

"Yes, your father is the founder and long-time CEO of NarrowGate Technologies, one of the largest and most formidable tech giants in Silicon Valley. His is a public company and run quite differently than yours. Is this correct?" Garfield asked.

"Yes and no. You would have to ask him for more details. However, as a publicly held company trading on the New York Stock Exchange, NarrowGate is subject to all the scrutiny and requirements of a typical public U.S. for-profit company," Sophie replied.

"But you replied yes and no. What is the no part referring to?" the other host asked perceptively.

"My father bootstrapped NarrowGate on his own with two minor partners. They knew what they knew and followed a pattern laid out for most U.S. businesses. Years later, he became aware of some of the philosophies present in long-standing Japanese companies, which he found compelling and in line with his beliefs.

"This means NarrowGate is indeed for-profit and aimed at meeting the needs of its shareholders. However, it is run with a clear intent to take care of its employees, provide great products and services to its customers, and treat its suppliers fairly.

"My father firmly believes that of the three stakeholders, the employees come first," Sophie replied.

"Very, very impressive Ms. Shriram. Clearly the apple does not fall far from the tree," Garfield added, amazed at the intelligence and maturity of this young entrepreneur.

"Sophie, you mentioned your mother. How has she helped you?" the other host asked.

"Guess who named my father's company?" Sophie replied.

"Your mother, I assume?" the host answered.

"Yes. Do you know what it means?" Sophie answered provocatively.

"No. I have not heard the story. Please tell us," The host responded leaning forward with interest.

"Enter by the narrow gate, since the road to perdition is wide and many take it; but it is a narrow gate and a hard road that leads to life, and only a few find it.[14] This quote is from the Gospel of Matthew, chapter 7. The context is a sermon by Jesus who is teaching and admonishing his disciples. It follows immediately after the Lord provides the golden rule, 'Always treat others as you would like them to

[14] Matthew 7:13-14

treat you; this is the meaning of the law of the prophets.'[15]

"My mother suggested the name, *NarrowGate,* so this same admonishment would be incorporated into everything my father did at his company," Sophie responded wondering how she was so easily able to bring forth these Gospel passages.

"Amazing! You are also good friends with Sarah O'Malley, the daughter of former President Sean O'Malley, are you not?" Clearly Garfield was uncomfortable and wanted to switch subjects.

"Yes," Sophie replied.

"How has her father's passing affected her?" Garfield questioned.

"I would like to thank you all for your kind invitation and allowing me to showcase some of our newest items from our collection. I greatly appreciate the access your show has given me to an audience I might not ordinarily reach. We will continue to work hard to provide fun, affordable, high-quality clothing to young women with hopes to do right by our employees every day," Sophie replied.

"Thank you, Sophie Shriram! CEO of Sophie's LLC. Very impressive! Very impressive!" exclaimed the other host while the audience applauded and cheered. With that the director cut to a commercial break.

Knowing the cameras were not recording, Vanessa Garfield growled, "You didn't answer my question! Who do you think you are?"

"I'm Sophie Shriram!" And with that, she got up and left.

[15] Matthew 7:12

# 35

# VISITORS FROM FRANCE

The show aired two weeks later. Everyone was gathered to watch it at Sophie's parents' home. When it finished, Sophie's father and mother were shedding tears of joy, and Jean was hugging her tightly.

Hank was the first to speak. "Sophie, I cannot tell you how impressed I am by your performance on that show. You were teaching them and teaching me too! I learned some important concepts from your interview. Well done and congratulations!"

Sarah added, "Sophie, you are simply amazing! I could not be more proud."

Sophie was taking it all in and especially awaiting her father's voice.

Her mother added, "That's my daughter! You set a fine example for your company. I was already proud of you. I am not surprised in the least."

"Sophie! You are simply wonderful!" Jean cheered.

Then all eyes turned to her father, the CEO of one of America's greatest companies. What would he say? What critique or advice would he provide to his one and only daughter?

"My dear Sophie, I love you!" is all he could emit between sobs of joy. Then he put his arms around her, and they cried together for a long time. He whispered, "We should both thank the Lord for your amazing gifts, my precious daughter."

She whispered back, "I already have. Plus, I thanked Him for the gifts of you and Mom, too."

Then the phone rang. It was Uncle Ronnie and Uncle Jack on a conference call, yelling, hooting, and hollering their praise for their precious Sophie.

After the excitement died down, Jean made an announcement. "I am happy to let you all know my parents will be visiting from Bordeaux and wish to meet you, Mr. and Mrs. Shriram."

Sarah immediately looked in Sophie's direction and noted her joyful smile, but also that she was avoiding eye contact.

"This is wonderful news, Jean. We look forward to meeting them." Mother Miriam was truly happy at the news.

A short time later, Sarah approached Sophie on the patio where she was alone sipping a glass of French wine from Bordeaux that Jean brought especially for the occasion.

"Is something wrong, Soap? I noticed you didn't look at me when Jean made his announcement."

"I couldn't look at you," Sophie still averting her gaze.

"Why? What's wrong?" Sarah was becoming concerned.

"I didn't want to cry. I am so happy. I was worried I wouldn't be able to control myself."

"Okay, woah. I was hoping that was the reason. I won't say more. I could not be happier for you." Then they hugged each other for a long time.

Three weeks later, Jean's parents arrived from Bordeaux. Together with Jean, they met Sophie's parents for the first time at their home in Palo Alto. It was an important event in all their lives. Upon arrival and small talk, the three men proceeded to the back patio, while the three women went to the kitchen to finalize dinner preparations.

Rakesh invited Jean and his father, Phillipe, to join him for a drink, offering a variety of liquors and wines, including a wonderful selection of wines from Bordeaux.

"You know, Phillipe, it was not until Sophie became serious with Jean that I discovered the mystery of wine from your region of France. Up until that time, I was a beer and whiskey man," Rakesh remarked while taking orders from his two guests.

"This is interesting, Rakesh. Since Jean has been living in California I have begun to experiment with whiskey from... where is it? Kentucky, Bourbon County, at Jean's urging just for this moment. Would you mind if we tried some in honor of our first meeting?" Phillipe asked respectfully.

"Would I mind? Never! Your wish is my command." Rakesh prepared three glasses of fine sipping bourbon, then asked about cigars.

"Of course, I have not come without being prepared." Phillipe then presented Rakesh and Jean with fine Cuban cigars he brought with him from France.

"This is wonderful! Let us toast the great blessing of having Phillipe and Collette here with us today," Rakesh exclaimed with great enthusiasm.

Later, after a wonderful dinner, the two fathers found themselves again on the patio sipping another bourbon talking deeply about their experiences and hopes for their children.

"Rakesh, I have to say I was quite surprised to find that not only are you Catholic, but you also have an American accent. You really are simply an American, aren't you?" Phillipe asked with genuine interest.

"Not only am I an American, I'm from Boston! That means I'm double American through and through!" he laughed. "I've rebelled against becoming a Californian for thirty-five years, but I must admit this is God's country with the Pacific Ocean, coastal mountains, redwood forests and Sierra Nevada mountains. We've been quite blessed," Rakesh said reflectively while sipping his nectar of Kentuckians.

"This is our first time in America. We look forward to exploring it with Jean and Sophie this coming week. I must also say how much we love Sophie. She is truly special. I told Jean, 'I think Sophie will be a wonderful mother someday,' after her first visit to Bordeaux," Phillipe replied.

"This is high praise, indeed! Sophie was very impressed by Collette after visiting while at university and has told me how much she has learned from both of you, including the art of sewing and dress design from Collette." Rakesh was very comfortable with Phillipe, and it showed.

"Sophie is perceptive. Collette is the brains of our family. I'm a simple carpenter who was lucky enough to convince his son to get a university education. Luckily for both of us, he must have inherited his mother's intelligence. Otherwise, he'd be pounding nails like his father," Phillipe laughed.

"Then we have something very much in common. We would not be sitting here if it weren't for Miriam. She's the brains of our family, too. She steered me in the right direction and is my rock. The only talent I have is hard work and persistence. Any luck I've had along the way has been due to Miriam."

"Yes, we are lucky men, indeed. However, we are not in your league Rakesh, when it comes to wealth. You oversee one of the world's great companies. I am a simple carpenter and Collete is a seamstress. We do not have much to offer Sophie in this regard," Phillipe added looking up at the stars.

"Dear Phillipe, I consider cash to be simply a resource like intellectual property, plants, equipment, brands, and such. Profits simply reflect a company's well-being. Any cash that results is to be cared for and used to the advantage of the company, its employees, and shareholders.

"A long time ago Miriam convinced me that great affluence is not a worthy objective, and so we have lived modestly and put any excess wealth we developed towards the use of the company, the Church, and our community. Don't get me wrong, we live comfortably, but neither Miriam nor I believe we should hold tremendous assets nor bequeath them to Sophie.

"She must follow her own path, not towards riches but towards God. We believe inheriting great wealth would inhibit this journey rather than enhancing it," Rakesh responded.

"I cannot believe this!" Phillipe gasped.

"Does this mean you are disappointed, Phillipe?" Rakesh asked.

"No, Rakesh. Just the opposite. I could not be more pleased with your response." Phillipe leaned forward and raised his glass of Kentucky nectar for a toast to a family he could truly admire.

The following morning at breakfast at their hotel, Phillipe, Collete, and Jean were discussing the events of the previous day.

Collete asked, "Phillipe, what did you think of the Shriram's?"

Looking directly at Jean he replied, "You should marry that girl."

Later that day, Jean called Rakesh to ask him if he and his wife were available for him to stop by that evening. They were, and upon arrival, Jean asked them, "I seek your permission to ask Sophie for her hand in marriage. Would you approve?"

Rakesh and Miriam turned and looked at each other then back to Jean, simultaneously saying, "Yes!" Then, together they all hugged.

Jean called Sophie, who was just getting off work. "Hey Sophie, you're coming to dinner with me and my parents tonight, right?"

"Yes. You already knew this. When do we meet?" Sophie answered.

"I'll pick you up at six-fifteen, OK?"

He met Sophie at her front door. She was dressed in a smart *Sophie's LLC* outfit, looking cool and relaxed.

Getting down on one knee, Jean asked, "Sophie, you are a gift from God to me. I love you with all my heart. Will you marry me?"

"What?!" Sophie was in shock.

Jean, still kneeling, looked up and presented her with a diamond ring.

Sophie started crying. "Yes," she whispered, barely able to speak.

# 36

# WOMAN'S INTUITION

Sophie and Jean were married at their local church not long after completing their Pre-Cana marriage preparation classes. Their wedding was concelebrated by their local pastor and Uncle Jack. Jean's parents were happy to travel again to California for the blessed occasion. Rumors and speculation were rampant in the media regarding the scope of the reception, and many of the critics were left wanting after witnessing a modest party at the church banquet hall, albeit the hall built primarily through funding from the NarrowGate Foundation. Not surprisingly, Sarah was the Maid of Honor, while Hank served as one of the groomsmen.

After the reception they found themselves talking to Uncle Ronnie and Father Jack about all they had experienced in the time since their trip to the Continental Divide Trail in Colorado.

"I would have never guessed in a million years where that trail would end up taking me," Hank said, while drinking a beer and smoking a cigar.

"Me neither," added Uncle Ronnie. "Who could make this up? Two Army grunts who served in the same unit years apart lucking upon the Shriram and O'Malley families, and so far, we haven't been excommunicated."

"So true. Think about it from my perspective. I grew up in the

Bible Belt. I go to the University, meet Sean O'Malley and Rakesh Shriram. It is because of them that I couldn't shake this feeling I was called to be a priest," Uncle Jack chimed in, puffing one of Rakesh's finest cigars.

"Yes, how did you come to that decision?" Sarah asked.

"Rakesh told me I should be a priest while we were drunk one night camping in the woods. We'd only known each other for a couple months, and he told me he thought it was my calling. I asked him how he knew and he said, 'I know things!'

"We were kids, but I knew he was right, even though I wasn't Catholic, yet. I wanted to be a preacher from an early age. Then the idea of being a priest came on stronger once I joined the army. An Army chaplain helped me discern and approach the Jesuits. The thing about those two galoots was their lives revolved around God, whether they knew it or not. It was just innate, and thankfully they set a good example for me to follow. They never made fun of me, either. They did just the opposite!"

"Me too," Ronnie joined. "I might not be here above the sod if it weren't for Sean and Rakesh, and you too, Jack."

"I'd like to propose a toast?" Hank asked.

"Please do," Uncle Jack replied.

"To the Shriram and O'Malley families, especially Mrs. Shriram, also known as Mother Miriam, and Mrs. O'Malley, may she rest in peace. Two great families. Two women to be admired," Hank toasted.

"Amen!" Father Jack responded.

"Hooah!" Ronnie grunted.

Together they all clinked glasses, and Sarah noted how reverently these three men regarded Mother Miriam and her own mother, Maggie.

Later that evening, Sarah asked Hank, "What do you think

about all of this today?"

"It was a great day. Jean and Sophie are a match made in Heaven. I especially like what Mr. Shriram had to say at his opening toast for the reception. How did he put it? 'Let's make sure we don't take this for granted this Sacrament of the Church. Real grace has been bestowed on Sophie and Jean today. Let us all pray for them as they embark on their journey together as one.'"

"I could not be happier for them. I'm really glad you were here with me, *Hanky Pooh*." she laughed.

"What!? You're not hanging that nickname on me!"

"Too late! Angie and I both like it," Sarah laughed and took off running across the backyard toward the Shriram's kitchen to say goodnight to everyone.

The next morning, Hank was having breakfast with his mom and asked what she thought about the wedding.

"T'was truly a wonderful wedding, Hanky Pooh!"

"What! No way. Sarah's not going to get you to call me that, too." Hank's face reddened with embarrassment.

"Too late, me boy! Ha ha! Not to worry. I'll let Sarah decide on your new nickname." Mary grinned. "As for what I thought about the wedding, I'll say this—the Macron and Shriram families are wonderful. I noticed how much the fathers enjoyed each other. What did you think?"

"I had fun. Say, what do you think of Sarah?" Hank asked knowing his mom could see through any façade he might erect.

"She will make a fine mother," Mary answered directly.

"That's it?" Hank asked incredulously.

"Is there higher praise I could give?" Mary answered coyly.

"Hmm." Hank was annoyed.

"OK, my son. Let me tell you what I really think about Sarah. She is special, very, very special. Why? She is herself, no matter what. Caring, humble, smart, demanding, all the many gifts she has been given are extraordinary. But, most importantly, she loves you!"

"I'm going to ask her to marry me, Ma."

"I'll be praying for you and Sarah with hope and faith in God's perfect will."

Later that day, Hank arrived at the Shriram's house. Rakesh was surprised by the visit.

"Hank! I'm surprised to see you here. Is something wrong?" Rakesh asked, waving for Hank to come in while calling for Miriam.

"I'm sorry to surprise you, but I have something I have to ask you." By this time Mother Miriam had joined them in the foyer. Together they went to Rakesh's study.

"I know it has been just over a year since I met Sarah," Hank said, his eyes steady on them. "In that time, I've come to love her with everything I've got, and I think she loves me, too. I would like to ask for your permission and blessing so that I may ask her to marry me."

Rakesh and Miriam looked at each other in astonishment then turned to Hank. "Yes!" they cried together. Then they all hugged. With that Hank left to find Sarah.

# 37

# CHALLENGE ACCEPTED

Hank assumed she was home because her car was parked in its usual spot, but she did not answer her door. Then he figured she might be out for a run, and this might not be the best time, but it was a two-hour drive back home, and his mission was confirmed. He intended to execute his plan.

A short time later, he saw her return but decided he should wait until she had time to get herself fixed up. There was a sports bar down the street that seemed like the perfect place to wait.

While sipping his beer, a man sitting next to him asked, "How 'bout those 49ers? Think they can go all the way?"

"Why not? The quarterback is solid, and their defense is in the Top 5. The main question for me is the coaching staff. I don't see them making adjustments during the game. They're too predictable."

"I couldn't agree more. Hey, my name's Charlie Thomas. Good to meet you." He extended his hand and gave Hank a firm handshake.

"Hank Carson. Nice to meet you, Charlie."

"I haven't seen you here before. You new in town?" Charlie asked.

"Yeah, sort of. I live in Merced. My girlfriend lives down the street. I'm waiting for her to get showered up because she just got back from a run. She doesn't even know I'm here. I'm fixing to ask her to marry me."

"What? No! Don't do it!" Charlie laughed.

"I know. I know. But when you know she's the one, then you might as well go for it," Hank replied.

Charlie nodded. "You're right, Hank. I've been married for forty-eight years. My buddies and I joke all the time about wives and marriage. Truth is, I wouldn't know what I would do without her."

"I hear you. I got a spring in my step after I met this girl. I'll be the luckiest guy in the world if she says yes."

"I stopped working quite a few years ago. My career goes back a ways. I remember a time when things were different when it was a man's world. I was working in Chicago, and our office was one hundred percent men. There was cursing, off-color jokes, fooling around, going to bars after work, late-night dinners. You know, prototypical 'Old Boys' club stuff. Then one day, three new hotshot women were assigned to our project. They were competent and tough. Things changed overnight. Truth is most of us guys didn't want to be cursing and drinking after work. We wanted to go home to our families. We didn't want that old boys' stuff, but none of us had the guts to stand up to the peer pressure we put on ourselves.

Charlie dropped his voice to a whisper. "Yeah, nothing is better than having good women on your team, in your corner. They're bedrock. Without 'em, we'd be in deep you-know-what. But don't tell anyone I told you so."

"I won't. I hear what you're saying. This girl is really special. Way smarter than me. I am scared to death that I'm simply not worthy of her," Hank added.

"I felt the same way when I was your age. Want some advice from an old pro?" Charlie asked seriously.

"Sure. I can use all the help I can get."

"Step up to the challenge! Shift to another gear. If this young woman is as impressive as you say she is, then you need to rise to the occasion and make it your life's work to exceed her expectations, not just now, but fifty years from now and then some, Lord willin'. You'll both be better for it," Charlie answered confidently.

"Damn," Hank breathed.

"What's that mean, Hank?" Charlie asked, leaning towards his new, young friend.

"It means thanks. It means I agree. It means I accept the challenge," Hank replied.

"Good man. Go get that girl!"

With his heart pounding, Hank texted Sarah and asked if she had time to talk.

She texted back, "Sure," but was very surprised when Hank suggested they meet at the park across the street from her apartment.

He'd never seen her look more beautiful as she walked across the street. He noticed her smile when she saw him and hoped he wouldn't blow it. She sat down on the bench next to him.

"I can't believe you're here, Hanky Pooh! What a great surprise." She was as happy as he'd ever seen her.

"Yeah, well I've been doing some thinking and planning and I've got something I want to say to you. It has to be done in person," Hank said seriously.

Surprised and now becoming concerned, Sarah asked, "Is something wrong?"

"I've spoken to my mother, who I trust more than anyone. I've confirmed and gotten approval from Mr. and Mrs. Shriram," Hank replied.

"What are you talking about?" Sarah was even more concerned.

Then Hank got down on one knee and looking up said, "Sarah

O'Malley, you are the most beautiful and wonderful girl I've ever met. I love you with everything I've got and will make it my life's work to live up to your expectations. Will you marry me?"

"What!?" Sarah was now weeping.

After what seemed like an eternity, and his eyes watering with emotion, Hank asked again, "Will you marry me?"

"Yes," Sarah whispered, and then repeated louder, her eyes wide and watering. "Yes!"

Hank gently took her hand in his, glanced up at her a moment, then slid a diamond ring on her ring finger.

Both were startled and turned to face the sound of cheers from at least twenty-five people who Charlie Thomas had told to stand on the sidewalk to witness the momentous occasion.

Together they walked towards the happy sound and the rest of their lives together. Interestingly, Charlie was nowhere to be seen.

# 38

# PRAYERS ANSWERED

Sarah stepped outside the bar and called Sophie, who was at the airport awaiting a flight for her honeymoon to Japan with her husband of less than twenty-four hours.

"Hi, Sophie. Are you looking forward to visiting Japan?" Sarah asked.

"Yes, of course. We already talked about this last night," Sophie replied wondering why she was getting a call to talk about her trip.

"Well, we'll have something else to talk about when you get back," Sarah responded with dramatic effect.

"What?" Sophie asked a bit out of breath after walking to her departure gate.

"Hank asked me to marry him about a half hour ago."

Sophie screamed and called Jean over. They put the phone on speaker mode and both congratulated Sarah at the fantastic news. Sophie was crying. Jean said he had to physically hold her up, she was so overcome with joy. The girls agreed to plan things out upon their return.

Sarah and Hank enrolled in the Pre-Cana marriage preparation program at Sarah's local parish. They met with her pastor multiple times, as well. Timing for the wedding was coordinated with President Petrov to accommodate his schedule so that he could attend. Father

Jack was to concelebrate. Uncle Rakesh would stand in as the father of the bride. Mother Miriam would support Sarah in every way possible. Sophie would be Sarah's matron-of-honor, and Jean would be Hank's best man.

One day, Father Jack called Sarah to ask if it would be okay for him to visit her and Hank, well before the wedding. She readily agreed and together they set things up, coordinating his visit with Rakesh and Miriam, as well.

Sarah met him on the appointed day at a small café near her apartment for a late breakfast.

"I've been meaning to ask you a question, Sarah," Father Jack started.

"Go ahead. Shoot." Sarah looked up wondering what had brought her father's good friend all the way from Virginia to check on her.

"Remember on the trail up in the Rockies you wanted to talk about praying?" asked Father Jack.

"Oh, yes. I remember. I was pretty angry, too. I regret that now," Sarah replied.

"As I recall you were wondering about why your dad prayed for your mom's soul, hoping she would be in Heaven. You also questioned why we pray at all. *What good is it?* I recall you asking me," Father Jack continued.

"Then I tried to meditate and ended up praying instead," Sarah replied.

"I remember that. That's why I've come to visit you. Here is my question: how is your faith, Sarah?"

"I thought you might be coming to ask me that question. Here is my answer. Since I saw you last, I've cried more than I ever thought I could. I was angrier than I ever thought I would be. I became aimless and sad. I was listened to, hugged, and prayed for by many people. I met a man on a trail who I love. He loves me. Soon we will be married. I went to Confession for the first time in many years. Now I go to Mass every Sunday, and I pray all the time. Instead of being angry, I am thankful for everything – the good, the bad, the many blessings I've been given. I don't take anything for granted. I can't thank God enough."

"Amen. Praise the Lord," Father Jack whispered.

Sarah shifted her position and fiddled with her napkin. "Can I ask you another question, Father Jack?"

"You know you can."

"How would I know what my vocation is?" Sarah asked.

"Great question! You must use all of your senses, your wisdom, your faith. You have to accept removing your attachments to things of this world, placing yourself in the hands of our Lord. Then you ask for direction and listen for the answer. You pray, ask, and listen.

"Then you test your understanding by speaking of your vocation to people you trust. Listen to their response. Pray some more. Ask your Guardian Angel for assistance to help you know. Then go accordingly, acting upon what you believe to be God's call, doing your best, all the while praying and listening to the results.

"In my case, I had an idea of what I should do that would not go away. No matter what I did. No matter how long I went. The idea remained and told me I should be a priest. Eventually, I realized it was more than my own desire. I was being called by the Lord."

"Would you be surprised if I told you I keep hearing, 'I want you to be a mother'?" Sarah asked.

"No. Not at all," Father Jack replied.

"I can't shake the guilt, though."

"Please explain."

"The CEO of my company says I'm his rising star. I just got a big pay raise and a retention bonus. I went to college for this. I learned from my dad, from Uncle Rakesh, and from my grandfather how to be a businesswoman. I feel it would be a waste to not go for it. I'm good at it, too, and I like it."

"Hmm. Then let me suggest that tonight when you're lying in bed preparing to go to sleep, imagine yourself in two scenarios. The first is you're married to Hank and are blessed with children. You've left your job to provide your full and complete focus towards raising them. The second is you're married to Hank and together you've decided to postpone having kids so that you can concentrate on your career. You move up in rank, pay, and prestige in your company earning respect in the community and your industry. Give yourself adequate time to imagine both scenarios. Then ask yourself which gives you more joy."

"I already know the answer," Sarah replied.

"Which is?" Father Jack poured more coffee. They both liked it black.

"Being a mother would give me way more joy than being successful in business." Sarah sat up straighter.

"Then why the guilt?"

"I've worked so hard. I don't know. It is hard to explain."

"So, are you telling me God wants you to serve him by being an ace businesswoman?"

"Actually, I think he wants me to be a good mother. I keep coming back to that when I think about the future."

"Got it. Motherhood makes sense as your primary vocation. Imagine the purpose God had in mind for you when he formed you. Another way for you to think about this is to imagine that God provides a long life for you and blesses you and Hank with children.

For the rest of your life, you will be a mother and wife, which are your primary vocations. Does this make sense?"

"Yes," Sarah replied as she poured more coffee for them both.

Father Jack continued. "The Irish have a saying, 'If you want to make God laugh, tell him your plans.' So, imagine a future where many things will happen to you and Hank. You can't predict the things you will experience, good or bad. Has He not prepared you for what is to come with your education, business, and life experience? Perhaps there will be another way he will ask you to serve Him in the future. You will have to be attuned to this possibility. I would worry less about not fulfilling your potential in business as much as I would about missing God's call."

"Can I tell you a secret, Uncle Jack?" Sarah whispered.

"You know you can," he replied then took a long sip of his coffee savoring it along with her humility.

"Nothing would make me happier than to be a mom. I'll put everything I have into it! What you said makes sense."

Father Jack simply smiled savoring his coffee and the intelligence of this talented young woman while thanking God for both.

The big day came and went with all the usual stresses, strains, joy, and reflection. Press coverage was muted and focused mainly on the visit from President Petrov, who was three months retired from his presidency, as planned. To Sarah's surprise, he brought his wife, Sandra, along with their son, Ivan. Sandra was especially funny with a sharp wit and an uncanny ability to get everyone at her table to laugh raucously.

Father Jack tried to give his shortest homily ever, but this was not possible, given the importance he placed on the occasion. Later at the reception, Rakesh and Victor gave wonderful toasts, each claiming to be Sarah's godfather.

As Hank's mother, Mary, stood to speak, the hall suddenly became quiet.

"I'll have you know I called up me cousins back in Castleplunket and had them ask around about Sarah's family, the O'Malley's from Castlerea, which is but a stone's throw away from where I grew up don't you know. Shocked I was to find out the whole family seemed to have been criminals."

Everyone gasped in astonishment!

Mary continued, "Locked up for one thing after another until they got kicked out of Ireland and shipped off to America about 1885. It was while they were on the boat comin' across that they conjured up the story about the potato famine causin' them to take the low road. I couldn't believe my ears! I says to me cousin, 'Are you sure you got the right O'Malley's?' And she says back to me, 'Sure, I am.' So, I called up Hank and suggested he reconsider marrying into a criminal family. To which he tells me, 'Ma, you're daft in the head. It wasn't her father's family who was from Castlerea, it was her mother's!'"

Everyone was laughing hysterically at this diminutive Irish woman, who had them all in the palm of her hand.

"So, I says to Hanky Pooh, would you mind tellin' me what her mother's maiden name was?

"'Mind?', he says, 'I'd have to be an eejit to support your criminal investigation.'

"Well, that satisfied me. You always want a man to defend his woman's honor. You know it could be that Mrs. Maggie *Carlos* O'Malley came from rough, Castlerea stock, but I doubt it. Yes, Hank, I did find out her maiden name and know all about her family. But this is all in jest. Please let me turn serious for a moment. Let there be no doubt that Mr. and Mrs. O'Malley sure turned out one fine lass in Sarah, who I now treasure as me own daughter. What joy!

"It is my hope and prayer that I can make her parents proud and meet their high standard whilst I still have time on this Earth. Will you join me for a drink, then? To Sarah and Hank. May the road rise to meet you!"

# 39

# SMOKY REFLECTIONS

Later that evening Rakesh, Phillipe, Victor, Ronnie, and Father Jack found themselves at Rakesh's house sipping sixteen-year-old Macallan scotch in Sean's honor. Phillipe then produced more hand-rolled Cuban cigars. They were ceremoniously lit by Rakesh, who claimed to be an expert in the art. Looking up he whispered, "We sure have come a long way from the days of Schlitz and Swisher Sweets, haven't we Sean?"

"Jack, your homily was spot on. Not sure why you didn't weave in some *Monty Python & The Holy Grail* quotes, but I'll let it slide. It was a terrific wedding," Ronnie observed.

"They are a match made in Heaven, boys," Father Jack replied.

"Indeed. Hank seems made of the right stuff. Sarah would not accept anything less," Rakesh added.

"I feel fortunate to be here with you men and to be part of this wedding celebration," Victor said.

"You four men will play an important role for these two newlyweds. It is clear to me Sarah has a special relationship with each of you, which is a great blessing," Phillipe observed.

"She's been through a lot in the last few years. Her faith was tested and remains. I look forward to seeing it develop further in the years to come," Father Jack replied.

"Hank's mom is a pistol! Sharp. Funny. Not to be underestimated," Rakesh said while trying to blow a smoke ring, which seemed easier in his younger days with his favored Swisher Sweet cigars.

"Indeed. Indeed. I'd like to propose a toast in her honor," Victor said.

They all came together. "To Mary Carson of County Roscommon. Pure bedrock. A woman to be admired. A mother to be honored. May she live a long and happy life while her enemies sprain their ankles always one step behind her!"

"Amen!" Rakesh, Jack and Ronnie yelled in practiced unison.

"Amen." Phillipe added.

"I didn't know a Russian would be skilled in the art of Irish blessings," Father Jack Martin laughed in his well-honed Irish accent.

To which Victor replied, also with an excellent Irish accent, "Ah, surin' I learned a few things as a young spy in Dublin."

All four men stopped and looked at Victor in surprise. Then he laughed hard and added in a brilliant French accent, "*Je n'oublie pas les français,*" and then translated, "I don't forget the French, either," for Phillipe's benefit.

"A man of many talents! I'll drink to that," Rakesh hailed as he raised his glass and puffed his cigar.

"Where do you go from here, Victor?" Phillipe Macron asked, feeling totally comfortable with these formidable yet humble gentlemen.

"This is a great question, Phillipe. I wonder if I need to know, as being with Sarah, Hank, Sophie, and Jean reminds me of my younger days when I did without planning, following my instincts and reacting to come what may.

"However, I suppose my dear wife, Sandra, would not appreciate this style of living. So, I am taking time to discern the path forward staying open to how I might be most helpful." He chuckled.

"I think the world has benefited much from your discernment thus far, Victor. I will pray for you, hoping your next phase of life is rewarding and fun." Father Jack proclaimed.

"I've got an idea for you," Ronnie chimed in with a smile.

"This ought to be good," Rakesh warned.

"What do you advise, Colonel Gardner?" Victor asked, taking on his well-practiced persona of the formidable President of Russia with his thickest Russian accent.

"I think you should develop a university course and teach it at Stanford, Oxford, University of Moscow, and University of Beijing."

Victor was surprised this was not a joke suggestion, "What subject should I teach?"

"Peace through Bourbon," Ronnie replied.

"Now you're talking boy!" Victor now changed to a flawless American accent to everyone's astonishment.

"Oh, yes, I was also a spy in New York City for two years. Ah, but those were the good old days," Victor laughed. Then he switched to another language and confused all four men.

"Ah, so, I see you do not speak Mandarin. Let me translate in a British accent. Would you mind pouring me another scotch, dear Rakesh."

Phillipe asked, "How did you come to convert to the Faith, Victor?"

"My grandmother planted the seed of faith deeply into my heart when I was a boy. Sean O'Malley caused me to remember where it was. It is as simple as that." Victor poured some scotch into Phillipe's glass.

"I understand your grandmother was a devout Jew who survived the holocaust," Phillipe added.

"Indeed. She was a great woman. Fearless, intelligent, and wise.

She taught me well, but I got caught up into a system. My father was a very powerful man. Then I heard Sean's speech before he became president. I could not believe my ears. To hear a man speak this way was unusual to say the least. Then he came to visit me as his first order of business after becoming president. I've come to believe his question to me was inspired by God." Victor savored his cigar and scotch.

Phillipe leaned forward. "What question did he ask?"

"He asked me if I was evil," Victor replied, and took another sip.

"Incredible! How did this make you feel?" Phillipe asked.

"I wanted to kill him on the spot. I could not abide this level of disrespect. I started to plot my revenge immediately. Then, later that night, I had a dream. My grandmother spoke to me saying, 'Answer his question!' I woke up in a cold sweat and knew the answer: 'Yes, I am evil. I have let you down, my Babushka. I am a disappointment even to myself.'

"Then at our next meeting, which was held in secret in New York, Sean told me something I could not believe. He said he thought I was a good man. Later he would tell me his instincts told him to trust the influence of my grandmother, who he knew was a devout Jew. He was right! Then he taught me about the Faith. Afterwards I devoured everything I could to learn about Christianity, especially the Catechism of the Catholic Church. I contacted a local Catholic priest and asked him many, many questions. Most importantly, I saw an example of faith in action in Sean O'Malley.

"I came to understand Christianity as the fulfilment of Jewish prophesy and covenants. I was convinced my Babushka would approve and found myself praying that she was with Jesus, her *Melekh Mashiach*, in Heaven."

Rakesh was stunned by Victor's candor. "I cannot imagine your family and political allies were supportive."

"My wife and son converted soon after I did. I think they were convinced mostly by my newfound happiness. My political allies were struck with fear. My political adversaries were licking their chops. I had to put those things into God's hands and push forward. Luckily, we were able to engineer a real democratic process for the first time to enable a peaceful transition of power."

"You received a Nobel Peace Prize in the process," Father Jack added.

"Indeed. God works in mysterious ways. Former spy makes good. Let me change the subject to Sarah and Hank and let me also include Sophie and Jean. How can we help them?" Victor smiled, happy to think about these two newlywed couples.

All five men looked around at each other. Then, the carpenter, Phillipe Macron from Bordeaux, France, answered, "We follow St. Joseph's example, being mostly quiet, listening for God's call, ready to act when needed."

"Amen!" Father Jack, Rakesh, Victor, and Ronnie cheered in unison.

# PART III

# 40
# CAROLINA CONFESSION

Hank set up his mobile home in preparation for Sarah, mostly by tossing things out and moving tools and other gear to his storage unit. They both agreed it made more sense to live in Merced because of his business. It would take many more months to merge the rest of their lives after the wedding, but those are the details that come along as part of the matrimonial ride.

A few months after the nuptials, Sarah found herself heading to Charlotte, North Carolina, for a project and took the opportunity to catch up with Uncle Ronnie, as was their custom. She met him at the spectacular Carolina Hotel in Pinehurst, home to one of the world's greatest golf courses, Pinehurst #2, which was designed by famed Scottish golf course architect Donald Ross.

Uncle Ronnie demanded a hug and got one. "It is good to see you, Sarah. You look fit as a fiddle!"

"You know I am, Uncle Ronnie. You taught me to never go soft." Sarah regarded Colonel Gardner, twice awarded the Silver Star for valor, as her model for honor, integrity, and manhood. For her, he was indescribable. Wonderful. Mysterious. Demanding. Loving. Pious. Caring.

Likewise, Sarah was someone he would die for.

They proceeded to the Tavern for lunch, which would include

Uncle Ronnie's favorite hushpuppies, which he savored, along with sweet tea while listening to Sarah bring him up to speed on Hank, Sophie, Jean, and all the goings-on back home in California.

"Remember the last time we were together here in Carolina, Uncle Ronnie? You suggested we go on the hike, and you promised to tell me a story about my dad that might help me put things in perspective. We never got the chance because of his stroke. I was hoping you could tell me the rest of the story."

He suggested they move out to rocking chairs on the veranda. It was a warm October day in Carolina. A cool breeze was bringing in the faint smell of decay that portends fall colors and the onset of winter.

"I recall our conversation like it was yesterday. You were rightly struggling with things. I reckon they included anger at losing your mother, confusion, and perhaps dismay at how your dad was handling the loss of his darling wife and doubts about matters of faith. Am I on the right track?"

"Yes," Sarah replied looking out towards the beautiful grounds of the hotel nestled amid the great southern pine forest of the North Carolina Piedmont.

"Your father was rigorous in learning his faith. He never stopped learning about Catholicism along with other religions, philosophies, and cultures. He was voracious in his desire to learn. God just happened to be his favorite subject. Did you know he read the Bible every day after he became President?"

"No." Sarah wondered how much she didn't know about her dad, irritated that he was quiet about so many things.

Uncle Ronnie continued. "Did you know he once thought the Church was full of it and overstepped on many topics?"

"What! Are you serious?" she gasped.

"Your Grandfather encouraged him to challenge his

understanding, and so he delved into the origins of the Bible, its reliability, and the history of the early Church. He scrutinized much and came away satisfied.

"He learned to love going to Mass, and over time, he developed a deep love for God and His church, not so much because it was His great commandment but because of the many blessings he'd received, especially the love of your mother and you coming onto the scene.

"One day many years ago, before you were born, he said to me, 'Ronnie, the most important thing in this life is learning to love God—to really love Him. It's all downhill after that.'

"He didn't know it, but I was really struggling. What he said hit me hard. I told your dad that I didn't know how to go on. I told him I was so lonely it hurt. The only thing I had was my Army career, which did not seem to be enough. Then your dad asked me, 'Do you love Him?'

"I knew what he was asking, but I was mad, so I said, 'Love, who? How can I love someone I can't see? Someone I haven't met. Someone who made me gay. Someone whose Church says I can't fall in love and get married. Someone who made me not fit in. Someone who made me feel ashamed. How am I supposed to love someone who did all this to me?' Before your dad could reply, I added, 'How would you know anything about what I'm going through? Sure, you say *you* love God but look at how lucky you are. You've got Maggie. So, go screw yourself before you answer my question with your Roman Catholic malarkey.'"

"Are you kidding? You must've been very sad, Uncle Ronnie." Sarah was listening intently, hanging on every word.

"More than you will ever know. Your dad's response shocked me. He said, 'Ronnie, I love you like a brother.' He hugged me for a long time. Then he whispered, 'You might be mistaken about me, though. You're right, I'm beyond lucky to have found Maggie. Blessed is more like it. But don't think you're the only one who knows loneliness. I know what it means to not fit in. You might not see it, but I've gone through similar challenges. I'm still going through them. Yes, Maggie and I are married, but we have not been able to conceive a child. We may be reaching the end of the line on that count.'

"Your father continued, 'Also, I've got many issues of my own, which you know nothing about. I struggle and constantly pray I may overcome them. I keep sinning, though. I keep praying for all I'm worth so I can move beyond these faults and improve my character. However, none of what I've experienced compares to what you've been through with your homosexuality. I know you are carrying a heavy load. I don't know if I could carry it, myself, either.'

"Then I asked your father, 'So, if all you say is true, how come you still love God?'

"Then your father told me this story: 'When I was eighteen, I had an encounter with our Lord that I cannot explain. I was desperately lonely. I went on a retreat and prayed for help. One night I was awakened and could not sleep. I got down on my knees and felt His presence. I felt his arms around me, holding me. I cried until I could cry no more. I felt His love that night, and it has never left me. In fact, it continues to this very moment.'

"'Despite this,' your father continued, 'I still struggled with loneliness and sinfulness. I followed the wrong path and was punished severely, but never did this feeling of love leave me. I was simply given a gift I did not deserve. So, I don't know how to fully answer your question. Why do I love Him still? Because of my loneliness. Because of my sinfulness. Because of the punishments and challenges resulting. Because of the gifts I've been given like intelligence, faith, Maggie, you, Jack, Rakesh, my mother, and father. Because of ailments, deficiencies, and injuries. Because of the beauty of the Blue Ridge Mountains and the Shenandoah Valley. Because of strawberries, blueberries, and raspberries.

"Your dad continued, 'Why do I love Him still? Because I've received grace I didn't deserve that has enabled me to get on the right path. I thank God for everything. All of it. The good. The bad. Everything.

"'Ronnie,' he said, 'I also asked Him to help me learn how to love Him. Back in college, I was desperately lonely. I was at the end of my rope. All out of options. I didn't know what to do. I prayed to Mary, Jesus's mother, to intercede on my behalf so I could be less lonely. One day I went to the church near campus and prayed hard to Mary for her help and intercession. Afterward I went to the cafeteria. As usual, I sat by myself. Then I looked up. You were standing there and asked, 'Mind if I join you?' Yeah, how could I not love God after he gave you to me?'

"Sarah, girl dear, I was crying hard when your dad told me this."

Sarah whispered, "I never knew."

Uncle Ronnie continued, "We were young men when he told me this. Your father was newly married and struggling with his business, not understanding why he and Maggie could not conceive. I was newly promoted and struggling with my command.

"Up until that point, I thought your dad had everything. Then I realized we were both being tested, developed, sharpened.

"I thought, '*If Sean can learn to love you, then maybe I can, too.*'

"I started to see my pain and suffering in a different way. I read about some of the great saints of the Church and wondered how to 'offer up and join my suffering' to Jesus in hope that I might become more loving and faithful.

"I prayed hard to God, asking Him to help me truly love him. This turned out to be the greatest gift your father ever gave me. There is a Gospel parable in Matthew about the pearl of great price. Do you know it?"

Sarah nodded.

"It's a good one. Faith so strong it leads one to truly love God not out of obligation but just because of everything, which is my pearl of great price."

Sarah said, "Back when we were talking and planning the hike, you said this might help me understand where my dad was coming from. Dad saw Mom's passing as something that was meant to develop and sharpen him?"

"No. He saw your mother's illness and passing as part of God's will and struggled mightily to understand it. Eventually he just resigned himself to accept it. He had to trust Him.

"His faith and love of God were not diminished. He told me both were necessary for him to get through the tragedy. His only mission after her death was to be strong for you."

"And, then God took him from me, too," Sarah whispered. "Why?"

"Do you know the Book of Job from the Old Testament?" Uncle Ronnie asked.

"No. I'm afraid not," Sarah moaned knowing there was no good answer to her question.

"Your dad sure did." Uncle Ronnie decided to let it end there, entrusting her to God, who hadn't answered Job when he asked God a similar question way back when.

# 41

# DECISION TIME IN MERCED

About six months after the wedding, Hank noticed a change in Sarah and became concerned. She was not as positive and sure of herself. Normally patient, she seemed to snap at small annoyances. He doubled his efforts to avoid things he thought might set her off, like walking into the house without dusting himself off, or beginning to eat before she sat down at the table. Despite his attempts, the stress level seemed to keep rising. He even mentioned it to his Ma, such was his concern.

Mary studied her boy. "Have you asked her about it? What does she tell you?"

"She snaps and says it's nothing, but I know it's something. I guess I'm doing something wrong, but she won't tell me what it is."

"Perhaps I know how to help. Why don't you invite yourselves over here to dinner so that I might have some time alone with her?"

So he did.

Mary planned for her specialty—Irish Stew with homemade biscuits. More importantly, she asked Sarah over early to help with the meal preparation, presumably to teach her the tricks of the stew trade.

While they were cutting up vegetables and preparing the broth, Mary asked, "How are you doing, Sarah?"

"Fine, I guess," Sarah answered wondering why her new Ma was worried about her.

"I like to pre-cook the carrots a little in a pan with butter. Don't ask me why. I guess I learned to do this from me mother, God rest her soul."

"Hmm," Sarah replied.

"OK, Sarah, let me come clean. Hank told me he's worried about you. Is something wrong, dear?" Mary turned and looked into Sarah's deep blue eyes.

"Oh, well! Uh, I've got to quit my job, and I don't know how, and I'm worried about how we'll get by without my salary, and I don't know what I'll be doing after I quit, but I know I can't be a good wife and mother traveling as much as I do, and I don't know how to tell Hanky, and I'm worried he'll be disappointed in me."

"Is that all?" Mary exhaled in relief.

"What? Isn't that enough?"

"Dear Sarah, you can do no wrong by your Hanky. You just tell him what you're going to do and why. He'll stand by you and do what is necessary. Oh, and by the way, you needn't worry about money, and not for the reason you're thinking."

"How can I not worry about money? Our income is going to go down by a lot. Remember, I'm working for a Silicon Valley company."

"Trust me. Just talk it through with Hank." Mary hid a grin, happy this was Sarah's only concern. "I think you'll be surprised. Why don't you go meet him and walk back here together when you're ready. I'll finish up the stew. It'll keep fine until you return."

Sarah held Hank's hand as they walked down the street to Ma's place.

"What? You're going to quit your job, are you sure?" Hank asked, not believing his ears.

"I think so. I'm gone three to four days a week for work. It just doesn't seem right."

"Hot damn! I get my Sarry all to myself! Yeah! I'm really glad you're going to quit. Yeehaw! This is better than Christmas!" Hank yelled while jumping higher than Sarah thought possible.

"You're okay with this? What about the money?"

"What about it? We'll figure it out. Don't worry."

"Hmm," Sarah sighed.

"What?" asked Hank.

Sarah laughed. "Here I was worried about how you would react, and it turns out I was worrying about something that was going to make you happy. Men! Who knew?"

"Yeah, but now I'll be giving you a new project to do in the meantime," Hank said mysteriously.

"Oh, really, what's that?" Sarah leaned in close.

"We've got to find a bigger house. This place we're staying was good for me, but now we've got to find something we can grow into."

"One step at a time Hanky Pooh. Let's save as much as we can and take things as they come, but yes, I like the idea of finding a good house." Sarah had stopped walking. "Plus, I'm going to give my boss six months' notice when I resign."

"How's about one month notice?" Hank took Sarah by the shoulders, staring into her deep blue eyes.

"Three months! Plus, we can use the money," Sarah pleaded.

"Deal! I'm going to have to push hard on this new idea I've been working on. If it works, then we'll be rolling in the dough!" Hank started walking and then started skipping, suddenly transformed into a young boy. "Hurry up, Sarry! I can smell the stew and biscuits!"

They skipped the rest of the way to Ma's holding hands.

Hank couldn't wait to tell her the big news.

# 42

# TAKE TWO, HIT TO RIGHT

A month later, Sophie called Sarah to ask if she and Jean could visit. When they arrived, Hank took Jean to his workshop to show him his latest idea. Hank's "workshop" was spread out between his backyard, his truck, and his storage unit. Nevertheless, Jean was easily able to understand Hank's concept.

"*Oui,* Hank. I think I understand what you are proposing. Let me ask you a question. Have you documented your idea in writing?" Jean asked positively.

"Nope. Why would I?"

"Because I think your idea is novel. Why should you not patent it? If so, then you must document your idea and get someone to sign and be willing to uphold your claim that you invented it on a certain date. You must also include any co-inventors who helped you develop the idea," Jean replied while starting to imagine many uses for Hank's invention.

"OK, let's do it. Will you help me document this and be my witness?" Hank asked excitedly, happy Jean was seeing potential in his idea.

"Of course. Let me get a fresh lab notebook from my backpack."

The boys worked well into the evening documenting Hank's

invention. Jean took measurements and made rudimentary drawings. Together they signed and dated each page of the notebook. He then provided Hank with contact information for an intellectual property (IP) attorney.

"Hank, you must not divulge this publicly until you submit your patent application. The IP attorney will need to do a 'freedom to operate' investigation and help you write the application. I will take these sketches and convert them into engineering drawings and specifications. We must also build a working model and also document how to make it. By the way, what do you call it?"

"That's a good question, Jean. I've never called it anything. For me it is simply a means to make a house more energy efficient," Hank replied.

Jean's and Hank's phones rang simultaneously. Sophie, Sarah, and Hank's mom were out searching for them and had become concerned when they were not found in all their usual places, namely the backyard smoking cigars or Scruffy's enjoying a beer.

"Why would you look for us at Scruffy's when we're busy inventing the Dynamic Home Energy Shield?" Hank asked Sarah with a laugh.

"What did you say?" Jean had stopped talking to Sophie and was looking at Hank with his mouth wide open.

"Um. Er. I think I said Dynamic Home Energy Shield." Hank was equally astonished he had spoken the name of the thing he'd been imagining, brooding about, testing, and fixing for well over two years.

"Yes! This is a great name for your invention, Hank! Brilliant!" Jean shouted.

"Why is Jean shouting, Hanky?" Sarah asked.

"Oh, it's nothing." Hank tried to change the subject, not wanting to get Sarah's hopes up. "We're starving. Where do you want to meet for dinner?"

Sophie and Sarah had just finished an intense conversation that included planning a visit to Mary's place for consultation.

"Let me understand what you are asking me Sophie," Mary began. "You say you want to remain as the CEO of your company, while also becoming a mother, God willing. Is this so?"

"Yes, Mother Mary. It turns out my brand is very valuable, and I think I'm really good at being a CEO. But I also want to be a mother, too. I've sacrificed a lot to get Sophie's off the ground. Do I have to give everything up?" Sophie asked earnestly.

Mary was sitting in her favorite chair in her reading room at the front of her exquisitely manicured mobile home unit looking fondly at Sophie and her daughter-in-law, Sarah on the couch. "One question is all I'll ask before I render my answer to your question. How does God want you to serve him?"

"I don't know. Running Sophie's comes naturally for me. I love Jean and would do anything for him. We both want children." Sophie was very comfortable with Mary Carson, who she sensed was smart as a whip from the moment they first met.

"Sophie, dear, let me provide an analogy that might help you decide. Supposin' you had to swim across a river. Your objective is within sight on the other side. What do you do?"

"I gauge the flow and my ability. Then I walk upstream of my target and start swimming, working with the current and not against it," Sophie answered.

"Spot on. You're right! Life is like a river, dear girl. It can sweep us to wherever it wants to take us if we don't know where we're heading. Worse yet, we can work against it and miss our objective if we're not thoughtful and honest about our capabilities and where we're starting from."

Sophie sat up straighter. "So, are you saying I could figure out a way to do both? I can be CEO of Sophie's and raise a family?"

"Do you think God is asking you to serve him by being CEO of Sophie's, LLC?" Mother Mary responded.

"Hmm. No. I think He wants me to be a loving wife to Jean and a good mother to our children, if we have them," Sophie answered.

"Is that all He would want from you, given the many gifts you've been given, like intelligence, fortitude, and piety, which are apparent to all who know you?" Mary asked provocatively.

"I'm not sure," Sophie answered with humility.

"To my way of thinking, your first priority as Jean's wife is to help him get to Heaven and see our Lord face-to-face. Supposin' you have children, your new first priority is to raise them so they can get to Heaven, as well. Sorry, Jean, you take second fiddle, as a mother's first priority becomes her children. This work is most intense when the children are young and continues in different ways as they grow and mature. Regardless, motherhood is a vocation that lasts a lifetime.

"Your role as mother might be incompatible with being CEO of Sophie's for a time. However, is being the CEO your real mission? Or aren't you aiming to provide a good company for your employees, good clothes for up-and-coming working women, and a good example of faith and piety to everyone who knows you?"

"Yes," Sophie said quietly, reflecting deeply about Mother Mary's perspective.

"You own the company, right?" Mary asked provocatively.

"Yes," Sophie replied respectfully wondering where this wise woman was taking her.

"Then why not set it up so you can fulfill your roles as wife and mother where you ensure you meet your obligations to Jean and your kids without compromise. If you do it right, won't Sophie's still be there when the kids are ready for you to take on a different role in the company?" Mary asked.

"Oh my gosh! The answers to my questions become so much clearer when I let go of my personal ambition. You're right!" Sophie answered.

"Amen," Mary whispered.

*Amen.* Sarah thought, reflecting on the wisdom of her dear mother-in-law and her amazingly smart and talented friend, who was like a sister to her.

"I know what I have to do next!" Sophie stood. "I've got to talk with my dad about how best to set-up Sophie's so I can take on a different role if, and when, the time comes for me to become a mother. He'll know exactly what to do, or if he doesn't, he'll know who I should talk to. Let's find the boys and take Mother Mary out to dinner to celebrate."

Sophie knelt down next to Mary's chair and hugged her for all she was worth.

After dinner and dropping Mary at her home, Sarah asked Hank, "Are you okay if I become a stay-at-home mom?"

"Yup. Why do you ask?" Hank replied while focusing on pulling his truck out of his mom's driveway.

"Because I'm pregnant," Sarah said, slyly knowing she might cause him to wreck.

"What? What! Yeehaw!" Hank screamed at the top of his lungs, just like a kid again.

# 43

# FATHER RAKESH

Sophie approached her father and conveyed the perspective and advice provided by Mary. Rakesh was struck by Mary's wisdom and thought it possible to set up Sophie's company in such a way.

"Are you sure about this?" Rakesh asked gently.

"Am I sure about what? Setting up the company where I'm not the CEO anymore, or becoming a mother?" Sophie asked while looking off into the distance, staring at her father's prized old-growth cypress trees on the edge of their backyard.

"Let me be more specific because perhaps I can see a little further down the trail than you. Setting your company up to continue without your direct involvement as CEO will not be easy. It does not mean it is impossible or even improbable. It simply means it will take more time and require more attention than it might seem. Of course, the most important element is the people you choose to lead it. Let's take a walk, my darling, and properly examine all that is required. It is a beautiful day outside!"

Rakesh pulled on his windbreaker and donned his Tilly hat while informing his lovely Miriam that he and Sophie were going for a walk. She voiced an admonition to which he replied, "Yes, Master!" hoping to get a laugh but instead receiving a scowl.

Sophie knew she was in for a lecture when her father called her "darling." but she also knew he would have an important perspective and provide essential help if she were to navigate these new and interesting waters. Just then, she remembered the river analogy from her talk with Mother Mary.

"Do you recall the story of original sin from the Book of Genesis?" Rakesh asked with a smile, happy to be on a walk with his brilliant daughter.

"We have to go back that far for you to help me figure out how to keep Sophie's running while I'm out on maternity leave?" It was Sophie's turn to be provocative.

"Ha ha! Of course we do! This story is vital! It is also a story that is repeating itself every day in our society."

"How so?" Sophie asked, wondering where her interesting, thoughtful, caring father was taking her.

"Do you know anyone who has suggested you follow 'your truth' or something like that?" Rakesh queried.

"Yes."

"Do you know anyone who has left their husband or wife to find themselves because they felt trapped and unable to reach their full potential?"

"Yes."

"Genesis 2."

"What?" Sophie stopped and looked up at her dad, who was tall, lean, and vibrant, with penetrating eyes that could look right into one's soul.

"'You are free to eat from any of the trees in the garden except the tree of knowledge of good and evil. From that tree you shall not eat; when you eat from it you shall die.' This is Genesis, chapter two, verses sixteen and seventeen. I cannot emphasize enough how important these verses are. It is not by chance I have them memorized.

"We must know this story and understand it, for it is a key that unlocks a way to see the world more clearly." Rakesh began to walk again.

Sophie raised an eyebrow at him, intrigued. "Explain."

"We can understand this passage if we consider the four senses of scriptural interpretation. I've discussed them with you before but let me repeat them. They are the literal, allegorical, anagogical, and moral senses.

"As you know, to properly understand Scripture, we must take these into account, and this is what the Church does for us. Thus, we can see in Genesis the initial relationship between God and humans is direct and wonderful. Adam and Eve are in Paradise, literally with God. So, what does it mean then, that we should not eat of the tree of knowledge of good and evil?" Rakesh asked professorially.

"It means we must not disobey God," Sophie responded with confidence.

"Yes. Additionally, we learn we are not to think of ourselves as God. It is not for us to determine what is good and evil. This is God's responsibility. Our standard for what is good and evil comes from God and not from ourselves. What happens if we do this?" Rakesh stopped and looked directly at his daughter.

"We die?"

"Indeed. Our sin brought death into the world. For us to understand the ramifications, we must imagine what Heaven is like, because this is what life was like before we disobeyed God and sought to exert our own wills over His. It is almost impossible to imagine the damage done by sin except we can see it with our own eyes every day.

Sophie nodded. "I did not understand this passage as fully as you are conveying. This raises a question. How do we know what God's standard is for good and evil?

"Ah! A great question. In a real sense, God wrote the standard in our hearts, and we know it naturally in our consciences. Over the course of time, God revealed these standards to us through the prophets, most notably Moses and the ten commandments. Despite this, we kept compromising or ignoring them to pursue our desires. Eventually we lost the true understanding of what they meant, and in the case of the Jewish Pharisees, they became *too* scrupulous, following the letter of the law while neglecting what God truly intended. Eventually God sent us His Word directly, in the form of His son Jesus, to teach us His way fully and completely, and to provide a path to overcome death due to sin.

"We are nearly two thousand years after Jesus's death and resurrection, so how do we know today what is good and evil? The answer is Jesus left us the Catholic Church, which cares for the deposit of faith left to His apostles and conveyed through Scripture and Tradition. This is the Magisterium of the Holy Catholic and Apostolic Church. It is trustworthy because it is guided by the Holy Spirit and leads us to Heaven," Rakesh explained.

"But the Church is so messed up," Sophie moaned.

"How so?"

"Hello! Priestly sexual abuse," Sophie answered adroitly.

"Sexual abuse, whether by priests, scout troop leaders, teachers, preachers, coaches, and so forth, has been around since the fall of man. Cover-ups, terrible bureaucracy, graft, nepotism, bad popes, bishops and priests, schisms, and many other serious, sinful abuses come with the territory of a human-led organization. I don't trivialize these. Nevertheless, the Church survives despite them." He paused for a beat, and then said, "Let me ask you this: where is the Church wrong on matters of faith and morals?"

"How about gay marriage and not allowing women priests?"

Sophie asks earnestly.

"We can dig deep into each of these topics, and we will. However, let me answer your question with something for you to ponder: Do you fully understand the Church's teaching on sexuality, human life, and marriage? How much of your concern with these subjects is based on your understanding of actual Church teaching found in the Catechism?"

"I guess most of what I know about the Church's teaching is from the media, friends, people I know, and what I hear at Mass." She gazed off a moment, realizing she had spent very little time learning about her faith from reliable sources.

"You sound just like me when I was your age. I understand, but I also recommend you continue to learn about your religion and the mystical body of Christ we call the Catholic Church. Back to the subject at hand. I am worried for you and women of your generation. Information spreads quickly nowadays, but this does not mean it is true. Manhood, womanhood, motherhood, and fatherhood have been obfuscated, questioned, and diminished by ignorant, and in many cases, nefarious people purporting standards that are self-referenced or self-serving.

"Why do we question or look past Church teaching, which is clear on most, if not all, of these matters, and conclude the Church is 'messed up,' while trusting influencers?" Rakesh asked.

Sophie frowned. "I guess I just assumed the Church is messed up. I don't hear or read opinions that support the Church's teaching."

Rakesh nodded. "Popularity and volume do not make something true. The forces are strong that tempt us to turn against the truth, just as in the Garden of Eden. Don't let yourself be fooled that things are different today."

"Is there not good intention behind efforts to put women on

equal standing with men?" Sophie asked.

"Yes, definitely. The problem with evil is that Satan is very cunning. So, we must be wary when endeavoring to improve the standing of women in society that we are not duped. For example, I have seen many examples where women over-emphasize the importance of reaching career potentials at the expense of familial responsibilities. The same is also true for men, by the way. I stand before you guilty of the same and have confessed my sins and repented deeply.

"Over-emphasizing the importance of a career can lead to diminishing the importance of motherhood, fatherhood, and the family as the foundation of society by substituting the state as the primary means of raising "*offspring*" aka "resources" such that men and women may slake their ambitions and predilections unencumbered.

"Further still we should be wary that this same force might also cause us to diminish the role of fathers or the wonderful differences between femininity and masculinity. Satan is like a judo wrestler. He uses momentum to his advantage to throw us off balance."

Sophie stared at him, open-mouthed. "Are you serious? You think people believe the government can supplant the role of fathers and mothers and the importance of the family?"

"Yes. Not only that. I think some want this. Look into the history of socialism and communism. There is no surprise that those philosophies find much common ground with feminism, using it as a long lever to advance their godless designs," Rakesh answered succinctly.

"Why?"

"Because Satan knows if he destroys the family, he will win many souls for his evil intents."

Sophie stopped walking and stared directly into her father's eyes with real concern. "You can't be serious?"

"I am very serious."

"You think people who support gay rights, women's rights, and a woman's right to choose don't believe in God or are influenced by the devil?"

"I think many of them lost the trail, to use a hiking analogy. They may believe in God but might be ignorant of His reality. They might not believe in the devil and may have lost, or never had, fear of the Lord. Losing the trail also means they likely do not believe in the authority of the Church to teach on these matters, which seems to be the de facto position we find ourselves in. Ask yourself this question: why don't they believe what the Church teaches on these matters?"

"Maybe it's because they're not Catholic," Sophie retorted.

"Does that matter?"

Sophie narrowed her eyes in confusion. "What? Of course it matters."

"What a person believes does not change the truth. It only helps determine if their understanding of reality is accurate or not," Rakesh replies.

"I will answer your important question, but before I do, it really is worth thinking deeply about why people, especially Catholics, pick and choose or outright reject Church teaching on matters of faith and morals.

"I believe evil forces cause people to think the state can supplant the role of the family and that homosexual marriage and abortion are moral, for example. These are not new forces. These are not even new topics. They were foretold in Genesis Chapter 2. Even today, Satan continues to proffer, 'You certainly will not die if you eat this fruit.'

"Adam and Eve had a direct relationship and friendship with God, yet they chose to believe Satan and fell to the temptation of thinking *they* could determine what was good and evil for themselves and be like gods."

Sophie sighed. "OK. You've taught me a lot, but what does all of this have to do with me asking for help to set up my company for the possibility I might become a mother?"

"My darling Sophie, you are amazingly blessed with intelligence, business acumen, and so many other wonderful qualities. Your mother and I are very proud of you and not surprised by your business success. Yet here we are in a world full of sin and death, which started back in the days of Adam and Eve. Here we are father and daughter talking about setting things up so you can be a mother and also keep your company. Your best defense against the temptations of the devil is your faith and intellect.

"The things you hear me saying to you this morning may sound incredible. Who talks this way anymore? Why start a discussion regarding your company with the Book of Genesis?

"For us this should not be unusual because we are Christians, but I suspect it is unsettling because we live in a secular world. All the signals we receive from popular sources would have us think the world operates without God. Without angels. Without fallen angels, namely the devil and his demons. Where the Church is, as you say, '*messed up*' with no authority. Even more, the authority to determine what is moral or immoral is now defaulting to individuals who use phrases like 'it's all good,' 'your truth,' and 'my truth.'

"Despite this, and at the risk of offending you, it is my responsibility, as your father, to help you see reality so that you may pick the right path, not just now, but in the future, long after I am gone. You may not believe or understand all I am telling you now, which is why Jesus left us the Roman Catholic Church. It is there for you, and I encourage you to use it to develop your knowledge and understanding of your faith and supernatural reality.

"Am I barking up the wrong tree? Is any of what I am saying making sense?"

"Yes. It is hard, though." Sophie deeply respected her father and knew she needed time to take this all in.

"So be it! Here we are talking about your life's journey, your true vocation. Please bear with me, if I ask one more question."

"Go ahead." They were both well practiced in her father's way of teaching by challenging her to think for herself. She knew she could challenge him if she thought he was mistaken, and he would expect her to do so. As he said many times, 'Let us be, rather than seem.'

Rakesh looked up at one of his neighbor's majestic cypress trees wondering if this species might have been present in the Garden of Eden, as he asked, "What is the primary responsibility of a mother?"

"A mother must protect and nurture her children and do everything she can to ensure they go to Heaven," Sophie answered.

Rakesh stopped suddenly, stunned by his daughter's response. Overcome by joy, he took her by the shoulders and hugged her tightly, leaning on her to keep himself from going to one knee. Then he whispered, "Let's go home, my darling daughter, now we're ready to develop the plan to ensure your company is set up properly!"

# 44

# MOTHER MIRIAM

Sarah arrived later that day at the Shriram's cozy cream-colored California cottage for her monthly afternoon tea and biscuits with Sophie and her mother. For Sarah, this was a treasured tradition beginning after her father passed. For Miriam this was what she lived for. Having Sarah and Sophie together was a blessing beyond words.

"Good afternoon girls. Who will say grace?" Miriam began.

"I will," Sophie jumped in, blessing herself with the Sign of the Cross, in the name of the Father, the Son, and the Holy Spirt. "Dear Lord, thank you for the blessing of my wonderful mother and my BFF, Sarah. Thank you also for my father, Professor Doctor Shriram, I guess. Amen."

"You guess?" Sarah chuckled.

"Ugh. You don't know the half of it," Sophie sighed.

Miriam also laughed. "Do tell!"

Sophie moaned dramatically. "I asked Daddy to help me configure my company, so in case I have children, it is set up correctly. Before he did this, he had to take me back to the book of Genesis and give me a primer on original sin."

"What does Genesis have to do with setting up your company?" Sarah asked, wondering how there could be a connection.

"Devils!" Sophie replied dramatically.

"You're serious?" Sarah asked.

"Dead." Sophie hoped to increase the mystery.

Meanwhile, Mother Miriam sat back sipping her Bengal spice tea, with a hint of Napa Valley honey, and smiled at her daughter's beauty, intelligence, and acting ability.

Sophie turned. "Why are you smiling, Mom? You seem to be enjoying yourself too much."

"Keep going, dear. I'm interested to hear what your father told you."

"He said the devil is at work and has caused many people to lose perspective where they think they set their own standard of right and wrong. They pursue their career ambitions, setting them at a higher priority than being a mother or father. He said I should trust the Church's teachings on matters of faith and morals and continue to learn about our faith to better understand reality and serve the Lord."

"That's it?" Sarah asked.

"No. He said he is worried about me and women in general because our secular world and feminism, taken too far, have created an expectation for us that diminishes the importance of motherhood, fatherhood, and the distinctions between men and women. Secularism and evil forces have caused us to think the Church is messed up and has no authority on matters of faith and morals. I think there is a lot more to his concerns, but we did not have time to get into all the background," Sophie replied.

"What do you think of all of this, Mother Miriam?" Sarah asked with genuine interest.

"Did I ever tell you about my Aunt Deepika, Sarah?" Miriam asked.

"No."

"I remember Auntie Dee. She was fun!" Sophie jumped in.

"Yes, she was! Auntie Dee was my father's older sister. She was brilliant and eccentric. I was like a daughter to her, as she was not able to have children and never married. One day, several months after she passed, I received a letter that was addressed to her, as I was executor of her estate. It was from a woman who was a good friend of Auntie's but had not known of her death. I called her, and upon hearing of my relationship and her passing, she started to chuckle, which I found unsettling, to say the least. I asked her why, and she replied, 'I can appreciate why you would find that strange, but you must know that I already felt she had passed on some time ago. You simply confirmed what I already knew. Hearing your voice caused me to recall how your aunt and I became friends. It is an interesting story because at first, we were bitter rivals. I used to hate your aunt. Maybe that's why I laughed.'"

Mother Miriam took a sip of tea and then continued. "I was surprised and taken back. On the other end of the phone was an elderly woman who seemed bright and capable. I asked her to tell me the story.

"She hired my aunt as *her* assistant in 1957. They were working at a publishing company focused on the medical industry. She said Auntie Dee was very smart, aggressive, and ambitious. It was not long before she knew she should be working for her and not the other way around, but several years of tension would ensue before this occurred. All the while Auntie Dee was pressing for authority, and control and pursuing her ideas with incredible skill and determination, which impressed this woman even though they were rivals. Eventually, Auntie Dee became her boss.

"Then one day, they went to lunch and Auntie confessed to being extremely lonely and depressed. The woman was shocked because up until this point, she thought Auntie had everything going on. Then she confessed to Auntie that she was out of her league when she hired her. After their roles were reversed her life became better because she was able to balance her work and home life. This was the beginning of their great friendship.

"She said, 'We wasted almost five years in a rivalry that should never have been and was borne out of selfish ambition and immaturity on both of our parts. Later, when we were in our seventies, we would laugh about how naïve we were. I thank God for your aunt. If it weren't for her, I would never have known what life could really be like.'

"I sat there stunned after she hung up. That phone call changed my life," Mother Miriam concluded.

Sophie leaned forward. "Wow! I am shocked and amazed, Mom. I never knew this about Auntie Dee. She seemed amazing."

"She was a great hero to me, girls. Hearing this woman's perspective and relating what my auntie told her made a big impression on me. Up until that point, my first priority, above all else, was my research and clinical practice, but if I'm honest, it was really that I was hoping to gain fame and fortune in my field of psychology." Miriam stared out at her favorite rose bush that she favored above all her other plants in the garden next to her patio.

"What do you think of Uncle Rakesh's concerns, Mother Miriam?" Sarah asked.

"Hah! Rakesh! My Rocky!" She laughed. "I never knew he was going to be such a worry wart in his older years."

"Yes, and I get the benefit of his worrying," Sophie moaned.

"Do you know my name really isn't Miriam?"

"What?! You're not serious," Sophie yelled. "You've got to be joking. OK, what's your real name?" Sophie could not believe what she was hearing.

"Usha. My real name is Usha Sambanthamurthy. My family came from the southern part of India near where your father's family is from," Miriam related.

"And you're just now telling me your name is not Miriam, when I am twenty-seven years old because?"

"Because I want to." Miriam smiled and poured more tea for all of them.

"Is there anything else you want to tell us?" Sarah asked with a knowing smile but not knowing where Usha/Miriam wanted to take them.

"I had a big crush on your Uncle Ronnie back in the day," Mother Miriam winked.

"What?!" Sophie and Sarah both screamed in unison like twin sisters.

"Uh huh. I met him while I was working in an outpatient clinic at the Veterans Administration. He was a hot-shot soldier who claimed to have no issues resulting from his recent combat experience except for shrapnel in his back, shoulder, and arm, but I knew he was covering up. I was a young clinician working my first job at the V.A. When I saw Ronnie, I came undone, which was very unprofessional, I know.

"Eventually, he confessed his secret, and we agreed to be friends. Then he introduced me to his crazy friend from Boston, whom he called Rocky. Little did I know Rocky was short for Rakesh, and the rest is history." Miriam's eyes could not contain her joy at revealing this secret to her girls.

"I had no idea!" Sophie cried.

"What, you didn't know I was a Hindu?" Miriam asked with a wink.

"What?!" both girls screamed again in unison.

"I was raised by my parents in the Hindu tradition, which I

deeply love. They were not too happy that I was going to marry a boy not of their choosing, though. However, after they met your father, they could not stop themselves from loving him. My father and his dad were of the same age and got along famously. I had to agree to raise you in the Catholic faith, Sophie. Your father made this very clear when he asked me to marry him," Miriam explained.

"I always thought you were the one who got Daddy to be a devout Catholic," Sophie said.

"Ha ha! You could be right, but it was your father who caused me to convert to the Faith. He started to teach me about it after we started dating. He was my Confirmation sponsor, too. Miriam is my Confirmation name. It means Mary in Hebrew and would have a similar sound to how Jesus, or Yeshua, pronounced His mother's name. I have a very great devotion to Our Lady," Miriam explained.

"No one calls you Usha. That name isn't even on your driver's license," Sophie noted.

"A woman needs her secrets," Miriam smiled.

"Are there any more secrets you wish to share, Usha?" Sophie asked with a wink.

"Your father's not wrong with his concerns," Miriam replied.

"I know Daddy cares about me, but I'm not a kid anymore," Sophie observed.

"He knows this. I suspect he is hoping to arm you as you embark on the next part of your life's journey. Plus, a father always worries about his daughters, and sons, too, I suppose.

"It is hard for us to imagine a different way, but we must. Imagine what it must have been like for the early Christians. They were weird! One day they were Jews or pagans. Romans or Greeks. The next they were following The Way of Yeshua. Why? Why would they do this and risk martyrdom?

"I bet hearing your father talk of the temptation in the Garden of Eden, the Devil, evil and morality made you uncomfortable, no?" Miriam asked.

"Yes. I told him it was hard to take in," Sophie admitted.

"You girls have the benefit of being raised by devout Christian parents who continued to learn their faith while you were growing up, but you should not assume other people are like this, especially world leaders and other influential people," Miriam added.

"Ignorance of our Faith abounds. Perhaps this will change in the future as people realize that true happiness doesn't come from having cable TV, fancy cars, careerism, or seeking one's own truth."

"So, where does happiness come from?" Sarah asked provocatively, fully comfortable that Miriam was up to the challenge.

Sophie spoke up. "Let me try to answer, OK, Mom?"

Miriam smiled. "Sure, my love."

"Happiness comes from loving Jesus with all you've got, and doing your best to serve Him to your full capability."

"Well said, Sophie! Let's also be clear about what we mean by love. In this case, love is not a feeling but an action. It is charitable and results in the selfless willing of the best good and the truest happiness for another person, so much so that one is willing to give up one's time and treasure or even one's life for them. We're not talking about romantic love here. True happiness emanates from a love of Jesus that is so deep it causes us to be willing to sacrifice and suffer, if we must, to serve His objectives and not our own.

"This kind of love implies that we do not need to be ambivalent, aimless, or self-centered, nor afraid, or hungry for wealth and power, nor disempowered by blind fate, or worried about death because God sent us His Word, through Jesus, to let us know there is a better way, and that God is waiting for us in Heaven." She paused a moment and glanced from one to the other. "You girls must be careful not to let your intelligence become an obstacle to your faith. As Jesus would say, 'Those who have ears ought to hear.'"

Sophie closed her eyes for a moment. "Hmm."

"How am I able to say such things?" Miriam asked.

Hearing no answer, she continued, "This is not a rhetorical question. It demands an answer. Think about it girls. How am I able to say this, and how are we able to have this conversation? How is your father able to relate his perspective to you, Sophie?"

Sophie shrugged. "I guess you both understand Scripture?"

Miriam turned to Sarah. "More than that. What do you think, Sarah?"

"It seems to me we're all very blessed with gifts that enable us to discern these things."

"What you both say is true, but it is incomplete. Think about the relationship between God and His people over time. From the beginning, He revealed Himself through His creation, prophets, and Scripture, yet we continue to rebel and sin. Prophets were killed, disregarded, and shamed. Some places were so corrupt they were obliterated, yet we did not hear God's voice, or if we did, we disregarded it in favor of our own.

"In the beginning was the Word, and in the fullness of time the Word was made flesh in the form of the Son of God, named Jesus. To properly understand this God-Word or God-man we must use our full capabilities to understand Scripture—literal and spiritual.

"How am I, a former Hindu able to say, 'We do not need to be aimless, ambivalent, anxious, etc.? How am I, a mother and wife, able to know God is waiting for us in Heaven, and He wants us to have abundant life with Him? How do the three of us know that happiness comes from loving Jesus? Loving the Word of God and seeking to do

His will?

"Think about this deeply, Sarah and Sophie. Ponder it for the rest of your lives, for we would not know any of this if Jesus had not left us His Church. Not only does this Church enable us to begin to understand God's Word, but it also enables us to worship Him and join Heaven and Earth together in the sacrifice of the Mass.

"We think Heaven awaits us only after we die, but this is a mistake. We can find Heaven in this life where the whole Church – in Purgatory, in Heaven, and on Earth join together in the sacrifice of the Mass. We can find communion with God himself in the Eucharist. We experience His saving grace through the Church's Sacraments.

"Thomas Merton, a Catholic priest and monk, once said, 'The deepest level of communication is not communication but communion.' The Church is necessary for this. It is why we have the Sacrament of the Eucharist.

"I think the reason your father is so worried, Sophie, is because society has lost its respect and appreciation for the Church. The Church is continually attacked from the outside with apparent impunity and from within by the horror of clergy sexual abuse, which is an especially hard challenge for mothers because every fiber of our beings is oriented towards protecting our children. Let's not also overlook how hard this problem is for all the good priests who innocently suffer as a result.

"Your father is not wrong about the devil, by the way.

"Jesus founded his holy, catholic and apostolic Church on Peter. We are able to say true happiness comes from loving Jesus and the desire to serve Him that results because of this and not despite it.

"God's Word is written in our hearts. It is written in Scripture. It is written in our natural world. It is written in love. It became a man named Yeshua, born to a woman named Miriam by the power of the

Holy Spirit.

"How can we begin to understand God's Word without His Church? How can we properly worship and express our love for Him without it? So, just as we should strive to learn to love Jesus, we should do so through his mystical body, the Church.

"Today I think it is harder for us to appreciate this because society has seemingly advanced with technology, sophisticated governments, news media, science, universities, capitalism, global economies, big companies, etc.

"What place does the Church have in this sophisticated, scientific world?

"I won't speak for Rakesh, but as a convert to Catholicism, it is nearly impossible for me to tell you how much I appreciate and love the Roman Catholic Church. I desire that everyone partake in Her teaching and sacraments. I mourn for those who are led astray, including Catholics themselves.

"Whoever has ears ought to hear," Miriam concludes.

An awkward silence pervaded for a minute, and then Sophie, who was shocked by her mother's passionate and thoughtful explanation, said, "Wow! I never knew you felt this way, Mom."

"Yeah, well, you think your father is the big cheese. I'm just a simple Indian girl named Usha who now goes by Miriam." She laughed, then turned to her daughter's friend. "What do you think, Sarah?"

"I've got a long way to go!" Sarah replied enthusiastically.

Miriam smiled. "Sarah, my dear, your humility takes my breath away."

With that, Miriam pulled both of her "daughters" together for a long and well-deserved hug.

# 45

# RANGER POLICY

Hank and Sarah were devastated by the passing of their dear friend, Jean Macron, inventor extraordinaire, who was praying hard that he and his dear wife Sophie would be able to celebrate their sixty-fifth wedding anniversary before he passed. He fell short by three days.

After hearing the news, they decided to visit Sophie at her home to lend support as best they could. This was much appreciated, even though Sophie's children and grandchildren were on hand and ensuring extra coverage in her time of need.

They were greeted by Sophie's eldest daughter, Mary, who welcomed them to her mother's home and asked if they would mind if she joined them for tea and biscuits, which was their longstanding tradition.

"Mind? Of course not, dear. You are part of our sacred tradition handed down to Sophie and me by Mother Miriam. Plus, you're a grandmother, yourself and this is what we do!" Sarah added as she went inside to familiar territory.

Hearing their arrival, Sophie made her way using her trusty cane and quietly greeted her friends, albeit looking weary and frail from lack of sleep.

"Would it be okay if we had our tea on the patio? It is sunny today, I think," she said as she hugged them both.

As they walked, she stopped, turned and took hold of both of Sarah's hands. "Sarah, I want to tell you a story Jean told me about you just a few days before he passed. I think Mary and Hank will enjoy it, also." With that she turned with Mary holding her free arm for support and made her way to the kitchen to arrange the tea and biscuits just as her mother had taught her.

Not much was said until they reached the patio. Then Hank whispered, "I still can't believe my best friend is gone. I miss him so much it hurts, but I figure I won't be too far behind."

"My dad sure liked you, Uncle Hank," Mary replied, carefully disregarding Hank's premonition.

"You know Mary, one of the smartest things I ever did was getting your dad to help me imagine new and different ways to build affordable, energy-efficient homes. Having him by my side was a stroke of genius on my part!

"As you know, back then he was working on technology to enable personal flying vehicles. His company had also set a goal to send zero waste to the landfill for its own operations, and this got Jean thinking, 'Why couldn't private, single-family homes, which are so prevalent in the United States, do the same thing?'

"Then he asked, 'Why not recycle it on-site versus sending it off to a central location where who knows what happens to it?' I thought this was brilliant, and so we began going to the landfill to get a handle on recycling. Turns out we became garbage experts while your mom and Aunt Sarah were having tea and biscuits with Mother Miriam on Sunday afternoons."

"Yes, and I recall you might have smoked a few really expensive cigars while you were watching the trash, which you tried to call *work* but we knew better." Sarah chuckled and smiled at Mary knowing she would understand the context.

"Haha! Then, about a year later, I remember seeing your first Emmaus brick and thinking, 'You boys might be onto something'," Sophie laughed seeming to gain energy from Hank's fond memories.

"It took Jean and I a while to conjure the machine to make the bricks, but the idea of a closed-loop system to pulverize and process household plastic, metal, and paper, forming it into a 'brick' was both of ours, and the business partnership that resulted was a great surprise." Hank added.

"What was this secret you wanted to tell me, Sophie?" Sarah asked as Mary poured tea for all of them.

"Ah, yes. I almost forgot. It was a story Jean told our children and me a few days before he passed. He started by recollecting how Emmaus Industries came into being, including going to the landfill with Hank. This was something we had heard many times over the course of our lives.

"Then he told us something new. It was an aspect of his experience that I never knew because I was so busy raising our kids and guiding Sophie's LLC during the formative years of Emmaus.

"As you know his last two weeks were a roller coaster, but as he told the story he sat up straighter in his bed and became very calm and looked at all of us to ensure we were listening. Then he said, 'There should be no doubt that the key to success for Emmaus Industries was due almost entirely to Aunt Sarah.'"

"What?!" Sarah gasped.

"I remember this. Papa was very sure of himself and wanted us to listen carefully," Mary added.

"He said, 'Once Uncle Hank and I got the technology working we filed a series of patents to protect our invention, but we would have gone nowhere had it not been for Aunt Sarah's business savvy and financial genius. She guided us with two philosophies that unlocked the potential for this extraordinary invention. First, she regarded money simply as a resource and not an objective. Second, she guided us to license our technology to competitors to enable broader adoption and global expansion. She simply kept reminding us to pursue the value this new technology provided to society instead of our own personal ambition.'

"Then Jean paused and made sure we were all listening and said, 'She was the best boss I ever had, too. It was a great blessing to have been guided by her over the course of my career.'" As Sophie concluded, she leaned back and savored her first cup of tea with a knowing smile.

"This is not a secret for me!" Hank cheered.

"I never knew Jean felt that way about me," Sarah whispered.

"He told our kids how you spearheaded the use of Emmaus bricks as a form of currency where individuals could deposit them with a central agency for energy or tax credits. He also told the story of how you collaborated with a Polish company to license their patents to incorporate a unique geometry that enabled the use of Emmaus bricks without mortar for building construction.

"He said, 'Hank and I were two carpenters who became manufacturing men only by the grace of God who gave us Sarah Carson to guide us and then, eventually, she became our CEO, when she was able.'

"She never got the credit for what may have been our greatest innovation, which was licensing the patents so the world could take advantage of the concept. This led to widespread adoption that enabled the shift from centralized to radically decentralized recycling.

"Business schools went on to analyze this transformation for years to come, but Uncle Hank and I didn't need anyone to tell us that our key to success was Sarah Carson."

"Amen." Hank whispered.

Sarah was sobbing deeply. Sophie came to her side and wrapped her in a blanket and held her tightly just as she had done many years before high on a cold, dark mountain.

After the funeral, the family gathered at the Macron home, which used to be Sophie's parents' cozy California cottage. Sarah was by her side, but it was Sophie's eldest daughter, Mary, who had taken charge of ensuring all went smoothly that day.

Jean Macron had gained the respect of his community and was considered a pillar of piety and humility. Sophie requested a small gathering at her home with family and close friends, hoping to avoid the inevitable loneliness for as long as possible.

Mary asked everyone to gather on the back patio, which included Sophie and her adult children—Mary, Phillipe and Joseph, along with their spouses and her seven grandchildren and six great grandchildren. Sarah and Hank were accompanied by their children Ronnie, Jack, Thérèse and Elizabeth, along with their twelve grandchildren and four great grandchildren. Also joining was their pastor and several close friends and neighbors.

After the pastor said a prayer, Sophie asked everyone if they would join her for a toast to her beloved Jean. As she gazed at her family and friends she was overcome with emotion and unable to speak. Seeing this, Hank came forward and put his arm around her shoulder and asked her if it would be okay if he proposed a toast on her behalf. She nodded affirmatively and continued to hold on to him for support.

Hunching his shoulders, Hank stood before them as straight as he could, but the ravages of time had taken their toll.

"Dear family and friends, I would like to propose a toast to my wonderful friend, Jean Macron, whose humility was an inspiration and whose ingenuity and faith literally saved my life. A good father. A loving husband. A faithful servant. May he see our Lord face-to-face."

There wasn't a dry eye amongst the adults, but then Thomas, one of Jean's grandchildren, asked, "Could you tell us how my grandfather saved your life, Uncle Hank?"

"Ahh, Tommy, are you sure you have time for this story?" Hank asked.

By this time everyone was gathering around Grandpa Hank, including and especially Sophie and Sarah, as neither had heard this story before. Mary Macron asked all of the children to sit down in the grass and be very quiet. Likewise, all of the adults found chairs and focused their attention on this loving, gentle man.

"I've never told this story to anyone, not even you, Sarry. Sometimes a man doesn't see the point. What's done is done. Learn. Move on. That was the Ranger way.

"I didn't like Luke DeVoe from the moment I laid eyes on him. I saw how he looked at my Sarah, and I didn't like it one bit.

"By the way, your Grammy Sarah was a stunner! I never saw a woman as beautiful in my whole life, except for Sophie Macron, who some of you call Mother Sophie, which is a wonderful name for a wonderful girl. I've known her for over sixty-five years. How Grandpa Jean and I got so lucky is a question for the ages.

"Anyway, this Luke DeVoe was a hotshot construction general contractor from the central valley. We were competitors and sometimes partners. He pretended to be my friend. Really, he was a bully who constantly let me know he was superior in every way. He drove a flashy truck. Wore fancy clothes. Too fancy for a real construction guy, if you ask me.

"One time we were out bowling—Sarah, myself, Luke, and some of our business friends. Luke got three strikes in a row and then claimed this entitled him to kiss all of the women that were with us. No, I didn't like that he kissed my Sarah, but that he kissed her on the lips for a long time was more than I could take. So, I decided I would meet him afterward to explain my feelings to avoid embarrassment to your Grammy Sarah."

Sarah and Sophie, sitting together, turned and stared at each other with wide eyes.

One of their grandchildren noticed and interrupted Grandpa Hank, asking, "Grammy Sarah, do you remember Luke DeVoe kissing you?"

"Yes, I remember, Natalie. What I don't remember is your Grandpa Hank meeting up with him after the bowling." Sarah was worried about where the story was heading.

"You wouldn't remember because I did it while you weren't looking. I went up to Luke DeVoe and told him I thought that kiss was too long. However, it wasn't what I said, but how I said it that sent the message I was ready to fight.

"His reply to me was, 'You're right, Hank. I apologize,' which took the starch right out of me. What could I do? I wanted to punch him in the nose, but how could I after he apologized? That made me even madder!"

One of the great grandkids asked, "You were going to fight him, Grandpa?"

"No one kisses Grammy Sarah on the lips except your Grandpa! That was Ranger policy back then and it still holds today. But I guess I would make exceptions for great-grandchildren," Hank answered with a wink. Then he continued. "I think most of you know about the Dynamic Home Energy Shield that Grandpa Jean and I invented way back a when. We got a patent on it, too. Your Grandpa Jean was very upset that I included him as a co-inventor on the patent application. He considered me as the inventor and himself as a helper to write the application, but this was not true.

"Your Grandpa Jean was a terrific engineer with over twenty patents to his credit. I had the concept right with that energy shield idea, but it couldn't be built as I had conjured it. Your Grandpa Jean was able to figure out a way, and this enabled us to commercialize it. Now, if that isn't co-inventing, then I don't know what is!" Hank gazed at the many faces of his family and then whispered the last bit to increase the mystery for the sake of the children. "Humility was the hallmark of my great friend, Jean Macron."

"You said Grandpa Jean saved your life. How did he do that, Grandpa Hank?" asked Jack, one of Sophie's great grandchildren.

"Oh, yes, let me explain. So, this Luke DeVoe was a nasty piece of work. Right after we introduced the dynamic energy shield, he copied it and started to market it as his own. Not only that, but he also filed his own patent application and sued me for infringement of *his* intellectual property. Can you believe this?"

"What does all that mean, Grandpa Hank?" young Jacky asked.

"It means Luke DeVoe was trying to steal our invention," Grandpa Hank answered.

"Woah! That's bad!" Stephen, another great-grandchild, shouted.

"You aren't lying, Stephen! First, Luke DeVoe kissed Grammy Sarah. Then he tried to steal Grandpa Jean's and my invention. What would he do next? I told Grandpa Jean I was going to meet DeVoe and have it out with him. Then Grandpa Jean asked, 'Hank, does this mean you are going to fight Luke DeVoe?' And I answered him, 'Not only am I going to fight him, I am going to make sure I wreck his fancy truck by smashing his face into it.'"

Grandpa Hank gazed out and could hear the great-grandchildren murmuring, but didn't dare look in the direction of Sarah, Sophie, Mary, Thérèse, or Elizabeth. He knew his women folk wouldn't look too kindly on his recollections, but the way he figured it, at ninety-four, who was going to stop him?

He continued his story. "Grandpa Jean had other ideas. He convinced me that physical violence was not the way to go, and this was not because he was a wimp. Far from it! Grandpa Jean was tough as nails! He's a guy you'd want on your side in a fight, believe me.

"That wasn't the only part of how Grandpa Jean saved my life because I was not fooling about taking DeVoe out to the woodshed. Who knows what would have happened? Maybe I would have gone to jail or worse, but the lifesaving was something more, much more. Grandpa Jean saved my life by his example of faith and humility. He set a standard for manhood that caused me to reach deeper and try harder to be a gentleman and a good father. He was the most honorable man I have ever known.

"But don't think we let Puke, whoops, I mean Luke, off the hook. On Grandpa Jean's advice, I went to his headquarters to speak with him. I asked him to reconsider his lawsuit and told him I had proof that we invented the energy shield three years before his claim.

"I'll never forget what he said to me: 'DeVoes don't back down to anyone, least of all the son of a mobile home park manager.'

"Thank God Grandpa Jean prepared me for that kind of response because it was all I could do to not jump across DeVoe's fancy desk.

"The next day, we filed a lawsuit against him for patent infringement. It took five years, but we won our case because Grandpa Jean had me document, sign, date, and get witnesses for all of my ideas, drawings, and specifications in my laboratory notebook. This ended up being the key piece of evidence, and the straw that broke DeVoe Industries crooked back.

"They had to write us a check for $1,000,000, too!"

Grandpa Hank was enjoying the look on Sophie's face as she saw the wonder and pride in her family's eyes as he told the story.

"I don't know if I should tell the next part of the story."

"Why not Grandpa Hank?" asked Natalie.

"Well, because it involved Grandpa Jean and I playing a prank on Luke DeVoe. We got the idea from YouTube."

"But, I think I'll leave it there because I don't want Grammy Sophie and Sarah to get mad at me. Plus, we knew we shouldn't have done it, but Grandpa Jean said, 'That's what you get when you kiss Sarah Carson without permission.' I was good with that policy, too!"

All eyes turned to Sarah after her son, Ronnie, provocatively asked, "What do you think of all of this, Grammy Sarah?"

Sarah chuckled knowing her son was looking to get a laugh at his father's expense.

"I ran into Luke DeVoe the morning after the bowling kiss," she whispered and paused for dramatic effect. All of the young children became very quiet while looking up to this diminutive, grand lady who they all cherished. Sarah noticed her Hank straighten up in his wheelchair, too.

"I had just gotten my grande-sized black dark roast coffee at Starbucks when I heard his voice ordering a fancy drink with caramel and who knows what else. He walked over after he paid and said, 'Hey Sarah, I'm glad to see you. What did you think of our kiss last night?' It was clear he was trying to antagonize me.

"I closed the distance and got right up close to him, which he seemed to like. Gritting my teeth I said, 'This is what I thought of it.'

Then I kneed him in the groin as hard as I could. He went down to the floor moaning in pain." Sarah paused as she heard the children gasp.

"Then he looked up at me like a scared little varmint. I told him if you ever speak to me again, I'll send Hank over your way to finish this business." Sarah then winked at her great-grandchildren and leaned back fully satisfied.

Grandpa Hank grinned. "Why, my darling Sarry, I never knew."

"A woman needs her secrets, Hanky Pooh."

# EPILOGUE

## 46

# A LETTER FROM SARAH

Not long after Sarah's passing, her eldest daughter, Thérèse, decided it was time to bring her siblings together. She also invited the Macron kids, but only Mary could join.

She asked everyone to a small Irish pub near her parents' hometown of Merced, which wasn't as cozy as one would find on the Emerald Isle but would have to do as Scruffy's tavern had long ago succumbed to the vagaries of time. The Guiness flowed at lunch, which was unusual, but not uncalled for, as it had become rare for the four Carson kids—Ronnie, Jack, Thérèse and Elizabeth—to get together. Mary fit right in, as she and Thérèse had become good friends over the years.

"As I told you I have a letter from Ma, and I wanted us to hear it together," Thérèse explained.

"When did you get this letter?" Ronnie asked.

"My daughter, Maggie, shared it with me two weeks ago, about a month after Ma's funeral. She had a special relationship with her Grammy Sarah."

"Before I read it, you should know Maggie received the letter not long after losing her job due to a layoff. She was also having trouble with Jacky, who had been struggling and was having to do community service for some mischief he caused. Her husband, Jake, was also having a tough time at work with a terrible boss. Maggie was at a low point, and Ma knew it.

"Why I share it now is because Ma and Pa have passed on. So too have Mother Sophie and Grandpa Jean. Likewise, our great Uncles Rakesh, Ronnie, Father Jack, and Victor have all passed, which means we're it. We set the standard from here forward. Now we're orphans, like Ma was when she was just starting out."

"I miss your Ma. She was indeed my mother's sister and like a second mother to me. She was my hero. I only hope I can make her proud in Heaven," Mary added.

"You're like our own sister, as if two weren't enough," Jack chuckled.

With her heart pounding and tears welling in her eyes, Thérèse read the letter aloud:

> My Dearest Maggie,
>
> I understand you and Jake have hit a rough patch with you losing your job, his nasty boss and your Jacky acting up, as young boys often do. All three situations bring back memories, which won't do you much good other than letting you know your Dear Olde Grammy has an inkling of what you're going through.
>
> So be it! Life happens, no? I know what you are thinking, 'You're not much help, Grammy!'
>
> This is not the reason I'm writing you, my darling granddaughter. I know you can handle what comes your way with aplomb. Instead, I write knowing I'm coming to the end of the line. I fear it won't be long now because my Hanky is gone, and I miss him so!
>
> We had a good life, blessed beyond measure, really. I

could go on and on reciting the tragedies, maladies, lucky breaks, adventures, and joys we experienced but won't. I could also recite many lessons learned along the way, but who learns anything from someone else's life lessons?

Here's what's to know from your Dear Olde Grammy's perspective that might be of some benefit as you continue life's grand journey.

I had a very good father. I was mentored and loved by four very good men who I called uncles because my father regarded them as his brothers. I met a very good man, named Hank, who asked me to marry him and gave his life to me.

I read the actions of their lives like a letter, a love letter no less. Grammy Sophie told me of your grandfather's physical strength when he was needed up in the Rocky Mountains after my father was evacuated. I saw it firsthand, myself, many times and then later noticed how gentle he became as he aged. My Uncle Ronnie was a real-life hero, and I am convinced he is a saint. Father Jack was perhaps the most courageous of all, giving his whole life over to serve us as a priest. Victor Petrov changed the world by setting Russia on a course towards peaceful democracy. Uncle Rakesh... thinking about him takes my breath away. Perhaps the smartest of all, he was a genius in business but became even more learned regarding our faith and a great teacher of both.

Yet, your great-grandfather's and your grandfather's greatest calling was to be dads. My dad (your great-grandfather) set a standard for me and held me to it. I saw your grandpa do the same, but I also saw him cuddle your mom and change her diapers without complaint. He took to being a father like a duck takes to water. I see the same with your Jake.

How is this possible? These rugged, brilliant, action-oriented men are also wonderful daddies able to see deep into their daughters' hearts, praying for them and doing what is necessary, up to and including being willing to die for them without hesitation.

Don't we know the answer? We're mothers, after all. We've given birth to boys and helped to raise them into men.

I remember when I was a little girl walking with my father down a quiet country lane back in Virginia like it was yesterday. It was the shank of the evening on a warm July day with the honeysuckle and manure smells adding the mystery and nostalgia of a thousand years.

I was kicking a small rock along as he told me he thought he might be able to prove the existence of God by ruminating on the wonders of blueberries, strawberries, and raspberries, imagining how majestic the creative force must be to have conjured up three fruits, each so tasty on their own but mysteriously different, neither complementing nor interfering with one another.

Thinking aloud, he said, "How could anyone deny the existence of the Almighty if they really thought about how strawberries seem tailor-made for shortcake, while blueberries fit right handy in muffins, and as if that weren't enough, throw a few raspberries in some sweet cream, and if you're still not convinced, then you probably won't believe in miracles, either."

My Daddy was laughing and serious at the same time, so convinced he was of his metaphysical imaginings.

My father... I yearn to be with him in Heaven. I never got to tell him I loved him because he died in the night. We prayed the Rosary together just before. I guess that will have to do until I see him again.

Oh, my dear Maggie, are we not blessed by God to have been given good husbands and wonderful children to help fulfill us?

My Hanky never had a real father, which was one of the reasons why he liked Grandpa Jean straightaway. Your grandpa understood that Jean was raised by a good family. He was a wonderful example. I also know Uncle Rakesh gave him someone to aspire to because he told me many times, "Uncle Rakesh is a real man." I could not agree more.

It was your grandpa's mom, Mary, who held him to a high standard and expected him to be a good dad, which he was. My Hanky struggled with marriage a bit early on. Me, too. We figured it out together as we went along.

The other thing I learned after we got hitched was how much Hanky loved and respected his mother. It would be impossible to describe this in words, but you might come close if you ponder the Church's thinking on Mary, the mother of God.

Then I learned how much he loved and respected me. What's funny, thinking back to when we met, is how I thought all these tough construction guys considered women to be second fiddles. I was dead wrong on that.

I'm rambling, sweetie... Let me leave you with a few final thoughts, if you will allow.

Whether you're anxious or afraid, ambivalent, sad or happy, whether your faith is strong or faltering, you know the way. Taking in God's word leads us to believe He wants us to live humbly and simply while being loving for all who need us.

His trail is not found on a map. It is found in a person.

He once told us his name was I Am.[16] He grew up poor in a little hill town and knows what life is like. He's never left us, either. We can't see him right now, but we know He is here in spirit because He left us a Church where we can be in communion with him through the Eucharist.

It is a great mystery. A great adventure! You were made for this!

Love,

Your Grammy Sarah

[16] John 8:58

# SARAH'S PRAYER

# TEACH ME YOUR WAY

Dear Jesus, please teach me Your Way.
Help me to live in the present when I am scared.
Remind me to be humble always and everywhere.
Help me to simplify when I am worried.
Remind me of Your presence when I am sad.
Let me hear Your Word when I am ambivalent.
Feed me Your Eucharist when my faith falters.
Have mercy on me when I feel proud.
Let me appreciate Your glory when I am happy.
Help me to be present, loving, and wise
for all who need me.
And, in everything I do, please give me strength to
remain on Your way.

Amen.

# ABOUT THE AUTHOR

William E. Bullis brings over four decades of work experience spanning the computer and medical device industries, working in the fields of I.T., research and development, and manufacturing. A lifelong Catholic, Bill lives near Pittsburgh, Pennsylvania, with his wife of thirty-nine years, Leslie. Together, they raised three children. *Am I Really Catholic?* is his debut novel.

Made in the USA
Middletown, DE
14 May 2025

75527046R00168